Praise for Beverly Rae's *Running with the Pack*

"Running with the Pack is a fun romp of a read with plenty of action and one spicy couple."

~ *Joyfully Reviewed*

"The ongoing conflict between the Hunters and the Pack provide lots of action and excitement to keep the reader on the edge of their seats. The characters, even the bad guys, are well developed, and there is always a touch of humor mixed in with the passion and romance…I recommend this to all those who enjoy hot Alpha males, and exciting action along with the happy ever after."

~ *The Long and Short of It*

"One thing you will get from a Beverly Rae book is not only a hot, sensuous, highly erotic story but a bundle of laughs too. Oh, this talented author knows how to tickle the funny bone and has her characters mouthing off one witty comment after another."

~ *Love Romances and More*

Look for these titles by
Beverly Rae

Now Available:

To Fat and Back
Touch Me
Wailing for Love

A Cannon Pack Romance
Howling for My Baby
Dance on the Wilde Side
Running with the Pack

Para-Mates
I Married a Demon
I Married a Dragon

Wild Things
Cougar
Wild Cat
Clawed

Magical Sisters
Magical Sex

Print Collection
Magical Mayhem

Running with the Pack

Beverly Rae

Samhain Publishing, Ltd.
11821 Mason Montgomery Road, 4B
Cincinnati, OH 45249
www.samhainpublishing.com

Running with the Pack
Copyright © 2012 by Beverly Rae
Print ISBN: 978-1-60928-400-8
Digital ISBN: 978-1-60928-361-2

Editing by Jennifer Miller
Cover by Angie Waters

This book is a work of fiction. The names, characters, places, and incidents are products of the writer's imagination or have been used fictitiously and are not to be construed as real. Any resemblance to persons, living or dead, actual events, locale or organizations is entirely coincidental.

All Rights Are Reserved. No part of this book may be used or reproduced in any manner whatsoever without written permission, except in the case of brief quotations embodied in critical articles and reviews.

First Samhain Publishing, Ltd. electronic publication: February 2011
First Samhain Publishing, Ltd. print publication: January 2012

Dedication

Twenty years ago, I paid thirty dollars to join a singles newsletter and found the love of my life. He healed my heart and made me see that love was possible the second time around. This book is dedicated to all the lovers who found each other through unusual circumstances.

Chapter One

"Ooh, come on, honey, nip at me."

His grandmother called him "honey". Daniel Cannon blocked the disturbing image and nipped at the woman's sensitive nub. Brenda squirmed in delight again, but he held her, controlling how much she could move. He stabbed his tongue inside her pussy, pleasuring her, giving her climax after climax. Using his thumbs, he parted her, took a breath and dived in again. She thrashed around, clutching at the comforter.

"Ah, you're going to make me come. I, oh, oh, yes, yes!"

She jerked, tried to pull away from Daniel, but he brought her back. First blowing on her warm skin, then pressing his mouth to her swollen nub, he drove her to a higher frenzy. He'd make her enjoy another one, an even bigger climax. Sucking harder, he drew her into his mouth to flick his tongue faster and faster against her soft skin. Her juices flowed even more this time. Coming up for air, he rose on his elbows and checked for the rapt expression he knew would be on her heated face.

"Was that good?" Not that he doubted it for a minute, but women liked it when he asked. He didn't love this female any more than he had all the others, but that didn't mean he didn't want her to have a good time. She'd given him what and how he'd wanted it, providing him temporary physical relief along with momentary emotional respite, so giving her a few climaxes was the least he could do.

"You're so nice to ask but, honey, that was amazing. No wonder you're the leader of the pack."

"I share that honor with my brothers." That was why she was with him, of course. Every female within a hundred miles knew he needed a new mate, was expected by the pack's council to take another mate to replace the one he'd lost. *Lost.* They made it sound like he'd misplaced her like a set of keys instead of finding her murdered by shifter hunters.

"Sure, I know Jason and Devlin, all the terrific Cannon brothers. But I know you're the best. That you're the alpha-alpha."

"I think my brothers would debate that." He crawled on top, but when she tried to wrap her arms around his neck, he broke her hold. "No. I want you on your knees."

"Ooh, goody." She got onto her knees, hands planted toward the headboard, and wiggled her butt at him. "Come on, honey, stick it in."

Damn, how he wished she'd stopped calling him that. Daniel gritted his teeth, fingered her to loosen her up, and pushed into the ample backside of the female shifter. Brenda grunted at the force of his thrust and dropped to her elbows, spreading her butt cheeks wider for him. He repositioned his stance, leaned back and held on to her buttocks. Keeping his gaze on the tangled dark hair spilling over her shoulders, he concentrated on not letting the image of Torrie pop into his mind. However, as it had happened with previous willing sex partners, as soon as he tried to block Torrie from his mind, the vision of her sweet round face, framed by her glistening black hair, thundered through him. He groaned at his failure.

"I'm glad you like it, Danny. I've—ugh—been dying to get you into bed for such a long time."

Danny. Hell, he hated that almost as much as "honey". The fact that she'd mistaken his agonized groan for an excited one didn't surprise him. The female had the perfect body—round and lush with major junk in the trunk—but she couldn't boast much in gray matter between her ears. He'd chosen her the same way he'd chosen the many women before her—they had all been ready, willing and able. Yet not one had helped distract him from the loss of his love, his mate.

Torrie's face came to him again, smiling and laughing. He saw her playing in the woods with their two children, doling out venison for the evening meal and, painfully heartbreaking, holding open her arms for him during the cold night. Growling, he wiped her from his mind and focused on pounding as hard and fast as he could into Brenda.

"Yeah, honey, that's good. Why don't you spank me? I am such a bad, dirty girl. Hit me, Danny. Make me cry."

Although her names for him annoyed him, he still sought to please her, so he slapped her ass, each slap producing a squeal of delight. Too bad each squeal made his desire for her fade. Frustrated, he pushed her away.

"Suck me. I need you to suck the skin right off my dick." He grimaced at his tone. He'd never have spoken to Torrie that way. But this wasn't making love, this was sex, pure and simple. Besides, Brenda seemed to like it.

"Ooh, I'd love to." Brenda spun around, her face full of excitement, and gripped his cock. Rubbing his pre-juices over his dick, she tossed her hair back, tilted her head and swiped her tongue over his balls. "Lie down, honey, and let Brenda make you come." She licked her lips, deliberately tempting him. "I can't wait to taste you."

Part of him wanted to throw her out of the apartment. The other part, however, the one aching for release, begged to keep her. He ran a hand over her hair. Trying not to hurt her feelings, he got onto his back and spread his legs for her. "Then drink it up. But stop calling me honey. Okay?"

Surprise flickered across her features. "Oh, sure, h— Uh, I mean, sweetie."

He sighed and gave up. Like "sweetie" was so much better than "honey". Putting his hands behind his neck, he let the woman work on him. If nothing else, Brenda was better at blowjobs than the others, but it still boiled down to the same thing. The women hoped to become his second mate, replacing Torrie in the pack's leadership. He drew his lips back in a soundless snarl. If only it were that easy. But no one could ever replace Torrie. Not in the pack and certainly not with him.

Brenda tugged on him, drawing him in and out of her mouth like a pro. Cupping his balls, she fondled him, coaxing the climax. His shaft hardened again, growing thicker and oozing from the tip. "You taste so good. Do you want to get on top?"

"No. Keep doing what you're doing." Since Torrie's death, he'd found fucking anyone missionary style difficult. Something about the position, the nearness of her face to his, the proximity of her fangs and a possible bite—a very intimate act during sex—was way too much. Instead, he kept the sex dog-style, his climaxes coming with blowjobs.

The pressure built up, tensing his body, readying him for his release. Reaching down, he moved Brenda's hair out of the way to watch. "That's it. Use your mouth and your tongue, but watch the teeth. Ah, yeah, good girl." She really was a likeable girl. A twinge of guilt hit him. "You're doing great, Brenda."

Brenda increased her movements, pumping him at the base of his cock while running her tongue around the tip. Her thumb played with the tender skin of his mushroomed cap, calling his climax to the end. With a shout, he thrust his hips upward, driving his shaft deeper into her mouth. He sighed, ready for the release that would give him those precious moments when he could clear his mind of Torrie. The female hung on, drinking him in until he fell limp against the comforter.

"Did you like it, Danny?" Brenda slid up to snuggle against him and run her fingertips over his sweaty chest. "Would you like me to stick around so I can do you again? I could stay all night if you want." She batted her eyelashes at him. "Plus, I make a mean omelet. After morning sex, of course."

He almost cringed, but it wasn't like he shouldn't have expected it. Poor girl had no clue that he didn't intend to call her again, much less ask her to stay the night. "That's very nice of you to offer, but no thanks. In fact, I need to get going. Um, so if you'll get dressed..." Prying her hands off as gently as he could, he slipped from under the sheets and started gathering her clothes. She pouted, not making a move to get out of his bed. He closed his eyes and prayed she wouldn't want to cling.

"Are you sure I can't stay? I don't mind waiting until you come back." She pouted her lips even more, then added sad eyes to her all-too-transparent routine.

"Nope, no need for you to hang around here. Sorry." Not giving her any more time to argue, he dressed, tossed her a halfhearted smile and headed for the door. "Shut the door when you leave, okay? It'll lock on its own." He heard her whimper followed by the beginnings of another protest, but he was already closing the door behind him. Fortunately, the elevator was waiting and he hurried inside, mentally urging the door to close.

Daniel welcomed the brisk fall air by dragging in a long breath and taking in the smells of the city. Although he preferred the natural fragrances of the forest, the pungent city aromas had one advantage. They didn't remind him of home—or of Torrie. The night was starting to cover the city with a soft mist of darkness and fog, making it the perfect time to run. He hurried to the back of the building, undoing his clothes along the way. Within minutes, he stashed his clothing in a beat-up duffel bag he kept behind a Dumpster and completed the transition to wolf. He stretched, enjoying the feel of animal muscles and bones, then broke into a sprint.

Running gave him an escape, the rhythmic motion and the sound of his padded feet ridding him of thoughts of Torrie. But even that mental refuge was losing its effectiveness. Recently, his thoughts had started wandering again, taking him back to that awful day last year.

"Torrie? Where is she?"

"Daniel, don't go over there. You don't want—"

Daniel broke away from the shifter trying to hold him and rushed to the form lying in a shallow hole in the wet-soaked forest ground. His heart pounded in his ears, dulling the noises of those around him to a low roar. The hardening stone in his stomach warned him, but his heart and head fought against accepting what he saw.

"No." Groaning, he fell to his knees, his mind already losing the battle against reality. "Torrie."

It wasn't Torrie. The battered form wasn't his woman, his love, his life. He drew in a ragged breath and shook his head as if he could physically deny the horror. No, the nightmare wasn't real, wasn't right in front of him. Torrie was safe. She was visiting a friend in the city.

"Daniel, she's gone."

He reached out and placed a hand on the mutilated wolf face with the strangely lifeless eyes. Saliva congealed in a path from her mouth, down her chin and onto the ground.

"The hunters must've caught her alone."

He blinked, refusing to hear the other werewolf. Who was speaking? Why wasn't he saying she'd be all right? She had to be all right. "No, this isn't her. She was on her way to the city."

"We think she made it to the city, Daniel. That's where they must've shot her before bringing her body out here to…"

Rage, pure and deadly, broke through the pain-filled fog. "To the edge of the forest to dump. Like a piece of trash. Like roadkill. Is that what you're telling me?" He heard the confirmation in the other shifter's silence. "No, this is all wrong. You're wrong. This isn't my Torrie."

"Daniel, look at her paw."

Daniel did as he was told, thinking he could prove his pack mate wrong. He lowered his gaze to her left rear paw. Her paw glared obscenely white in the midst of the surrounding dark circle of blood. Torrie's coloring was unique, a single white paw setting her apart from other shifters. Choking back a sob, he stroked the paw, comforting her, searching for the slightest bit of warmth. Her body, too cold, was already stiff, destroying the tiny flame of hope left in his heart. The reality of her loss, the bleak future that stretched out before him, made him shudder under the bright sunshine. But the grief was short-lived, moving over to welcome the fury he'd felt earlier. Shifter hunters had done this. Anger flooded through him, surging hatred that fueled strength through every muscle, every tendon. He bellowed his pain, his rage, into a ferocious roar, frightening birds in the nearby trees into flight.

After several minutes or hours—he didn't know or care which—a hand touched his shoulder and he jerked, fangs breaking through gums, ready to tear flesh. Any flesh would do until he could find the ones responsible for this terrible deed. His growl had Maxim, his pack mate, stepping away. Maxim stared at him, pity drawing his homely face longer. "I'm sorry, Daniel."

Anguish blazed through him like a brushfire sweeping over dry grasses. He needed to hurt something, someone. He hurled *his body at the shifter and wrapped his hand around Maxim's neck. Other shifters tried to tear him away, but his rage gave him the strength to toss them off. Maxim struggled, pulling at him, striking him, but he barely noticed. Nothing hurt more than the agony inside and he had to get it out. He tightened his hold on Maxim, determined to trade someone else's life for Torrie's.*

If someone hadn't struck Daniel over the head, sending him into blackness, Maxim would have died that horrible day.

Daniel's gut twisted, tightening against the memory. He'd nearly killed a friend. And yet, Maxim and the pack hadn't held it against him. Many of them had lost family to the hunters, too, and knew the kill-lust that accompanied the grief. Daniel ran faster, deeper into the city, fleeing the torment that ran with him.

Suddenly, the scent of fear assaulted him, slamming him to a stop. He dragged air into his lungs, testing the smell. What the hell? Did he really smell that? Or was that a remnant of his memory? He lifted his head, closed his eyes, and checked again. The scent, unlike any other, wafted into his widened nostrils. No, he wasn't mistaken. Someone—a female—was in danger. He hesitated only a second to confirm the direction he needed to go, then took off at a hard run.

"Come on, people. Pick up the pace." John Rawlings, leader of the hunter group, quickened his speed. The other hunters grumbled, then followed his order.

Lauren Kade pounded after them, her boots slapping a flat rhythm on the pavement. "What's the use, John? We're out of silver bullets anyway."

"It'll die eventually, if we pump enough regular lead into it. I'm sure I hit it at least once." He cast her an irritated look. "And yeah. Thanks for screwing up my last order."

"I said I'm sorry several times." *Not.*

John raced around the corner of the alley, his hand sliding along the brick wall. Using the momentum of the turn, she nudged another hunter out of the way and closed in on John. She caught a flash of gray from the werewolf a few yards ahead of them moments before it disappeared into an adjacent alley. Silently, she urged the shifter to run faster.

Lauren reached the front of the group, glanced over at John and was hit with inspiration. Granted, it wasn't much of an idea, but none of her other schemes would work in this situation. She locked the safety on her rifle, then let out a cry.

Making sure to dart to the side and away from her fellow hunters, Lauren grabbed her leg and went down. She pushed her gun away from her and screamed louder.

"Lauren!"

"Man, er, woman down!"

"John, hold up. Something's wrong with your girlfriend."

Lauren grabbed her leg and rolled toward the others. She glanced past the hunters coming to her aid to see John jogging in place, eager to continue the hunt. He turned his head in the direction the shifter had gone, then back to her, and repeated the movement.

Figures that John would want to keep going. Biting her tongue, she kept her irritation from boiling over. John cared more about killing the werewolf than about her. But that was okay since she cared more about the shifter getting away than about her so-called boyfriend. Their relationship had started downhill last year, but she hadn't let him know how she felt. Keeping their relationship, after all, was part of her cover.

The hunters gathered around her, asking her to tell them what was wrong, doing their best to render aid. At last, John strolled over and knelt beside her.

"What happened?"

Super. No *"Can I help you, babe?"* Not that Lauren should've expected any real concern. But she'd expected at least a sincere attempt at faking it. She rubbed her leg and let out as pitiful a moan as she could muster. Right now she had to think of the escaping shifter. The longer she stalled the hunters, the better the shifter's chances.

"I don't know. I was running along and, without warning, this pain shot through my leg. The next thing I knew, I was face first on the pavement."

John nodded but was already turning to gaze in the direction the shifter had gone. "Uh-huh. Yeah, that sucks." He stood, leaving her reaching for him. "Charlie, take care of her, okay? Guys, let's get going before the beast gets too far ahead of us."

The man had a cold streak in him. She'd thought about breaking up with him ever since she'd come to see shifters for what they really were, but she'd cared for him. Maybe one day he'd understand what she now did: shifters were humans, too. However, the lack of consideration for her injury—fake or not—cinched the deal. Shifters or no shifters, she was so over him.

Nonetheless, she'd have to take her time until she could ease her way out of the relationship while still remaining part of the group.

"No, John. I need you." Like hell she did. He started to move away, but she grabbed his pant leg and held on. "Stay with me."

Damn, she hated to beg, but she couldn't think of anything else to do. Short of throwing her naked body at him. Hell, even that might not stop him. She could almost see it now.

Lauren tore material, popped buttons, ridding her body of every stitch of clothing. The hunters leered at her, but John stood quietly gazing at her naked body, not showing any indication of arousal.

"John, take me. I'm yours." She pushed her breasts together and flicked her tongue over a nipple. "What are you waiting for, my big, strong hunter-man?"

John shook his head. "Not now, babe. I have a shifter to kill." Ignoring her protests, he waved for the men to follow him and took off at a sprint, leaving Lauren naked and alone.

John shook her off. "Charlie will stay to keep you company. We'll come back for you once we've caught the animal. Good thing I shot it or we wouldn't have a chance in hell of catching it now. We still may not."

Only her agonized—and totally dramatic—scream kept him from striding away. "Oh, my God, I think I'm dying." She'd better watch it and not take the dramatics too far. After all, Meryl Streep she wasn't. But then again, Meryl never had to act with the likes of John. Whimpering, she put on her saddest look, aimed it directly at him and hoped he didn't have a defense against her pitiful face. If the man didn't take the bait, she'd have to seriously consider trying the buck-naked idea.

The urgency in his expression faded, replaced by resolute resignation. "Aw, crap." Kneeling by her side, he ran his hand along her leg. "Can you walk?"

"I-I don't know." Lauren grimaced, then changed her expression to a stoic one. With a sigh, she gripped her someday-to-be ex's arm and tried to stand.

"Good girl. You made it. See? All better, right?"

Little did he know. She took a step—or rather a contrived hobble—and whined. "No, I'm not all better. It really hurts, John." Was it her acting that sucked? Or just him?

"Maybe she needs to go to the hospital?" Luke, the quiet one of the bunch, gave her a sympathetic look.

"Oh, gosh. I don't think so. I mean, it's not that bad." She leaned against John and beseeched him with her best doleful eyes. The things she'd do to save a shifter! "I just need a little TLC from my big, handsome man. Please, John, take me back to my place. I'm sure with some ice or heat or whatever you're supposed to do with sprains, I'll be fine soon enough. Especially if you're taking care of me." She had to trust that the shifter had plenty of time to get away. Unless its wound had slowed it down—or worse.

"Oh, all right. If that's what you want. But stop the bitchin', okay?" Again, John's attention drifted toward the dark alley where the werewolf had gone.

What did she have to do to get this guy's full attention? Perform magic? Give him a BJ? She placed a hand on his cheek and pulled his focus back to her.

"Ooh, John, it's really hurting. Take me home. Now. Puh-lease?" Batting her eyes, she flirted, promising him more than she ever planned on giving him. God help her if he tried to take her up on her promise. For extra benefit, she lowered a pitiable look on Luke.

"Go ahead, John. The creature's gone anyway."

"Luke's right. We'll have to continue the hunt some other night." Charlie grumbled under his breath.

She kept silent, watching John's decision play out on his features.

At last, he let out a frustrated groan. "Fine. Let's call it a night, men."

Score one for the shifter and zero for the hunters. Lauren nodded, acting disappointed and guilty at the same time, and let John wrap his arm around her waist to steady her on the way back to their vehicles. With their goodbyes said, she scooted into John's Jeep.

"Hey, is your leg doing better?"

"Huh?" She glanced down. Not thinking, she'd tucked it under her other leg in the half-cross-legged position she always used. "Yeah, it is. Maybe I just wrenched it a little." She made a show of stretching out the leg and flexing her foot. "It still hurts but not nearly as much as when I stand on it. I'm sure I'll be fine once I get home and off my feet for a bit." John's brow furrowed in thought and she had to smother a smirk. Maybe she was a better actress than she thought. Either that, or he was dumber than she realized.

"Yeah." He slid into the driver's seat. "I'm glad you're feeling better."

Lauren inwardly winced at the softness in John's eyes. Here was the man she'd once liked. The man she'd, at one time, wanted more than anyone else. But she couldn't stay his girlfriend much longer. Too much had changed between them. Too much had changed in her.

Hell, now she felt like a real jerk. John still cared for her. Could he help it if he hadn't figured out that shifters weren't the evil beasts everyone thought they were? She hadn't known either. At least not until she'd gotten close to the werewolf she'd killed. Maybe if he'd seen the terror in the werewolf's eyes, actually spoken with her, he'd understand like she did. Maybe then he'd help her keep them safe. Or at least stop hunting them. She reconsidered telling John about her change of heart but, like the thousands of times before, decided she couldn't take the risk. If he didn't understand, he'd kick her out of the group, destroying her chances to help the werewolves.

Each hunt was getting harder to sabotage and she was running out of ideas. So far, she'd managed to thwart their hunts by planning ahead, but now she was resorting to stunts like pretending to hurt her leg. She smiled, remembering the stunned expressions on the hunters' faces when she'd anonymously alerted the cops to their dangerous hunts. If one of the cops hadn't been a friend of John's, the hunters might have ended up in jail. That one trick had kept the group off the streets for three months until the heat finally died down. Maybe she should try calling the police again.

"Lauren, are you okay? You drifted away for a minute."

She placed her palm on his cheek again. But this time she meant the endearing gesture. "Yeah, I'm good. I just need some rest." But the rest would have to wait until she found the wounded shifter.

Chapter Two

John hung around, waiting to make good on Lauren's earlier flirty promise. But she wouldn't sleep with him, hadn't slept with him for two months. How could she when she planned on dumping him? She finally pushed him out the door an hour later, then peeked from behind the curtain and watched him hop into his Jeep.

Good. Now she could get a move on. Although the likelihood of finding the wounded shifter was iffy at best, she had to try. Failing to keep the hunters away from the werewolf before John had shot it frustrated her, and she owed it to the shifter to help as much as she could.

Lauren shrugged on her jacket, picked up the satchel she kept filled with medical supplies and extra clothing, then slipped into her battered-yet-trusty Beetle. Night was in full swing and although the moonless sky would make it more difficult for her to find the shifter, it would also give her cover, hiding her from any other hunters searching for prey.

Making sure no one was around, Lauren slipped the gun over her shoulder, darted into the dark alley, and prayed she could get the werewolf to listen to her. She found the location where she'd had her "accident" and continued into the adjacent pathway. Breathing in the cool night air, she paused, gathered her bearings and took her best guess as to where the shifter had fled. Her flashlight's beam streamed across the ground, and she moved slowly, checking for blood spots and finding enough to help her track the animal. Thankfully, however, the red splotches weren't as big as she'd feared.

"Where are you, shifter? Don't worry. I don't mean you any harm." Like a shifter would believe her after seeing her with a group of hunters. Still, she hoped she'd get lucky and the werewolf wouldn't recognize her. Lauren pushed on, scanning the area in case the wounded animal hid behind stacks of boxes, crouched and ready to attack. She hunched her collar around her neck, shielding herself from the cool night air. Putting one foot in front of the other, she gripped her rifle and prayed she wasn't too late.

A low growl froze Lauren to the spot, and she cautiously turned to face the threatening sound.

"Hello? It's okay. I won't hurt you." Her nerves jangled, bringing a giggle to the surface. *Oh, shit. Not now. At least act as though you're not scared.* The answering growl, louder than the first, did nothing to calm her nerves. "I know you saw me with the hunters, but I'm not one of them. In fact, I helped you get away and I'm here to help you again." She waited, the silence worrying her more than the fierce growls. She giggled, her nerves taking over. "If I had a hunting license I'd tear it up. Would that convince you?" Another weak titter escaped her. If only she could stop giggling whenever she was frightened. "Sorry. Bad joke." Going all in, she took a deep breath and decided to take a big leap of faith. "I'm going to come over there, okay? Again, I won't hurt you. Will you promise not to hurt me?"

"I don't promise scumbag hunters anything. Go away while you still have your skin."

Although that wasn't the answer she wanted, at least it was an answer instead of an attack. She bit her lower lip to keep another giggle from popping out, then pushed away the fear edging along her backbone and took a step forward.

"Will it help if I put my gun on the ground?" She dropped her satchel and gently placed her rifle beside it on the dirty payment, then raised her arms, palms facing toward the unseen shifter. "See? No gun. Now, will you let me get closer?" What else could she do to get the werewolf to believe she meant her no harm? "I'm Lauren and I'm a friend. How about telling me your name?"

"Why the hell would you want to know my name? To put it on a nameplate under my hide?" After a long period of quiet, the shifter let out a tortured moan. "Do yourself a favor and stay away."

At least the shifter hadn't tried to attack her. If, that is, she was able to.

"I'm only here to help. I know you don't trust me, but I'm telling you the truth." Maybe if she'd worn a mood ring... Another giggle escaped her. Damn.

"I saw you with them."

"You're right. I was with the hunters and I admit it. But I'm not really a hunter. I go on hunts with them so I can try to help people like you." She took a step nearer, then paused, waited for the shifter to tell her to stop, then took another step. "Are you able to come out from behind there? Or do you want me to come to you?"

"First you laugh at me and now you want to get closer? You must have a death wish, hunter."

Lauren heard the pain of the human inside the animal. She smiled reassuringly and forced herself to relax. Or at least look like she was. "I can see how you'd think that. And I'm sorry about the giggles. But I can't help it. I do that when I'm nervous." So much for acting relaxed.

Knowing she risked her life, Lauren walked around the boxes and peered into the darkness. Brilliant amber eyes locked on to her, making her pulse jump in an uneven rhythm. She had to keep the connection and make her believe. She wasn't sure how long they stared at each other but, at last, the werewolf blinked and crawled from behind her barricade. Lauren knelt beside the animal and flashed her light along its front flank. "Where are you hurt?"

"Why? So you can shoot me in a different spot?"

A deep breath helped to calm her down. "I put my gun down, remember?" All she could do was hope the werewolf would sense her sincerity.

The shifter answered with a guttural sound, then motioned with her head toward her rear flank. Lauren swung the light on the area and resisted the urge to gasp. Blood covered her, tracking a bright path from her hindquarters and down her leg to run between her claws. Abruptly, an image of another wounded shifter broke into Lauren's memory.

Blood oozed from the fatal wound, gushing from the open hole in the werewolf's chest with each labored pant she took. Her breath came out in ragged puffs, spittle inching from the corner of her jaw. Cold horror filled the werewolf's eyes and a defiant snarl drew back her lips. Her ears lay back and she tried to lift her head, tried to get up, but couldn't. Other bullet wounds scattered over her lean body drew the strength from her, spilling her life's blood to the ground around her, but she held on.

"No, please!" Her breaths, harsh puffs of air, accentuated the anger behind her words.

Lauren had known werewolves could speak, yet she hadn't believed it until now. Her pulse quickened. She certainly hadn't expected to hear such a human voice coming from an animal. The shifter's plea wrenched her heart. She reached out to touch the dying shifter, to apologize, to give her comfort. If only she'd known the truth...

Lauren jolted at the touch on her shoulder and snatched back her hand. She could sense John lifting his gun to aim, knew she needed to stop him, but couldn't. "No, John. Don't."

The echo of the rifle's retort shook her.

Lauren squeezed her eyes shut, hoping that at least in her memory's eye, she could block out the vision of the shifter's face shattering into bits of blood, flesh and fur.

"Go away."

Lauren's shudder worked the memory out of her body so she could finally open her eyes. Retrieving the duffel bag, she held up her hands at the shifter's warning growl, then carefully dug out the disinfectant and gauze, placing them on the ground beside her. "I need to clean and bandage your wound. Will you let me? Although I know you heal faster in animal form, if you became human again, I could take you to the hospital."

"And how would you explain the gunshot wound?" The wolfish lips pulled back into a grimace. "Like I'd ever make it that far."

If only the shifter would be reasonable and let her take care of her. "Okay, if you don't want medical help, how about getting help from your friends?" She slipped a hand into her pocket and brought out her cell phone. "Give me a number and I'll call for you."

The shifter's laugh was low and mean. "Do you think I'm stupid? You want me to call my friends so you and the other hunters can ambush them."

"No, you're wrong." Putting the phone down, Lauren poured disinfectant over the gauze and pressed it to the wound. "You've got to let me help you. I don't want to see you die."

The werewolf let out a long moan, but Lauren took encouragement from the fact that she didn't say anything. Or was her wound sapping her strength too much to speak any longer?

"Get away from her."

The warning was more growl than words, but Lauren understood. Swallowing the sudden lump in her throat, she swiveled around to find a large black werewolf standing behind her, majestic and commanding. But it wasn't fear that overwhelmed her. *Holy shit, he's amazing.* Silky black hair covered his body with no marks of gray or white. The only color in his body came from his angry eyes and his long, white teeth. Her gaze slid down from the blazing amber eyes. Fangs. Big, mean, dripping-with-saliva fangs. She gathered her composure to speak. "I'm trying to help her."

"Like your kind helped her earlier?"

His voice, low and masculine, sent shockwaves through her. He lowered his head another notch and glared at her. Yet, somehow, she wasn't afraid.

She couldn't help wondering what his human voice would sound like. "No, you don't understand. I'm here to help her."

He glanced at the rifle on the ground, then tilted his head at her. "Is that why you brought a gun along? To help her by putting her out of her misery?"

She gritted her teeth and fought back a string of curse words. Forget amazing. Now he was just irritating. "Would it be on the ground if that were my intention? I don't know how long you've been watching, but—"

"Long enough." He snarled, pulling back his gums to show more fangs. "Get away, hunter, before I forget to restrain myself and tear you apart."

"You've got this all wrong." Lauren showed him the phone. "Do you think I planned on killing her with a cell phone? What? Am I going to talk her to death? You know, the old death-by-dial-tone execution method? Don't be ridiculous."

For a second, she would've sworn the animal smiled.

"There she is. Oh, my God, she's trapped between two of them!"

Three hunters, rifles at the ready, ran toward them with John in the lead. "Hang on, everyone. Hold your fire until she's out of the way."

Growling, the beautiful black werewolf took one look at the approaching hunters, then dashed past her. She gawked at the hunters, too stunned to do anything else.

"Move, Lauren. They're getting away." John roughly thrust her out of the way, slamming her into the alley's brick wall.

"Ow!" She recovered and rushed to grab her gun. "What are you doing here?" By the time she was up and running, the other hunters had passed her and were in hot pursuit of the two shifters who had a huge head start on them. Crap, hadn't they already done this chasing routine tonight? She let out an expletive and charged after them. "No, wait!" How had the hunters known where to find her? Had John doubled back to her home and followed her?

They pursued the shifters for another block with the hunters gaining ground. The growing bloodstains on the pavement quickened Lauren's breath and hastened her pace. From the amount of blood, the injured werewolf wouldn't last much longer. Lauren had to do something.

Skidding to a stop, she lifted her rifle and pointed it straight into the air. *Please, God, let this work without hitting anything.* The shot rang out, startling the hunters. They ducked and covered their heads, muttering surprised curses. The shifters, however, kept going, lengthening their lead, then disappearing around a corner.

"Are you out of your mind?" John stormed toward her, his face a mask of fury. "You know better than to shoot over the heads of other hunters. Or at least I thought you did."

"I-I'm so sorry, John. I didn't think. I just got caught up in the excitement." Did he truly believe she didn't know any better?

"What the hell are you doing out here anyway?"

"I thought that if I killed her myself, then maybe everyone would forgive me for screwing up the hunt. How did you know where to find me?" She studied his face, daring to catch him in a lie.

"I didn't." He shot her an exasperated look and shouted for the others. "There's no use going after them. They're long gone." Giving her another withering look, he added under his breath, "Thanks to you."

She smothered a self-satisfied grin and instead tried to appear as remorseful as she could. "I know, I know. Again, I'm sorry." He hadn't answered her question, but she let it go, hoping to avoid having to answer more of his questions.

"Tell that to them." John turned his attention to the questions of the others, leaving her to worry that she'd gone too far.

"How's Mysta doing, Tucker?" Daniel kept his voice low and his phone pressed against his ear. No need to let the humans surrounding him overhear his conversation. Especially when talking about an injured shifter.

"She's still out of it. Good thing you brought her to the house last night before she bled out. She's lost a lot of blood. Hopefully, she'll stay in werewolf form so she can heal faster."

"Has she said anything about what happened? How they managed to corner her twice?"

"Naw. She hasn't come to since last night and most of what she said then didn't make a whole lot of sense. Except that the woman found her. Her memory seems kind of mixed up after that."

Daniel gestured to Roland, the manager of The Lost Plate, one of many businesses the Cannon pack owned and operated, then slid into the big table in the back that was always reserved for pack members. The manager, a meek shifter, scurried to the table, clasped his hands and waited for Daniel to finish his phone conversation.

"Mysta was lucky to get away in the first place. But to get away a second time? Close to a damn miracle."

"Yep, she's one lucky shifter."

"Okay, then, make sure she gets whatever she needs." Daniel punched off the phone. "Tell me, Roland, how's business since the last time I was here?"

"Business is up, Mr. Cannon, even in this lousy economy. As you can see, this is our rush hour." He waved an arm toward the crowded room. "We're always jam-packed at lunch."

Daniel nodded and tried to pay attention to what the man was saying. "Good. That's what I like to hear."

Now if he could just get his mind off the female hunter.

"Can I fetch your regular lunch for you, Mr. Cannon?"

Daniel winced. "Roland, please. Haven't we talked about the canine references? No *fetch* or other offensive words."

Roland nodded vigorously and rubbed his hands, eager and ready to serve. "Sure, sure. I remember. I forget sometimes. Please forgive me." He sought out a nearby waitress, his hand shaking as he crooked a finger at her. "Sarah, get Mr. Cannon his coffee." He shooed the gum-chewing waitress on her way to retrieve the pot. "Black coffee coming right up, Mr. Cannon."

"My regular lunch would be great. Oh, and Roland—" Daniel quirked an eyebrow at the trembling shifter, "—will you please relax? I told you. As long as business is good, you don't have anything to worry about. And even then, you don't have to be afraid for your safety. You're one of us and I take care of my people." He checked the tables around them, then whispered, "I'm not the kind of alpha you need to fear. And call me Daniel."

Roland nodded again, his bright eyes shimmering with gratitude. "Yes, Mr. Cannon. Thank you, Mr. Cannon. I mean, Daniel."

Sarah returned to pour a cup of steaming coffee, then set the pot on the table for his exclusive use. Roland bowed as he backed away.

Being one of the leaders of the Cannon pack had its perks. Daniel sighed and watched the timid manager shuffle through the swinging doors that led to the kitchen. Roland's last pack leader had been a real asshole, turning the slight shifter into a wuss. No matter how often Daniel told him, the poor guy refused to believe that he wouldn't tear out his throat over the slightest infraction. Taking a sip, he let his mind wander and, like last night, was surprised at where it took him.

The female hunter's face had haunted him throughout the night, making sleep a precious commodity. The image of her, squatting close to the injured werewolf, struck him in the gut again. Not only because she'd approached Mysta alone, without her hunter friends—something he'd never seen a hunter do—but because of her body. She had all the curves he'd ever wanted in a woman and more. Although humans would probably consider her plump, he liked the roundness of her booty, the fullness of her breasts pushing against the material stretched over her bosom, the soft swell of her stomach. In fact, when he'd rounded the corner and found himself staring at her backside, he'd almost forgotten why he was there. Almost. Her hair was so curly. So silky. Or at least, that's how it had looked. He wished he could've touched it, could've run the strands between his fingers. Her eyes were an amazing mix of dark cocoa and the soft brown of a deer. From the second he'd seen her, she'd fascinated him.

Why the hell was he dreaming about a damn hunter? Yet he couldn't shake the knowledge that he hadn't thought once about Torrie in over twelve hours. Instead he'd fantasized about another woman, a hunter of all people. He dreamed of having her underneath him, sitting on top of him, bending over to open to him. A twist in his stomach warned him not to pursue this fantasy, but he didn't heed his internal alarm.

The huntress straddled him, her naked flesh shimmering with sweat. She grabbed his pecs, holding them firmly. Her breasts, temptingly perky, pressed together between her strong arms.

"Let me suck on them."

She leaned lower, her wavy locks falling to frame her enchanting oval face. He took a nipple in his mouth, keeping his eyes on her lust-filled ones, watching to capture the moment she climaxed—again. When she did, her eyelashes fluttered, her eyes softly closing as she savored the moment of release. She made a soft mewing sound, flaming the heat in his abdomen to an even higher pitch.

Growling against her breast, he slid into her and almost lost control when her walls closed around his shaft, gripping him, pulling on him. He kept his hands on her ample hips and helped her rise and fall against him, plunging deeper into her. She cried out and he clutched her firmer, first holding her to him, then forcing her to lean back. Bucking against him, she arched her back and held on to his legs.

He licked his lips, mesmerized by the small triangle of hair above her pussy that tickled the slickened skin of his dick. Pacing himself, he thrust in and out, over and over. "I'm going to show you what fucking is really like, hunter. Together, we're going to release the animal inside you."

"Make me yours."

He held his breath, caught unprepared for her request. "Do you want me to? You'll change. Become pack." Her breasts jiggled enticingly, drawing his attention away from her eyes. Palming them, he almost lost control, but gained it back before all was lost. Her eyes glistened, the lush russet lightening with amber. But how? She wasn't a werewolf. Not yet.

"I want to run with the pack, Daniel. Bite me and make me shifter."

He groaned, wanting more than anything to do as she wanted. "Are you sure?"

"Do it."

Daniel grabbed her by the back of the neck, rose and flipped them, putting her underneath him. His incisors broke through, his inner beast thrashing to take her and make her his. Her wild eyes stared up at him, then, with a soft smile, she turned her head, exposing her neck. Growling, he bent to her and sank his fangs into her. She struggled against him, her natural instinct to survive taking over, but that soon gave way. Instead, she clung to him, digging her nails into his back, keeping him to her neck as his teeth sank deeper, claiming more. Several minutes passed, then he finally released her. She lay arms thrown out, her auburn hair splayed against the white pillow.

"You're pack now." He licked the wound that was already healing. *"You're mine now."* Her silence unnerved him. *"Are you all right?"*

She didn't answer, didn't seem to hear him. Instead, she sat up, laid her head back and howled.

The fantasy broke apart, shattering her image into a million pieces and startling him back to reality. She howled? Talk about an idiotic daydream. Maybe Torrie's death had affected him more than he'd thought, in a different way than he'd thought. Surely fantasizing about a hunter was a sign, right? Was he starting to lose it?

He snarled, a tinge of lust layering his tone. The prim ladies at a nearby table, all of them pack members, turned to study him. The eldest lady watched him, considering him, amber flakes glistening in her dark eyes. Once he'd acknowledged her, she pointedly glanced around the room, taking in the many humans in the restaurant, a clear warning for him to take care.

When these ladies were around, he needed to watch his step. Even alphas weren't above the rules of the pack. The diminutive ladies couldn't harm him physically, but he'd rather face an army of hunters than get on the wrong side of a granny howler. The stories he'd heard about how they exacted justice made slasher movies pale in comparison.

"My sincerest apologies, ladies. I forgot where I was."

Her curt nod told him he was forgiven but that she wouldn't brook another slip. Daniel took another sip of his coffee and used the movement to glance away. Scanning the room, his gaze fell on the front door and he choked, then sputtered his drink, again drawing an unwanted scowl from the elder shifter. He quickly ducked his head.

What the hell was she doing here?

Trying to appear nonchalant, he raised his head and found himself caught in a gaze of rich velvet. Her eyes drew him in and chased everyone, everything out of his awareness. The hunter was beautiful. Even more beautiful than he remembered. He took her in, memorizing every curve, each dimple in her cheeks, the rise and fall of her chest. The dress she wore, although not too tight, still showed her womanly shape to mouth-watering perfection, shortening his breath. Her legs, taking up a good portion of her body, were strong and smooth and he instantly envisioned them wrapped around him, holding him tightly, never letting him go. She smiled at Roland, a simple smile of greeting, but it almost tore his heart out knowing her smile was for someone else.

She's a hunter.

Daniel closed his eyes, letting the thought take purchase and drive his desire away. Yes, she was a hunter and no matter what she looked like, how delectable she was, she was his enemy. Yet although his mind agreed, another part of him twisted in agony at the thought of never touching her. He gritted his teeth against the rush of desire and warned himself to think with the head on his shoulders.

He took a moment to dab the napkin to his mouth, smiled at the elderly ladies and hoped his legs would hold him. No way would he let a hunter dine at a pack restaurant. Not even when she looked like this one.

The expression on the approaching stranger's face had Lauren checking behind her. Surely he wasn't scowling at her. But with no one else near her, she had to accept that this incredible-looking man, dressed in black silk from his Italian shoes to his oh-so-form-fitting black shirt, was headed her way. His longish black hair curved under his ears, leading the eye to the kind of jaw line most men only wished they had, to a mouth any woman would spread her legs for a chance to nibble on. But it was his eyes that claimed her, forcing her to forget the toned, muscled body and dive inside them, searching for everlasting love. Or at least one helluva night of passion. If she disregarded the glare in those eyes, he was the stuff of wet dreams. The type of man romance novels were written about. The kind of man supermodels dated. So why the hell was he staring at her? Playing it cool, she dipped her head and quickly checked her clothes. Nope. No button undone. No stains. No tissue paper stuck to her shoes.

When she raised her head again, he was standing directly in front of her. Those breath-stealing dark eyes, surrounded by a golden haze, locked onto her and held her as securely as chains would have. Yet she wouldn't have fought for freedom. No, with him as her captor she would happily live her life chained to his bed. She clenched her fists, keenly aware of how much she wanted to flatten her hands against his chest. The thin silk material couldn't hide the firmness of him, the muscles rippling with his slightest move. If she could have undressed him right there in the lobby of the restaurant she would have. Not to mention what she'd have done to him once he was in the buff. She glanced at his crotch, then jerked her gaze upward, shocked at her bold move.

To cover both her frank appraisal and instant shyness, she stuck out her hand and lifted her chin. "Hi. I'm Lauren Kade. You seem to know me, but—"

"Get out."

His stern voice, rich and hauntingly familiar, shook her, sending a cold chill along her spine. Had she understood him correctly? Did he just tell her to get out? Suddenly, the trance holding her vanished.

"I'm sorry. What did you say?" Of course she'd heard him wrong. After all, she hadn't paid close attention. At least not to what he might say.

"I told you to get out. Your kind isn't welcomed here."

His words knocked the air out of her. She inhaled and slowly exhaled, taking time to recover. "My kind? What kind do you mean? My kind...as in dentists?" Was he a dissatisfied patient? But she'd never had even one patient complaint.

"You know what I'm talking about. Get out."

Talk about handsome and rude all at the same time. What the hell was wrong with this guy? Who the hell did he think he was? Acutely aware of everyone listening, she tried to bring civility to their conversation. "I'm sorry, but I don't understand. Did I do something to offend you? Perhaps you're mistaking me for someone else."

"Trust me. I know exactly who I'm talking to."

Why did so many hunks have to be such conceited schmucks? She checked the other patrons, found the answer to her next question, but asked it anyway. "Am I not dressed appropriately? I mean, lunch is hardly a black tie affair. I would think a dress would be suitable. And I do have shoes on." She smiled, hoping he'd lighten up at her joke.

"Your attire has nothing to do with it. I want you to leave. Now." His dark eyes flashed at her, his thick eyebrows falling toward his nose and chiseled features.

Was she getting punked? Lauren glanced around again, this time looking for her friend, Bobbie, who loved to play practical jokes. "Is Bobbie behind this?" She laughed, confident that she was right, and dashed toward the swinging door to the kitchen.

"Hey! You can't go in there."

"I bet she's hiding in the kitchen, right? Bobbie, the jig's up. You can't trick me."

She stalled, the doors swinging shut behind her, and gawked at the cooks. Two chefs and four waiters stared back at her. But no Bobbie.

"Oh, I get it. She's hiding." Dashing around the kitchen, she checked under tables, in cupboards and had her hand on the freezer door when someone grabbed her. She whirled to face the exasperating man. A very worried manager stood behind him.

His hand clenched around her arm did several things. First, it surprised her. Next, it hurt like hell. And lastly, it embarrassed her. "What do you think you're doing? Let go of me."

This man had gone from rude to ranking jerkwad status and the joke wasn't funny any longer. Why would Bobbie want this man involved in her prank?

"This isn't a joke and I don't know who the hell Bobbie is."

"Then I don't get it. If this isn't a joke, what's going on?"

His face was mask of contained anger. "You're acting like a chicken with its head cut off and I've had quite enough of this idiocy. You are not welcome." Taking her along with him, he marched her out of the kitchen, through the curious patrons and toward the front door.

Angry and humiliated, she yanked her arm from him, spread her feet wide and matched his combative stance. "Who the hell are you to decide who can eat here? I've dined here lots of times and I've never seen you before." She crossed her arms, challenging him to lay his hand on her again. "I think you're out of line, mister. Only the management can ask me to leave. Only Mr. Richmand can throw me out."

"I happen to dine here often as well and I've never seen you." He waved his hand around as though shooing a fly. "Which isn't important. I'm telling you in no uncertain terms that you don't belong here."

"Why the hell not? What sets me apart?"

The corners of his mouth tipped upward. Lifting one hand, he called out, never taking his eyes off her. "Roland, come here."

The meek man she'd come to like and know as the manager and owner of the restaurant rushed to stand beside the rude man. "Yes, sir?"

"I don't want this woman dining in this establishment. Ever." This time his voice was loud enough for the patrons in the remote accesses of the restaurant to hear.

Warmth rushed up her neck and into her face. If he talked any louder, the people across the street would hear him. Instead of voicing her retort, however, she kept her calm appearance, preferring to enlist Mr. Richmand's help instead of dealing with the insolent man on her own.

"I don't understand what's going on, Mr. Richmand. This gentleman seems to have a problem with me and I don't know why." She gave the manager a big "we're friends" smile and shared it with the other diners, sending them a clear message that she was the victim. "You know me. I've dined here lots of times. I've even brought my office personnel and celebrated promotions and the like."

Mr. Richmand, clearly unnerved by the man's obvious hostility, attempted to plead her case. "Yes, it's true. She's a regular. Perhaps there's something I could do to help?"

"Most definitely, Roland."

She dared to relax a little. Finally, the man saw that he was in the wrong. "Oh, good. I'm glad to see you've changed—"

"You can escort the lady out of my establishment."

"What? Wait. This is *your* establishment?" She looked to the manager, then back to the now not-so-handsome, ugly-because-he's-an-asshole man. "Are you kidding me? You're really throwing me out?" She tried to laugh, but the sound came out forced and tinny.

"If you're asking if I'm kidding, rest assured, I am not." Mr. Rude scowled at her. "Roland, do as I instructed."

"Yes, sir." Roland, a plea in his eyes, pointed at the entrance and reached to take her arm.

Lauren jerked her arm away, her heart pounding. "I do not believe this." She scoured the other patrons, hoping to find someone, anyone, to stand up for her. "This is so unfair. And possibly illegal." She had to try one last attempt. "And what will you do if I refuse?" She lifted her chin, squeaked out a soft giggle and stood her ground. "Because I do refuse."

Mr. Rude's eyes narrowed and his menacing smile grew. "You've got that all wrong, lady." He inched closer and sniffed.

Had he just sniffed her? Did he think she stank? She resisted the urge to lift her arm and check her armpit. No, she remembered putting on deodorant that morning. Besides, with the aroma of the food wafting through the restaurant, how could he tell? Owner or not, this guy was seriously messed up.

"As the owner, I have the right to refuse service to anyone I don't like." He paused, then smirked. "And, Miss Whatever-Your-Name-Is—" his smile morphed into a sneer, "—I don't like you."

Why didn't he like her? Yet the question on her mind wasn't the one that shot out of her mouth. "Is that so? Well, you lousy good-for-nothing jerk, I don't particularly care for your company, either."

"Then you shouldn't mind never coming again."

She opened her mouth to respond, but couldn't think of anything harsh enough to say. At least nothing she could say with children present. Instead, she held her head high and glared back at him. "Fine."

"Fine."

She had to do something, couldn't let him get away with treating her badly. Glancing around, her gaze fell on the waitress carrying a tray. Not giving her time to change her mind, she took a tall glass from the tray and dumped it over his head. Chin up, she waited for his reaction. And got nothing. What was wrong with this man?

"Are you finished acting like a child?"

His calm demeanor made her want to slap him. Instead, with nothing more to say and no alternative left, Lauren whirled around and marched out of the restaurant. Tears stung her eyes and she quickly wiped them away. No way would she cry and give him the pleasure of watching her through the window. He'd see her cry, bastard that he was, and then he'd laugh his ass off. Her phone rang, startling her. She choked back a sob, straightened her back, and answered the call. "Y-yeah, this is Lauren."

"Hey, babe, are you all right?"

Sheesh and she'd thought John was a jerk and a half. He was Prince Charming compared to Mr. Rude. "Uh-huh. I'm okay. What's up?" Struggling to keep the tears out of her tone, she warned herself to shape up. She wouldn't let some insignificant restaurant owner put her in a funk. After all, who was he to her? No one. Other than the sexiest man she'd ever seen. "Errr."

"Are you sure? You sound strange."

"Sorry. Ignore me. I'm having a tough day." She started walking, putting distance between herself and her former favorite place for lunch. "What's up?"

"We're going out again this week."

Lauren stopped to look at a clothing store's display, out of the path of foot traffic. "Already? We don't usually have hunts so close together." Once a month was the regular schedule and never two nights in the same week.

"I know, but some of the guys got to talking about last night and, since the hunt kind of got interrupted, we figured we'd go out again. You know, kind of a do-over."

Interrupted? She frowned, knowing she had been the interruption. Damn. She'd thought she'd have more time before having to come up with another way to botch the next hunt. "Crap."

"Does that mean you're not up for it? I mean, we'll understand if you want to bow out of this one."

She could hear it in his voice. He'd love it if she dropped out of the hunt. Maybe even out of the hunter group. Not that she could blame him. If she weren't John's girlfriend, the others would have never put up with her. On the surface, she was the most inept hunter they'd ever had. But that was part of her cover. In reality, she'd made a promise to herself. After watching the shifter she'd shot die a slow and painful death, she had to stay with the hunters and do anything she could to keep another werewolf from getting killed. That night had changed her forever and she couldn't pretend the hunts didn't exist. The memory blindsided her, rocking her on her feet.

The night exhilarated her. For the first time, she worked her way to front and center with John, leading the group in the chase after the shifter. They cornered the she-wolf in a dead-end alley, and Lauren felt so alive, so afraid, so powerful. John nodded at her, then stepped behind her to give her the first shot. Even now she could feel the weight of her rifle against her shoulder, inhaling then holding her breath seconds before she squeezed the trigger. She rolled her shoulder at the retort of the gun. Other shots came a second after hers, yet she barely heard them. The werewolf jumped into the air, blood shooting out of her body, and Lauren gasped at the sight. The slap of the shifter's body slamming to the pavement echoed in her ears.

Sounds and smells around her drifted into a mixed haze. Unable to move, she allowed John to drag her toward the shifter, his congratulations assaulting her ears.

And yet, although she'd pictured that moment in her head several times since joining the hunters, she was unprepared for the avalanche of emotions pummeling her. She knelt beside the shifter, saw the pain and fear in her eyes, heard the anguish in her voice and knew at that moment that she'd done a horrible thing. She'd killed a person, not an animal. Leaning over the dying shifter, she vowed to stop the atrocity from ever happening again.

Lauren shook the visions from her mind, bringing her back to reality.

"Lauren? Are you there? Lauren, answer me."

"Yeah, I'm here." She hated the idea of another hunt, but she had no choice. "Count me in."

The clawing at Daniel's gut, the intensifying yearning he'd struggled with, didn't lessen after Lauren's departure. Even eating his favorite meal, then ordering a stiff drink, couldn't shake the unsettling sensation. Lauren Kade. Her name fit her.

Strong, to the point, yet alluring. Her name played like a melody inside his head, accompanying flashing images of her face, her heaving chest, her burning eyes. If she hadn't been a hunter, if he hadn't seen her cornering the wounded shifter, he might've given in to the urge to whisk her into the back office and tear off her clothes.

Maybe he should take her as payback for the attack on Mysta. Daniel slugged back the last of his drink and groaned. Yeah, right. Like he could ever take a female by force. In his gut, he knew the real reason. Payback, his ass. He wanted her, plain and simple. Daniel hated it, but he had to admit that no other woman, shifter or human, had pulled at his lust the way this one had. At least not since Torrie.

She's a hunter.

If he reminded himself often enough, would it finally sink in and rid him of these ridiculous ideas? Shoving the empty glass across the table, he phoned Tucker to check on the wounded werewolf. "How is she?"

"Geez, man, didn't we just talk?"

"Tucker." Daniel lowered his tone. "Humor me."

His friend's sigh filled his ear. "She's about the same. I guess she lost more blood than we originally thought. But she's hanging in there. She was lucky it wasn't a silver bullet."

"Is she awake and talking yet?" Although he was sure he already knew what she'd say, he needed to speak with her. She'd gotten cornered, then shot. Same old story. Yet for some reason, Daniel had to hear every detail about the hunt and especially about the lovely hunter. Something about the way the hunter had squatted next to the injured Mysta didn't mesh with his image of a hunter ready to kill, but he couldn't quite grasp the idea just out of reach. If that didn't unnerve him enough, another question gnawed at him. If he saw her again, perhaps in a dark alley, what would he do? Hurt her or take her?

Chapter Three

"Damn, man, you are such a pussy." Tucker snickered at Daniel.

Daniel shoved against his friend's shoulder on his way back to flop on the couch. "I'm telling you. This sucker hurts like hell."

Tucker flipped his white hair out of his eyes, chugged the last of his beer, then grabbed Daniel's arm, tugging him to a standing position. "Come on, tough guy. I can't take any more of your bitching. We're off to the dentist."

"I don't like dentists." Daniel heard the whine in his tone and grimaced. He bet Tucker heard it, too. "Let's give it a day or two. Maybe it'll get better."

Tucker laughed and dragged him through the house, then out to the driveway. "Like I said, you're a pussy. Besides, how would you know you don't like dentists? You've never been to one." Tucker pushed him toward the passenger side of his beloved Jaguar, then slid into the driver's seat. "Look, man, it's not all that bad. Once you're pain-free, you'll thank me."

"I seriously doubt that." Daniel concentrated on the buildings and other cars, trying to keep his mind off his toothache and the stories he'd heard from werewolves who'd visited the dentist. "He's at least one of us, right?"

"Beats me." Tucker rolled his lips under, a telltale sign that he was trying not to laugh. "I pulled the name out of the phone book."

Daniel's rising panic zipped higher. "Are you crazy? A human dentist isn't going to know what to do with my teeth. This is nuts. At least find one of the pack's dentists."

"Unfortunately, the only one I know of is out of town. That leaves you in a bind, my friend. You can either suffer—which isn't going to happen since I have to suffer with you—or you can suck it up and go to a human tooth doc. Quit worrying about it. He'll probably think you've got big-ass teeth is all. But teeth are teeth, right?"

An excruciating sting shot through the left side of Daniel's mouth, making the entire side of his face throb. Tucker was right. He couldn't take this any longer, even if it meant seeing a human dentist. He palmed his cheek and muttered, "Are we there yet?"

Tucker swung his sleek black Jag into a parking lot in front of a modest one-story brick building. "Yep. We're here."

The receptionist did a double-take when they walked in, then focused her amber-colored eyes on Tucker. A smile covered her average-looking face, framed by blue-streaked hair. "Yes? May I help you?"

Daniel glanced at Tucker, who bestowed a large grin on the obviously attracted-to-Tucker girl. "Yeah. I'm in pain and I need to see the dentist. Now."

Her frown faltered a second before widening to match Tucker's. "Oh, I'm so sorry to hear that you're hurting. However, since you're not a patient of ours—"

"How did you know that?"

She hadn't taken her werewolf-colored eyes off Tucker for one second. Twirling a blue strand of hair around her finger, she batted her eyelashes and centered her attention on the bigger shifter. "Trust me. I would've remembered him." Her gaze darted to give Daniel a cursory glance. "Or you."

Tucker matched her, lust-filled gaze to lust-filled gaze. "Perhaps you could make an exception? My friend is a puss— uh, wimp—about pain and he's driving me bonkers." Tucker flashed a bright smile. "You know how it is, don't you? I can tell by looking at you that you're a sensitive person who feels other people's pain. So, please, how about it? Give the guy a break?"

"W-ell, I'd really like to help, but the doctor is booked for today. Perhaps we could get you in tomorrow morning? You'd come back with your friend, wouldn't you?"

Daniel fought against the urge to slam his fist on the counter and break up this instant love-fest. Not that he wasn't used to this situation. Tucker often caught women's interest because of his unusual coloring both in human and animal form. Most of the time, however, the women looked at Daniel, too. Together, he and Tucker made an impressive pair: one dark, the other light. "No, that won't—"

"Let me handle this, man." Tucker leaned over, getting closer to the bewitched receptionist. "I love your eyes, darlin'. That's a very unusual color for you. Am I right?"

She tittered under his flattery. The large intake of breath, then sigh couldn't enhance her flat bosom. "How sweet of you to notice. I, uh, like to wear different colored contacts. I mean, without color, the world would be so drab. Don't you think?" She ran her hands over her hair.

Tucker winked at her. "Oh, I do, I do. And what's your name, darlin'?"

"I'm Bobbie." She pointed at the name plate pinned to her uniform. "Bobbie Williams."

Bobbie? Daniel squinted at the nameplate. Where had he heard that name before?

"And tell me, Ms. Bobbie, why are you working behind a desk? A beauty like you should be on display at an art museum for everyone to enjoy."

Tucker had turned on the Rhett Butler charm. Not that it didn't work most of the time. Knowing when to get out of the way, Daniel stood back and watched the pro at work. If anyone could change her mind, Tucker could.

He would've laughed—if he didn't hurt so much—at the way she waved her hand around, playing with her hair, smoothing her uniform, doing everything she could to wiggle her ring-less left finger at Tucker. Subtlety was definitely not her strong suit. "Can we get back to the reason we're here?"

Tucker shot him a look, then rolled his eyes at Bobbie. "Like I said, he's such a lightweight." He reached over the counter and took her hand. "Darlin', I don't suppose there's any way possible to get him in to the dentist right now. I'd consider it a huge favor. One that I would love to repay."

With Tucker around, women didn't need candy to get their sweet fix. Daniel plastered on a pitiful expression—which wasn't hard to do since his tooth was killing him—and moaned.

Bobbie's gaze flicked to him, then back to Tucker. She tipped her head, glanced at the other clients waiting and whispered, "Let me see what I can do. The doctor and I are good friends, so maybe I can pull a string or two. Especially since I can see that he's in awful distress."

"Oh, he's definitely in distress. It's a real emergency." Tucker's tone dripped molasses. "You, Bobbie Williams, are an angel residing on Earth."

She blushed and hurried out of her office area, then down the hall. "I'll be right back. Now don't you go anywhere, okay?"

A few minutes later, Bobbie was back. Yet instead of returning to her chair, she rushed over to Tucker. If the woman had any bigger crush on the white-haired shifter, she'd drool on his shoes. With the barest of glances at Daniel, she announced her good news. "The doctor will see you now. Marla will show you the way."

"You, darlin', are amazing. I'll wait out here for you, man." Tucker slipped her arm through his and led her around the counter to her chair. "Bobbie and I will use the time to get better acquainted."

Bobbie's light laugh followed Daniel as he walked down the hallway toward the assistant motioning for him. He glanced in one of the cubicles and saw a young boy, earphones in his ears, rocking to music loud enough for others to hear. Once in the chair, Marla hooked a dental bib around his neck, patted him on the shoulder, then left him alone to wait for the dentist.

Instruments neatly arranged on the tray didn't do anything for his jittery nerves. "I hope this guy's good and not some hack."

"Well, I can't speak for this guy, whoever he is, but I think I'm pretty good at my job." A stool squeaked behind him. "But seriously. Don't worry. You're in good hands." Papers rustled. "You're Mr. Cannon, right?"

He froze. The voice, the one he'd heard repeated in his mind so many times since meeting her in the restaurant, was loud and clear—and only a foot from him. Daniel closed his eyes, heard the stool squeak to a stop beside him, then heard her sharp gasp.

"Oh, no, it's you."

I can not believe that jerk is sitting in my chair. Lauren scowled at him, willing him to open his eyes. When he did, she pointed all her irritation directly at him and iced her voice with sarcasm. "Hmm, imagine meeting you again. I was at your place of business and now you're at mine. Just goes to show you what a small world this is."

"You can't be the dentist. Tell me you only work here, then get the other assistant back." There was no love lost in his tone, either.

Lauren's sneer grew. "Sorry, bub. I am the dentist. Trust me, you wouldn't have made it to the chair if Bobbie hadn't talked me into it. Of course, I could still decide to refuse *you* service." She enjoyed his annoyed expression even more than her sneer. "You know how it is. I have the right to refuse service to anyone I don't like. And I definitely don't like you." She started to pull off the latex gloves, then paused. Could she let him walk out without at least trying to help him? What kind of dentist was she if she did that?

"Hey, that's okay by me. I wouldn't let you touch my teeth if you paid me." Daniel tried to unhook the dental bib. "Ow!" He clapped a hand over his jaw, scrunched his face and squeezed his eyes shut. "Shit, shit, shit, shit, shit!"

She had no doubt searing pain traveled the length of his jaw and into his head. Lauren leapt off the stool and pushed him back in his seat. "Hush up. I have a child in the next room and I doubt his mother would appreciate his hearing you cuss a blue streak."

"I don't give a crap. Besides, he can't hear us anyway with his music blaring in his ears. Take this damn thing off me." He tugged at the chain around his neck but only managed to tear the paper covering his chest. "Damn it. How does this stupid thing work?"

She slapped her hand over his mouth, effectively silencing him. Yet she was unprepared for the sizzle that sliced through the glove, into her fingers and into her hand. Jerking her hand away, she peered at her fingers, expecting to see scorch marks on the latex. "Holy shit."

"Uh, uh, uh, doc. No cussing. Remember?" He started to grin, but the grin quickly warped into a grimace with his next howl of pain.

"Ha, ha. Nice to see your agony hasn't squelched your sense of humor." Sheesh, she hated to see someone like this. But if anyone deserved a little pain to put him in his place, it was this guy. Still, if she denied him help, wasn't she acting like a jerk, too?

"Stay in the chair. You're definitely hurting so why not let me take care of it for you?" She arched an eyebrow at the suspicion in his eyes. "Hey, it's no biggie to me. Do what you want. But as a dentist, I feel it's my duty to at least offer to help someone in pain. Even a jerk in pain."

She waited, ready to let him make the decision. The next round of pain made the decision.

"Okay, get to work. But only because I don't have any other options."

Lauren thought of all the things she could do to him while he was in her care. She could pull the wrong tooth. Or tell him he needed dentures. Or drill into more than one tooth. Oh, she could be such a bad, bad girl.

Chuckling, she bit back a retort, picked up her instruments and motioned for him to open wide. She sighed. Too bad she wasn't really a bad girl. Instead, she was a damn fine dentist who wouldn't think of risking her reputation. Not even for some well-deserved fun. Not even for some super-duper good fun. She studied his teeth, unusual in their size and appearance, and quickly found the tooth giving him trouble. "I'll have my assistant get some X-rays and I'll be back after I've taken a look at them."

He groaned and this time, she didn't fight to stifle her grin. "Man up, Mr. Cannon. And stay put. I'll try to make this as painless as possible."

Cannon? Where had she heard that name before? She tore the gloves off and forced herself to walk—not run—from the room. After giving Marla directions, she slipped down the hall and into her office. Closing the door quietly behind her, she concentrated on breathing deeply and evenly.

What was it about this guy? Sure, he was infuriating, but it had to be something else. And why did his name sound familiar? He was devilishly handsome with movie-star charisma about him, but that wasn't it, either. Lauren dropped into her desk chair, her brow furrowed. No, he had a special quality about him that unsettled her but in a good way. A way she hadn't experienced in a long time. Not only did he ooze charisma, but his smell was familiar, too. Where had she smelled that scent before? Was it his aftershave? Accidentally, her hand bumped her mouse and her monitor lit up with today's emails. The first on the list was an email from John telling her when the next hunt was.

She froze, then inhaled as though trying to retrieve Mr. Cannon's scent to confirm her suspicion. That was it. He smelled like a shifter. She probably wouldn't have noticed it if she hadn't gotten so close to him, but that's what it was. She bolted out of her chair, her legs automatically taking her back to him. Thoughts exploded, tumbling around her brain, fighting for her attention.

Oh, my God, I have a shifter in my chair. Does he know I'm a hunter? If so, is he here to cause trouble? Should I get him out of here? Or do I pretend I don't know and treat him like I would anyone else?

She slammed to a stop outside the cubicle. He was still in the chair, moaning and groaning.

"Lauren?"

She jumped at the same time he did. "Oh!"

He twisted in the chair to glare at her.

Marla gave her a questioning look, then handed her an X-ray. "Here it is. I don't see anything wrong. Do you?" The young girl lowered her voice. "But they're awfully big. Don't you think?"

"Big?" Mr. Cannon lifted a cocky eyebrow, glanced at his crotch, then back to her with a twinkle in his eyes. "And the answer's yes."

Lauren plastered on a smile and answered both their questions. "No, I don't think so." She gave her assistant more instructions that sent her to the lab, then took her time returning to the stool beside him. She supposed shifters needed dental care like everyone else, right? So all she had to do was handle him like she would any other patient. Well, almost like any other patient.

"Mr. Cannon, I've looked at your films and I have to say that, from the way you were behaving, I thought you'd probably need a root canal. But that's not the case. You need to have a filling. A very small filling, at that. Overall, however, your teeth are in remarkable shape." For a human. But for a werewolf? Who knew?

"I know who—and what—you are."

Her mouth grew drier than a beach on the Fourth of July at the fierceness in his tone. "I, uh, figured you'd remember me from the restaurant. But don't worry. I'll help you anyway."

He sniffed and deepened his scowl. "You're a hunter."

She froze, an instrument poised in her hand. "You're a shifter?"

"As if you didn't know."

"I didn't then, but I do now." The man may be one fine-looking piece of manhood, er, shifterhood, but he was also a major headache.

"I can't believe I'm letting a hunter touch me." His scowl deepened until he gritted his jaw, then groaned in pain.

"Touch you?" She couldn't help lowering her gaze to his crotch. Her imagination took over, leaving her wishing she had him behind doors and not in her dental chair. That wasn't helping her. Better to keep her eyes on his gloriously masculine face. "Don't flatter yourself, Mr. Cannon."

"Okay, that did it. Pain or no pain, I'm out of here." He started to slide out of the chair, then stiffened and let out a yowl of agony. "Holy shit, that hurts!"

"Again. Knock off the obscenities and sit back down." She pushed on his shoulders, flattening him against the back of the chair. Then, with a look that told him not to argue, she pulled his chin down to open his mouth and swabbed the inflamed gum with a numbing agent. His eyes grew wide, then he relaxed and let out a sigh.

"Oh, yeah. That's better."

"I'm glad. But that's not going to last long and unless you want to have another flare-up, you'll stay where you are, Mr. Cannon. And trust me. The only thing I'll touch is your teeth." At his snarl, she dropped her instrument on the tray and toed the rolling stool, sliding away from him. "Of course, if you don't want my help, then all you have to do is leave. Either way, quit wasting my time and make up your mind."

He opened his mouth, probably ready to slam her again, and she prepared for a barrage of snide remarks. However, the howl he let out unnerved her more than anything he could have said. She lurched forward, half in an attempt to help him and half to get him to quiet down.

Pressing both hands to his chest—*muscles and muscles and more, oh, my*—to force him back in the seat, she saw something that was beyond comprehension. She had to be hallucinating. Or daydreaming again. Lowering her voice, she placed a palm on his cheek and whispered, "Is that a tear?"

For a second she thought he hadn't heard her. His eyes held her, amber flakes making them irresistible. His chest heaved under her hand, matching the quickened pace of her heart. Gently, he took her hand and covered it with his, then lifted his head to whisper in her ear.

"Get the hell off me."

She blinked, thrown by his soft tone with such harsh words, then yanked her hand away.

"Look, you're hurting and I can help." Crossing her arms over her chest, she tilted her head. "Will you let me help you or not?"

A clash of emotions warred across his face. "If this pain weren't so terrible, I wouldn't be anywhere near you."

"You already told me that." She closed her eyes, sighed, then shot him another exasperated look. "Let's be reasonable about this. You don't like me and I don't like you. But as a professional, I'm here to solve your problem." He had to be the most bullheaded man she'd ever met. "Come on, Mr. Cannon. Say it. Say you want my help."

His growl was more animal than man. "No, I don't want your help. But, damn it, I *need* your help. And it's Daniel."

"Want, need, it's all the same to me. So we're a go then?"

He gave a curt nod.

"Fine. Then sit back, refrain from howling or cursing, and let me do my job."

She turned her back on him, pretending to rearrange the instruments on the tray but mainly wanting to hide her grin.

Thirty minutes later, Daniel heaved a sigh of relief, not caring if Lauren and her assistant heard him. How had one small filling caused so much pain? Since it was his first filling, he hadn't known what a toothache felt like. Then to end up with a dentist who doubled as a hunter just made the whole thing that more painful. He opened wider, giving Marla more room to finish whatever the hell she was doing inside his mouth. Once again, she asked him to "Close tight, Mr. C" over the suction tube. His eyes, however, always came back to Lauren.

Damn, but she was beautiful. And sexy without being overtly sexy. Her curls fell forward to caress her cheek as she worked and he almost answered the impulse to twirl a strand around his finger. Her big soft eyes, hidden behind the ridiculous-looking safety glasses, highlighted her intelligence while giving her an innocent, almost doe-like appearance. That was enough to worry him, afraid his growing desire would soon attract attention. But then when she leaned closer and her breast brushed against his arm, he had to close his eyes and think about cauliflower to keep from grabbing her and placing her on top of his shaft. Thank God he hated cauliflower.

"I think that should do it. Take it easy with that tooth for an hour, okay?" Her stool squeaked as she rose.

Lauren's voice, now that it wasn't dripping with sarcasm or anger, was melodic, flowing. A voice any man would love to hear every morning for the rest of his life.

"Got it."

Damn it. Why did she have to be a hunter?

She hunched over the adjacent counter to write and his gaze fell to her plentiful backside filling out the white dentist coat. If she were pack, he wouldn't hesitate to take her. Fantasies of how he'd spank that lovely bottom, her pink flesh turning rosy, set his heart racing. Although the assistant took off the dental bib and muttered something about his leaving, he stayed where he was, enjoying the way Lauren eased from one foot to another, causing a corresponding sway of her ass. Damn, she was hot. Nicely curved in all the right places. And her scent was intoxicating.

He frowned, suddenly aware of a change. Although the smell had been faint, he remembered a hunter smell on her in the alley. Yet he couldn't detect the usual underlying stench of gun metal and sweat any longer. Now she smelled like flowers. Like lavender. He liked lavender.

"The numbness will wear off soon, Mr. Cannon. Bobbie at the front desk will check you out."

He had to force his eyes off Lauren to squint at Marla. "Okay. But I think the doctor and I need to have a private conversation first."

The curious assistant exchanged a look with Lauren who waved her off. "I'm not sure why you think so, but go ahead and take his chart to the front, Marla. I'll be ready for Mrs. Halloran in a minute."

Daniel hadn't planned it. In fact, he'd intended to tell her off, to warn her to stop hunting shifters, but the words never materialized. Instead, an intense heat ripped through him and he reached out, hooked the front of her blouse in his fingers and tugged her on top of him. Grabbing her by the back of the neck, he brought her mouth to his. Her hands clutched the front of his shirt, but she didn't push away. Hungry with the desire coursing through him, he thrust his tongue past her lips and found her delicious taste. She straddled him, her skirt hiking up to the vee between her legs. He ran his hand along her silky length until his fingertips pushed at the lacy thong under her professional attire. Groaning, he ripped the material aside and fondled the tender swell of her ass. She wiggled her bottom and he took that as a sign that she needed more.

Slipping his hand between her legs, he found her wet pussy and pinched her already hot nub between two of his fingers. Her wetness washed over his fingers, giving them the lubrication to plunge into her cave. His cock twitched in anticipation, making him yearn to replace fingers with shaft. Plunging in and out, he finger-fucked her, letting her choose the speed by how fast she moved her hips against his hand.

He'd known she was hot, but she was tight, too. Beyond tight. His dick strained against his slacks, wanting to dive deep inside her. Letting go of her neck, he waited for her to pull away, but she stayed. She wanted this as much as he did.

Lauren moaned into Daniel's mouth, then settled on top of him, her hot pussy pressing against the hard bulge in his pants. Her hands worked apart the buttons on his shirt, then swept under the fabric to rest on his pecs. Hating to do so, but wanting to get his pants undone, he let go of her and unzipped.

She arched her back, bringing her breasts to his face. His shaft free, he grabbed her breast and kneaded it, urging her to unbutton her blouse. "Come on, Lauren. I'm ready for you. Fuck me, hunter." His whisper was filled with lust.

Lauren moaned and tore off her jacket. Her breasts rubbed up and down against his face, driving him near the edge. He wanted to taste every inch of her, to rub her wetness on him. He yearned to slide his shaft deep inside her, to strain against her clenching walls, to feel his come shooting inside her. God, how he had to have this woman. Not as a plaything like the others and not as a diversion. She was more than a diversion. He sensed she could become an obsession. Warnings went off in the logical side of his mind, urging him to stay away, but his libido nixed those ideas, giving pure instinct control. He pulled her mouth to his again.

"Oh, my goodness. Lauren, what are you doing?"

"Wow, if that's how she fixes teeth, then let me hop in the chair."

Lauren stiffened, then scrambled off Daniel, clutching the lapels of her white coat together. She let out a small cry, her attention riveted to the hallway. He hurriedly zipped up, covering his protesting cock, and twisted around to find Tucker and Bobbie. Bobbie's gaping mouth hung open and Tucker's grin was wider than Daniel thought a mouth could stretch.

"Oh, my God, I-I—" Lauren tucked her head and put her back to the onlookers. "I can't believe you did that to me."

"*To* you? Like you couldn't have stopped me? Sweetheart, trust me, you were a willing participant. A very willing participant." Daniel raised a finger to Tucker, silencing him from making a snarky remark.

Lauren, her skin a mottled pink color, finally met his gaze. "You are a pig. No, a dog."

He couldn't help it. Lowering his eyebrows, he gave as good as he got. "No way, lady. I am no dog. I'm a wolf."

A mortified Lauren remained silent. Had she heard him? Bobbie, however, managed a quick recovery and, scooting past Daniel, took the distraught Lauren's hand. "Don't worry. The only people who know, who saw you, were me and Tucker." Leading the stunned dentist out of the room, Bobbie made a "phone me" gesture to Tucker, then blew him a kiss. Tucker pretended to catch the kiss.

His friend had apparently enjoyed their time together, much to Daniel's dismay. With his clothes straightened and his cock nearly back to normal pre-aroused size, Daniel trudged past him toward the reception area. "Not a word, man. Not a damn word." But Tucker's chuckle and question chased after him.

"Hey, wait a sec, Daniel. Did you call her a hunter?"

"This is not what I need after the day I've had." Lauren cradled her rifle in the crook of her arm and trudged alongside the other hunters. "I'd rather have curled up on my sofa with a good book."

John wrapped his arm around her. "Are you kidding me? A hunt always turns the day around for me. Besides, you're your own boss. You can do what you want. What could have made your day so bad?"

Like she did nothing but sit at her computer and watch funny videos on the Internet. Lauren started to tell him what had happened with Daniel Cannon, then thought better of it. He didn't have to know about her loss of self-control, or how she'd tried—and failed—to keep her thoughts off the ultra-sexy shifter for the rest of the day. She'd even called one of her male clients "Daniel" twice before Marla finally whispered, pointing out her error. "Oh, nothing special. The same old thing."

"That's what I'm talking about. How can your day have gone that badly when it's always the same each day?"

"Never mind." Lauren wasn't about to explain. What did it matter now anyway? She was fortunate that Bobbie and Daniel's friend were the only ones who'd witnessed her crazy sexual play with Mr. C. "John, have you ever met anyone named Cannon?"

John abruptly turned on her, his face scary in its intensity. "Where did you hear that name?" He took her arm, scaring her even more. "Tell me."

Lauren broke his hold and rubbed the fingerprints he'd left. "What the hell, John? What's with you?"

"Tell me where you heard that name."

"I have a new patient named Cannon and I couldn't shake the feeling that I'd heard the name before. Not that it's an unusual name or anything. Why are you acting so strange?" Had she said too much? No way would she tell him that her new patient was a shifter. Hell, she wished she'd kept quiet now.

"Is your patient a werewolf?"

Her breath hitched in her throat. "No. Of course not. Why?"

John's relief was evident in the tension flowing out of his body. "Good. There's a large shifter pack with alphas named Cannon. You've probably heard me mention them before."

Crap. Now she remembered where she'd heard the name. "Wow. Alphas, huh? More than one?"

"Yeah. Word has it that three brothers run the pack." John shrugged off his brusque attitude and returned to his normal demeanor, reassured that her patient wasn't a shifter. "So, you got a new victim, huh? Business must be good." John chuckled. "I don't know how you could do that."

She tensed. Had someone other than Bobbie and Tucker seen them and told John? "What do you mean? I haven't done anything—" She snapped her mouth closed, keeping "wrong" locked inside. Playing tongue-tag with another man was wrong. But playing Show and Feel with a werewolf was the ultimate betrayal to a hunter. Although she planned on dumping John, she had to keep playing the part of the faithful girlfriend for as long as she could. How else could she repay her debt to the werewolf she'd killed? "What are you talking about?"

"I'm talking about poking into people's mouths and messing with their teeth. Sheesh. I don't know how you do it. It's disgusting."

Relief washed over her, making her miss her footing. She fell into step behind him along with the other hunters and tried not to take what he'd said as a dig.

John held up his fist, signaling a full stop. He glanced around, his eyes scanning the dark alley. Throwing them a wicked grin, he put a finger to his lips and motioned for them to follow him.

Lauren dropped to the back of the group and switched her gun's safety to the off position. If she had to, she could cause a diversion from the rear easier than in the front of the group. Halfway through the alley, John went down on one knee, waited for them to do the same, then pointed to a dark corner where one building met another. She squinted into the blackness and hoped she wouldn't see what she feared most.

A small werewolf bent over the prone body of a homeless man. The man, wearing rags and shoes with holes in the bottoms, was either asleep or unconscious. His hand, however, firmly clutched an empty whiskey bottle.

The poor man had no idea that a werewolf stood over him. Could she wake the man up without scaring the werewolf into biting him? If so, would John and the other hunters hold their fire to keep from hitting the man? Inching forward, she touched John's shoulder to warn him against shooting while an innocent human was in the line of fire, but she was too late. A shot blasted the silence apart, jolting her and sending her stumbling to the side.

The werewolf's screech of pain echoed around the alley. Wounded, the shifter landed on its feet but couldn't stand. Blood ran down its hind leg. The werewolf tried to stumble away, but lost its footing and slumped to the ground.

"Gah! What the fuck is this? Help! Someone get this thing away from me!" The man dropped his bottle to scuttle away from the growling creature. The other men rushed to John, cheering and slapping him on the back. Two hunters helped the man to his feet and retrieved his bottle, then led him down the alley toward the street. Pointing his rifle at the snarling werewolf, John stood back, his chest out and pride oozing from him. "Say nighty-night, shifter."

Lauren slowly regained her feet, tears stinging the backs of her eyes. Why couldn't she have acted faster? Disappointment mingled with guilt, tearing a hole in her stomach. But now was not the time to wallow in her feelings. She gritted her teeth and took a few steps toward the sickening scene and the great white hunter holding court over his doting subjects.

"Wait! Don't shoot!"

John and the others pivoted to her without placing their backs to the werewolf. "What, Lauren?" His eyes flashed above his gleeful grin.

She clenched her fists, resisting the urge to slap the stupid smile off his face. "You promised me I could shoot first." Why hadn't she remembered to say that earlier? Had their discussion about Cannon thrown her off? But maybe she wasn't too late.

"I did? I don't remember that." John's brow knitted and she prayed he'd taken his dumb pill today. He wasn't the brightest man on the block and she could usually convince him to do what she wanted without him knowing she'd bamboozled him.

"Yeah, you did. Granted, you were drunk." She got the expected snickers from the group. "But a promise is a promise. And now you go and blow it."

"Seriously, babe, I don't think—"

"You don't think and I don't care, John. Just answer the question. Are you going to give me what I want or not?" She pouted in the way John couldn't resist.

Hoots and laughter surrounded her. "Yeah, John-boy. Give her what she wants or one of us might have to give it to her." John punched the loudmouthed hunter in the arm.

She strode to the group and positioned her body between John and the werewolf. "So the way I see it, you owe me the kill." She turned to face the werewolf and widened her eyes, hoping to alert him to her plan. "Let me be the one to put him down."

She watched the battle in John's eyes and knew how much he wanted to kill the shifter. But, with the heckling of the others, he had little choice but to give in.

"Fine. Just make it quick."

She blew him a kiss along with a sexy smile and waved everyone back. "You guys might want to step away. Uh, you know. I'm not that good a shot."

"Ain't that the truth?"

"Back up, dudes. You never know where her bullet will go."

At least her bumbling hunter act was still holding up. She almost shook her head in disbelief. Almost a year and they still hadn't caught on? Wow.

She stepped closer to the bleeding wolf. If he was as intelligent as she thought werewolves were, he'd catch on. At last his gaze met hers and she gave him a huge no-way-can-you-miss-this-signal wink. He blinked, then tilted his head. She wasn't sure he understood what she was about to do, but he knew she was up to something. She aimed a couple of inches above him, allowing for the discharge from the rifle to miss him.

Get ready, wolf. Taking a breath, she squeezed the trigger. The shot rang out and, after only a moment's hesitation, the werewolf yelped, jerked, then fell silent. Taking the dirty blanket the homeless man had used, she flung it over the body of the werewolf in feigned disgust. "Good riddance."

The hunters shouted and John lifted her to twirl her around. "You did it. You finally killed one."

"Finally? But I killed the female. Remember?"

"Oh, sure. Yeah. I forgot. Never mind." John released her and turned to his men. "Grab the carcass for Lauren, men."

"No!" Her shout stunned them into inaction, giving her a moment to think. "Uh, I mean, it's my kill, right? Then I decide what to do with the hide. And I've decided that I want to leave it right where it is."

"But why waste a hide you could hang on your wall?"

Lauren took John by the arm and led him away from the werewolf. "You know I don't like trophies on my walls. Besides, it's a scrawny thing." She adopted an evil expression. "And I want it to stay here. I want to imagine the rats having a feast. I think that's the best way to dispose of a vile creature like that. It's my kill, my decision, right?"

"Whatever you say, Lauren. I'm just so damn proud of you. Men, group together."

Lauren swallowed the bile in her throat and returned his hug but didn't follow the others as they circled around John. Instead, she paced over to the werewolf, then bent down and lifted a corner of the blanket, pretending to examine the head. "Stay still until we leave. If I can, I'll come back to help you," she whispered. She would've sworn the shifter's lips pulled back into a smile.

She turned to face the group and a movement above her brought her to a standstill. The beautiful black werewolf who'd escaped with the injured female werewolf crouched on the roof above her, his lips curled back to expose deadly fangs. She took a moment to appreciate his magnificent body, then abruptly dropped her eyes. If she drew attention to him, John would start the hunt again, thrilled by the chance to bag two in one night. The magnetic pull emanating from the mystical animal, however, drew her attention back, holding her spellbound. His eyes, brilliant amber, glowed against his black face and the dark night around him.

Lauren couldn't help but study him. His body was all muscles and packed action. This creature, this regal being, was more a true hunter than John could ever be. The werewolf tilted his head, reminding her of someone else. Suddenly, realization struck her, dazing her. *It's Daniel.* She smiled, a little embarrassed not to have made the connection before. She should have known. In either form, he had the same intensity, the same sexual pull, the same overpowering presence. She frowned. The same accusatory expression? But why was his fury focused on her and not the others? *Shit, he doesn't understand. He thinks I'm with them.*

Panic rolled through Lauren. She had to do something before John and the others noticed him. In the end, however, it was Daniel who drew their attention.

The werewolf on the roof turned toward the hunters and widened his snarl. A spine-tingling growl floated down to the hunters, and he crouched as though ready to attack.

Praying her idea would work, Lauren lifted her rifle, aimed and pulled the trigger.

Chapter Four

Daniel crouched, his body tightening but he ignored his first instinct to jump. The shot had come not from the hunters he faced, but from Lauren. Pain ripped through him, but it wasn't the pain from a gunshot wound. She'd shot at him and missed. This ache, however, was a different kind than that of any injury. This was a hurt of betrayal and disappointment. Granted, they weren't the best of friends to say the least, but he'd assumed they'd called an undeclared truce after their lip-lock. Or was that wishful thinking on his part? He scowled at her and sent a silent question. *"Why?"*

She opened her mouth as though to answer, then slammed it shut again. He gawked at her, the indecipherable glint in her eye drawing him in until, without warning, she raised her gun and pointed it at him—again. Growling, he didn't give her time to shoot and whirled away, rushing over the top of the building as several shots rang out.

He ran hard, outdistancing the hunters but unable to leave his own confused thoughts behind. The damned woman had tried to kill him. But why the hell would she help him with his toothache and get him hot and bothered, only to turn around and try to kill him? She'd known what he was and hadn't seemed to mind then. One minute she was sitting on top of him, her body pressed against his, and the next, she was trying to plug him full of holes. Were all human females so unpredictable?

Daniel slowed, morphing as he continued to trot toward his clothes hidden behind the Dumpster. Lauren, her back arched, her breasts thrust against his face, came front and center, blocking out the scene in the alley. He could still smell her scent: a light mixture of fragrances accented with lavender. He dragged in a long breath, remembering how his cock had come to full attention when she'd climbed on top of him. She'd rubbed against him, her heat matching the fire between his legs. His fingers had explored her cave, the grip of her walls, and he'd almost exploded with his lust. If he'd had more time, just a few minutes longer, he'd have slammed into her, bucking upward into her dripping snatch.

Yet, unlike the other women he'd had sex with since Torrie's death, he couldn't force Lauren from his mind. Instead, thoughts of her had invaded him often since their brief moment together, tearing at him, making him swell with desire. He'd gotten a taste of her, and now he wanted the full-course meal. He yearned to savor the silkiness of her skin, feel her pliant bottom in his hands again.

She's a hunter.

The admonition he'd tried so many times fell flat yet again. Somehow, her being a hunter hadn't deterred him from thinking about her, dreaming about her, wanting her. At least, not until now. She'd gone too far tonight, helping to kill a member of his pack, then shooting at him. A whimper filled his throat, but he forced it down.

Tyler was gone. Killed when he'd only wanted to help the homeless human. Tyler, whose heart was as big as the sky, lay dead in that alley. Daniel could almost see the hunters using his friend's lifeless body in a tug-of-war game, vying to take his pelt home and mount it on their wall. And Lauren was part of their group.

Daniel leaned against the dirty brick wall and hung his head. It was his fault. He shouldn't have let Tyler go into that alley alone. He should've ordered him to stop. But how could he have known the hunters would come out again tonight? They never went on hunts this close together.

He ground his teeth against the churning in his gut, dressed quickly, and decided it was time to take action. Instead of doing what the pack had always done—staying one step ahead of the hunters, hiding in the dark, avoiding confrontation whenever possible—the shifters needed to take a stand. The hunters would become the hunted.

Lauren's face, her brow furrowed, her eyes searching his, came to him, and the ache in his chest intensified. Snarling his determination, he shook as though physically ridding his body of her, freeing his mind of her face. He no longer had time for ridiculous yearnings. He had to act.

"I don't know why we didn't do this before now, Daniel." Tucker lifted his nose to sniff. Even in human form, their sense of smell was better than other humans.

"Shifters have always taken a defensive stance when it comes to hunters. For decades, we've countered their deliberate attempts to harm us with a peaceful, fight-only-when-forced-to-fight position. But those days are gone. We've lost too many good people." Good people like his Torrie and Tyler. Daniel breathed the dank air into his nostrils and attempted to separate the myriad of scents hanging over the human city into separate definable aromas. He closed his eyes and concentrated, refusing to give up after two hours of hunting. "Stay human until I tell you to change." Although they couldn't move as quickly and were less able to defend themselves, they also had less chance of getting shot.

"Maybe they aren't hunting tonight."

The disappointment in Tucker's voice bothered him. "Remember, we're not out to kill. We just want to wound them, to make them think twice. We aren't sinking to their murderous level. Not yet anyway."

"Shit."

Although Daniel sympathized with Tucker, he wasn't ready to step over the line. "And yeah, I'll bet my claws they're out tonight. I get the impression that this group gets together a lot more than the average hunter clan." A whiff of telltale gunmetal and human sweat tickled his nose. "We're in luck. They're close." He broke into a jog, knowing the six shifters would follow.

Daniel stayed cautious, moving noiselessly as he led his men toward their adversaries. At last, he could hear the hunters' voices, their laughter ringing in his sensitive hearing.

The hunters talked about the other night's hunt and the shifter they'd gunned down. Fury gnawed at Daniel and he silently damned them to hell. Crouching, he motioned for his friends to stay back, then peeked around the edge of the building. Five hunters stood in a loosely formed circle, their guns comfortably crooked in their arms or resting against a nearby Dumpster.

"I say we call it a night, John." A middle-aged hunter ran a hand over his weary face.

"Not yet. We haven't searched long enough." John scowled. "You getting too old for this, Walter? If so, you can always stay home and knit in your rocking chair."

Walter drew himself straighter and puffed out his chest. "No need to turn gray over me, John-boy. If your little girlie can keep up, I can. That is, *if* she can."

Does he mean Lauren? Daniel risked leaning farther out, but Lauren wasn't around. *Wait. His girlie?*

"Don't worry about her. She'll catch up with us. Anybody's boots can come untied." John glanced toward the other direction and shouted. "Yo, Lauren. Are you coming?"

Daniel crooked his neck, searching for her. Was Lauren dating the hunters' leader? He clenched his teeth and fought the revulsion constricting his throat.

Her reply echoed off the walls. "Yeah. I'm on my way. Hold up, will ya? I'll catch up."

"See? She's catching up. Let's get moving."

"But she wanted us to wait for her, John."

"I know, but she'll be fine on her own, Walter. Which is more than I can say for you." John slapped the older hunter's arm good-naturedly, hefted his rifle into the crook of his arm and guided them away.

"Why aren't we jumping them?"

Daniel resisted the urge to swat at Tucker's breath tickling his ear. Or was it his own irritation he wanted to swat? Why weren't they jumping the hunters? Instead, he hissed back, "I have my reasons. Take it easy."

"This doesn't make any sense. We need to—"

The thud of approaching footsteps hushed Tucker, and the other shifters crouched deeper into the darkness. Lauren burst into the alley, clutching her rifle, then slid to a stop. Slumping against the Dumpster, she lowered her gun to the ground, squatted and tugged at her laces.

"Oh, for Pete's sake. This frickin' thing won't stay tied." Oblivious to the shifters only feet away, she mumbled a few curse words and tightened her laces.

Daniel wasn't surprised to find Tucker and the other shifters smiling. But their smiles left him with an unfamiliar, uncomfortable sensation. "Don't think about it, men. We're after the whole group. Not one female. We'll skirt around her and catch up with the rest of them." Why didn't she hurry and leave? He scowled at her, wishing he could somehow warn her. Wondering why he wanted to warn her.

"Forget it, Daniel. Besides, she's asking for it. She helped kill Tyler, right? Then she deserves it just like the other scumbags do. Tyler should have his death avenged." Tucker had shucked his clothing and shifted, dropping to all fours and padding around the building's corner before Daniel knew it. The other men disrobed and transformed into their werewolf forms, giving Daniel no choice but to follow them.

Crouching into an attack position, Tucker and the others moved toward their prey and surrounded her. Hearing their low growls, she froze and slowly looked up, her features resonating shock. She was outnumbered and she knew it.

Daniel, still in human form, approached her and stood behind his friends. "Don't scream."

Her wide eyes locked on to him and he could hear the change in her breathing, her puffs coming out in short, harsh bursts with the quick rise and fall of her chest. He sniffed, catching her alarm, her surprise—and something else. The odd scent swept through his memory. She was panicked, yes, but more. She was aroused. And, startling him, he was aroused, too. Yet instead of pleasing him as he'd thought it should, her fear wiped away the attraction and made the whirlwind in his gut grow bigger, wilder. He didn't want her here, didn't want her afraid of him or his pack. Instead, he wanted her away from them, safe in his arms.

At last, she tore her gaze from his and looked at each werewolf, one at a time. She swallowed, her mouth working to form words. "W-what are you doing?" A giggle followed her question, out of place considering the trouble she was in.

He wanted to tell her that he'd keep her safe, but the others would never accept that. Hell, even he couldn't understand why he wanted to. When had she gained such control over his emotions? After one little grope session? Irritated, he forced his brain to counteract everything his body told him. "I would think a hunter would recognize a hunt."

She didn't react at first. Was she in shock? Then she blinked and tittered, realization lighting in her big eyes.

"That's right. I saw you on the hunt. The one where you shot at me. The one where you and your friends killed Tyler." At her wide eyes, he added, "Yeah, he had a name. We all have names and families. Does that make any difference? Does it make any difference that he was trying to help that homeless man? His name was Tyler and you murdered him."

Her mouth fell slack and her eyebrows dipped toward her upturned nose while those big brown eyes hooked him and dragged him inside her soul. Eyes that could rip out a man's heart and make it her own. He had to stop this fascination with this woman. Had to remember what she was. What she'd done. Who he was.

"No. That's wrong." She slapped a hand over her mouth, smothering yet another giggle.

What was all the giggling about? Did she think this was funny? He gritted his teeth, struggling to keep his annoyance in check. "Don't deny it. I was there, remember? I was the other wolf."

She nodded and stood up, slowly, deliberately not making any sudden moves. The tips of her mouth rose. "I know. I remember you."

"Then you can stop lying."

"I'm not lying." She took a step forward, making the werewolves growl. In a move he had to admire, she lifted her chin and faced them down. Deep breaths raised and lowered her chest, drawing his appreciation. She seemed calmer and, thankfully, she didn't giggle again. "I didn't shoot your friend. In fact, I helped him."

Daniel guffawed along with the half-growling laughs of his friends. "Wow. I have to give it to you. You've got balls." He scowled at her, no longer amused. "Oh, so you tried to help him? Like how you tried to help me by filling me with holes? Lady, you are one piece of work."

She didn't buckle under as he thought she would. Instead, she glared back at him, keeping her head high and ignoring the werewolves. The shifters closed the semicircle around her, tightening the trap. "You don't understand. If you'll give me a chance to explain, I'll—"

"You'll what? Tell us that you're working with P.E.T.A.?"

His sarcasm had the effect he'd wanted. The determination in her eyes flared. She definitely had nerve. Lots of nerve and sexy fire.

"Look, you jerkwad. If you'd open your ears instead of flapping your gums, you might learn something." She fisted her hands on her hips, challenging him. "Why don't you ask your other friend? She's alive, isn't she? Or at least she was when you two escaped." Her gaze flickered for a second, then fixed on him.

He had to give it to her. Bringing up Mysta was a gutsy move. "She's alive. No thanks to you."

"Damn it, you hardheaded hound. I was trying to help her when you came along and took over." Lauren waved her hand at the shifters. "I guess that's what you do best, huh? Take over? Play alpha?"

"I don't *play* at anything. And like I told you before, I am no dog. Too bad you didn't understand that or maybe you wouldn't be in the fix you're in now." Tucker shoulder-bumped Daniel, his subtle reminder that time was precious. "I know, Tucker. We need to get out of here before the others realize she hasn't caught up to them, then double back for her."

They needed to stick with the plan. A revised plan, however. Sure, he'd wanted to hurt a hunter tonight, but not this one. The command to attack Lauren stuck in his throat. "I don't want to risk the hunters coming back before we get this done." He silenced the pack's disagreement with one glare. "Take her back to the safe house."

They planned on kidnapping her? Lauren let out a giggle-turned-squeak and waited for whatever happened next. She backed away from the approaching werewolves to bump against the Dumpster.

Daniel's friends broke the ring to pace in front of her, never taking their eyes from her. She couldn't understand everything they said, but his command had thrown them as much as it had her. Suddenly, the white werewolf beside him changed, his legs elongating, his fur melting away, his face transforming into the man who'd accompanied Daniel to the dental office. A very nude man.

She dropped her gaze to the ground, looking away from his maleness. "You're kidnapping me?" No, this couldn't happen. "Seriously?"

Daniel's hand on her arm brought her head up and she stared straight into his emotionless face. Her heart pounded, her pulse raced. His eyes drew her inside, showing her the animal within him and drawing her down until she was sure she could feel his heart beating along with hers.

"Better to kidnap you than to kill you. Don't you think?" His low voice rippled through her, shockwaves of warm, liquid sex appeal. For a second, she forgot the werewolves, forgot the hunters, even forgot to breathe.

He blinked, breaking the trance he'd put her in. "Right now I'm not so sure." She giggled. Had he almost smiled? The brief flash of humor disappeared before she could catch it and keep it with her.

"Let's go." His hold on her tightened, shooting pain up her arm as he dragged her with him. The werewolves turned the corner and changed, then dressed with clothes hidden in a dark corner. Within seconds, they pushed on, forming a wall around her, like a rock star escorted off stage by security guards. However, she felt anything except safe.

She should scream. Maybe if she did, John and the others might hear her. Yet if she did, if she drew the hunters back, then the shifters could get hurt—or worse. Glancing at Daniel's hand on her arm, she wondered if his touch had somehow stolen her voice. In fact, every time she glanced at him, more of her panic eased away. He was so handsome, so masterful. She watched the others and couldn't help but compare them to him. Tucker may have him outdone in size, but Daniel exuded the personal power of a born leader. She hurried, keeping pace with his purposeful strides. Although it didn't make sense, having him close to her helped keep the terror at bay. If she kept near Daniel somehow she'd get through this.

By the time they made it to the black SUV, her chance to escape was gone. Tucker opened the door, then reached for her.

Daniel grabbed her, making her the meat in a shifter sandwich. She wanted to giggle at the idea.

Their bodies, those of hardened warriors, pushed against either side of her. She tucked her head, unsure of where to look. If she turned either way, her breasts would brush against a chest. Heat flashed through her and she struggled not to face either man. She was a captive, and yet all she could think about was sex. What the hell was wrong with her? Although perhaps thinking about sex was better than giggling at them again.

"Nothing happens to her, Tucker, got it? Take her to the house and keep her safe. I'll take care of her later."

He was leaving her alone with the pack? Fear burst to life again. "No, Daniel. Don't leave me alone…" The unspoken *with them* floated in the air. He stared pointedly at her hand on his arm. She yanked it away and tried to cover her embarrassment. "I mean, how do you know they won't do something to me when you're not around?"

"You have nothing to worry about." Daniel lifted his hand, nearly caressing her cheek, then dropped it. "They'll do as I say." He nodded, indicating the back seat. "Get in."

Tucker moved out of the way, allowing her to slide into the back seat. He followed her and she scooted to the other side of the vehicle, wanting to stay as far from him as possible.

"To the house, Luca."

The driver nodded and started the car. Lauren twisted to stare out the back window, hoping to implore Daniel to come with them. He stood on the street corner, his head cocked to the side, reminding her of the beautiful black werewolf, and lifted his hand to wave. Almost as though ashamed of the action, he dropped his hand quickly and strode back into the dark alley.

"Uh-hem." Tucker tipped his head toward the front of the car. "Relax. It's only a short drive."

Lauren inched closer to the door and placed her hand on the door handle. How had this happened to her? And more to the point, how was she going to save herself? Did she dare jump from the moving car? One look at the locked door shattered that idea. She sneaked a peek at Tucker who shot her another—*hungry?*—grin. Stifling a titter, she closed her eyes and sent a silent message to the one man who could help her—Daniel. It didn't make sense. John was the one who would help her, but she felt safer with Daniel around and she wasn't about to question her instinct. At least not yet.

The vehicle screeched to a stop a short time later. Dreading what she might see, Lauren peeked through the tinted window and blinked. An ornate metal gate swung open and the SUV continued down a long winding driveway lined on each side by beautifully manicured lawns and topiary. The grounds, however, were insignificant frames to the magnificent mansion at the end of the circular drive. Stately white columns stood guard at the front of the house while luscious greenery decorated its pristine white walls. Lights sparkled along the drive, a precursor to the brilliance of the lights burning brightly inside.

"Ah, home, sweet home."

"Are you kidding me?" Lauren followed Tucker out of the car and lifted her gaze to the top of marbled steps leading to the elaborately carved front doors. "This is a shifter house?"

"You were expecting something less? Maybe an oversized dog house?"

Tucker's grin mocked her, rushing the heat of her embarrassment into her cheeks. "I, uh, I don't know what I expected. Just not this."

"Yeah, it's pretty spiffy, huh?" Tucker waved his hand, motioning for her to start up the steps. "After you, m'lady."

Lauren led the way, only now noticing the men and women who stood guard around the house and yard. "Are you expecting a war?" She heard his growl and tried not to let it bother her—much.

"We're always at war. Or maybe I should say we're always the targets of a war by you hunters."

Moving through the intricately carved doors opened by two burly men, Lauren entered the grand foyer and couldn't keep from gawking. The largest chandelier she'd ever seen held court over the marbled entrance, casting glittering prisms of light to the three wide hallways and a winding mahogany staircase leading to the second story. A large room, beautifully decorated, waited to the left.

"This way."

She hesitated, wishing she could study the paintings and sculptures lining the foyer, then followed Tucker into the nearest hallway. "Is this where the pack takes all its prisoners?"

Tucker's engaging laugh would be contagious under different circumstances. "I guess so. Considering you're the first hunter we've ever brought here."

"So you've never had a hun—uh, human here?" Photographs of striking men and women of various time periods watched her as she doubled her pace to stay behind the large shifter. Without warning, he came up short and she had to sidestep to keep from bumping into him.

"I didn't say that." Tucker opened a door, allowing her to enter ahead of him. "Humans, yes. Hunters, no."

The room was twice the size of her apartment. Feeling like a princess—albeit a captive one—Lauren glided around the room, running her hand over the luxurious textures of the bedspread and loveseats. She continued examining the beautiful room, her senses taking in the rich and the subtle, yet colorful details. "Wow. I never knew shifters lived like this. I mean, I thought only royalty and movie stars lived in places this grand."

"I think there's a lot of things you don't know about us."

Her fingers slid over the marbled nightstand next to the king-sized bed and fanned along the heavy curtains on the window. What the hell? Pulling the draperies aside, she touched the glass almost as though she could wrap her fingers around the iron bars on the other side. Her heart plummeted. "Bars on the windows? Do you guys kidnap a lot of people?" She turned to find Tucker watching her. "Or are the bars to keep others out?"

"You're the first captive. We do, however, sometimes need a room where we can confine a new and uncontrolled werewolf."

She couldn't help but bait him. "You mean you use this room as a cage?"

He coughed, ignoring her jab, and added in a subdued tone, "So, how's your friend?"

"My friend?"

"You know. The cute one at the front desk of your office."

If she didn't know better, she'd swear he was blushing. "Do you mean Bobbie?"

His grin told the whole story. The man—the werewolf—was smitten with her best friend. She turned away to hide her smile.

"Yeah. Bobbie."

"She's good. Uh, she was kind of upset that you didn't leave a phone number. You know, for our records. Maybe you should give her a call."

"So you're playing matchmaker now?"

Lauren turned toward the sound of the voice. Daniel stood in the doorway, his face an inscrutable mask, his eyes boring holes into her soul.

What was it about this guy that unnerved her? She frowned as the real question took its place. What was it about this guy that turned her on? Granted he was handsome, but she'd known other handsome men. She slid her gaze down his hard-toned body. No, this was more than simple physical attraction. "Where did Tucker go?"

The space between his thick eyebrows puckered. "Tucker had other matters to attend to. More important than discussing your friend." He closed the door behind him. "I want answers."

"Oh, well, I thought they'd make a cute couple. Bobbie's into big—"

"You know what I'm talking about."

Lauren did, but she didn't relish trying to convince him of her innocence. "I already told you. I was helping your friend. Both of your friends." She had to make him understand. Not only to save herself, but having him believe her seemed important. "Don't you remember that first time I saw you? When the female was trapped and then you showed up? You both got away that night." She clasped her hands, zeroed in on him and urged him to hear the truth in her voice. "Both of you got away because I helped you."

"We got away on our own accord. I don't remember you stopping the other hunters. In fact, you should be thanking Mysta and me for not harming you. And now I'm supposed to believe you were trying to help Tyler, too? Is that the load of crap you're trying to feed me?"

Sometimes a head was just too hard to knock any sense into it. But she'd sure like to try knocking some sense into his hard head. "I'm not feeding you anything but the truth. If you're too bull-headed to know it, then there's not much I can do." She puffed out an exasperated sigh and took a different approach. Maybe if she could get him to concentrate on the first werewolf she'd managed to help, he'd listen to her explanation about Tyler. "How is your female friend? She was wounded, but I wasn't sure how badly. If you'll talk to her, she can tell you that I wasn't going to kill her. In fact, I put my gun on the ground and told her as much. How many hunters would do that with a cornered werewolf?"

He snorted, his derision rankling her nerves. "I wish I could ask her. Unfortunately, she hasn't come round yet, so I guess I'll have to get the answer on my own." His features hardened. "One way or another."

Chapter Five

Daniel studied Lauren, trying to detect any hint of deception and finding none. Even more surprising, she appeared genuinely concerned about the injured she-wolf's welfare. "I would've thought you'd be happy about Mysta's condition."

Lauren collapsed on the edge of the bed and a tear traced a path down her cheek. Was this a trick? His usual skepticism warned him to beware, but the way she hugged herself as though she were suddenly chilled had the ring of truth.

She took a shaky breath and exhaled, long and slow. "I am so sorry. I thought she was okay. Or at least, I'd hoped she would be. Damn it." She wiped away another tear and lowered her head. "I thought I'd helped her."

Was she telling the truth? Daniel moved to stand in front of the confusing hunter. "What do you mean?" She shook her head, unable or unwilling to answer. Instead of demanding a response, he sat beside her, his arm brushing hers. "How did you try to help?"

Not that he'd believe anything she said. He couldn't believe a hunter. Could he?

"I've tried to tell you. I'm not a hunter anymore. I used to be, but I'm not anymore."

"Then why are you with them? Why do you go on hunts? Why did you help kill Tyler?" She was either telling the truth or she was one helluva liar. But the problem remained. How could he know which one she was?

"I didn't kill Tyler."

He choked back his anger. "That still doesn't change the fact that you're one of them. That you cornered him just like all the others did. Maybe you didn't pull the trigger, but you're just as guilty." He pulled his lips back into a snarl. "So you're saying you didn't shoot him?"

"No. It's complicated. I may have fired a shot, but I didn't hurt him."

"Come on. What are you trying to pull?" She wasn't making any sense which probably meant she was lying again. Probably? No, no doubt about it.

"I used blanks."

"Blanks? But he wasn't moving." Could he believe this wild tale? Part of him sprang to alertness, ready to catch any sign that she was telling the truth, hoping she was telling the truth.

"John shot him first. But I convinced him to let me finish him off. Fortunately, Tyler understood and played dead when I shot him with blank bullets." Her eyes widened into pools of concern. "But I couldn't get back to him later to help. Didn't he make it back to the pack?"

"No."

If what she'd said was true, then Tyler would've made it to help. Some way, somehow. The fact that he hadn't shown up made her story more difficult to believe. Daniel's stomach churned as the knowledge of what he wanted to believe and what was true clashed.

She sighed and leaned against him. The touch of her against him sent shockwaves into his arm to streak down to his groin. Instantly, his cock awakened and grew. He gritted his teeth, telling himself to move away, but his body wouldn't listen. Instead, he reached out and placed his palm over her hand. At first she tensed, then rested more of her weight against him and laid her head on his shoulder.

"I need to make amends." She sniffed and wiped her nose with the back of her hand. "I need to help. To make up for the time when I did hunt."

"I don't understand." Her warmth seeped into him, lessening the anger he held for her. He drew in her heady scent, a scent filled with lavender. "Talk to me."

He wanted her to do more than talk. He wanted her to kiss him. He wanted to see her rock underneath him. To hear her cry out his name in the heat of passion.

The ache in his stomach churned, taking his lust to a higher level. Unsettled, yet not surprised at the idea, he wrapped his arm around her, enveloping her, giving her his strength. *Screw talking. I have to have her.* The force of his desire struck him hard, making him thankful he was sitting down.

"I'm a traitor." She laughed, a bitter, sad sound. "At least that's what John and the other hunters would call me." At last she lifted her head.

His heart beat faster, louder. He could live a lifetime looking into those eyes. But could he ever trust her? Could he believe the story she was telling him? If it were only his life that he risked, he'd gladly take the chance. But he had the pack to consider. "Go on." She placed her hand on his leg, making him wish she'd move it a few inches closer to his crotch.

"I sabotage the hunts. Whenever we corner a shifter, I cause a diversion and give the shifter a chance to escape. Or at least, I try to."

If only he could read her mind. Then he'd know the truth. Yet, he couldn't help but think that a small part of him had already made the decision to trust her. "So that's what you did that first night I saw you? The night you were with Mysta?"

"Yes. I faked an injury during the hunt, distracting the men. She got away, but I knew she was hurt so I came back later, hoping I'd find her."

A curl had fallen over one eye and he couldn't resist brushing it back, enjoying the slide of the silky strand over his finger. "And when I found you and Mysta?"

"I was getting her to trust me. Or at least I was trying to. If I'd succeeded, I could've found one of her kind—your kind—to get her to safety."

Maybe he could believe her. After all, he did remember her gun lying on the ground. If she'd wanted to kill the she-shifter, she could have done so easily enough. Damn, how he wanted to believe her. He wanted to think she was just another human and not a hunter. A very sexy, desirable human female he could take to his bed. His gaze swept over her form, lingering on the rounded curves of her breasts, then her hips. But he had to keep his wits. "And that's what happened in the alley with the homeless man?"

She shook her head, perhaps denying his accusation. "I swear I did help Tyler. But I don't know what happened after we left him there. I'm sorry you don't believe me, but I understand why."

"So you're sticking to your story?" He had to hear her answer. Had to hear her say it again. Maybe, if she did, he could believe her. He prayed to hear the answer he wanted.

"Yes, I pulled the trigger and shot blanks that I'd substituted for the real bullets. If I really killed Tyler, then why did I shoot over your head? I had a clear shot at you."

"Over my head, huh? It sure felt close enough to me." But then her shot hadn't hit him, had it? She could've shot wide.

"I have to make it look good or I'd get in trouble."

She ran her tongue over her lips. The action, so simple yet so sensual tore apart the last shred of his resolve. Groaning, he crushed his mouth to hers and pushed her back against the bed. She moaned, enveloping him in her arms. He kept her mouth on his and pushed his tongue inside. Her juices, so sweet, so different than any he'd ever tasted, tantalized his tongue, filled his mouth. This was more than a mere kiss. This was a promise of more to come.

Daniel groaned and laid his full length on top of her, loving how she felt underneath him. How long had it been since he'd had a woman in this position, her face so close to his? He knew the answer and shoved the thought away.

He wanted to kiss her lips, see her eyes when she came. She whimpered, driving his need higher. He pushed her arms above her head and held her two wrists with one hand. She struggled, enough to drive him crazy with hunger but not enough to get free. She didn't want freedom. He knew that as well as he knew how much he wanted her.

Daniel slid his tongue along her neck, traveling up the soft, scented skin until he reached her ear. Nibbling at her flesh, he slipped his fingers under the neckline of her shirt and tore it away. She gasped, bringing his gaze to her face. No fear lingered there. Instead, lust, pure and beautiful, raged in her eyes. He unbuckled her jeans, thrilling when she lifted her hips to give him room to push them down her sleek legs. Her thong followed to puddle with her jeans around her ankles. She toed off her shoes, then stepped out of her clothes as she tugged at his shirt to bring it over his head. His jeans were on the floor in seconds.

Her smile was full of knowing and power.

Daniel paused for a moment and wondered if she was actually the one in control. But his inner animal, rearing to the surface, didn't care. Not as long as he could take her. And he could. She waited, arms pinned above her head, for him to do what he wished with her.

He placed his hand on her shoulder, then let it glide along her arm, over the curve of the side of her breast, then back to cup her breast. Her tongue peeked between her lips and he flicked his tongue after hers, trying to catch it. He missed, then kept going, taking a long, torturous route to her nipple. Tugging the taut bud into his mouth, he sucked, tasting the sweetness of her against his tongue.

One wetness drove him to seek the other wetness between her legs. He palmed her mons, using his fingertips to coax the outer lips of her pussy. She opened for him, willingly, ready for his growing shaft, making yet another promise.

A shudder rippled through him, unnerving him in its intensity. No woman had made him feel this wild in human form. The truth froze him, taking his mouth away from his prize. But the woman beneath him wasn't ready to let him go. Grabbing him by the hair, she yanked him back to her, pressing her breasts and her lips against him. He moaned and gave in to her demands.

Their bodies melted together, leaving no room. He lay between her legs, opening her wider to rub against her pussy. Taking her bottom, he spread her cheeks, running his fingers in the warm cleft.

Daniel traced a trail with his tongue down her neck, nipping as he went along, each nip harder than the last. Lauren tilted her head, showing him her throat. He answered with a low rumble that said nothing but meant everything. The sound, so primal, drew his emotions out of hiding, opening the way to the wolf within him. She clutched him, her urgency building his.

Arching her back, she gave his mouth her breast again. Soft murmurs drifted to his ears, sweet words urging him to go farther, take more. He rolled his tongue over her nipple and rubbed her pussy, sinking his finger into her cave. Daniel suckled her nipple harder, driving his finger deeper until she gasped and squirmed.

He entered her, adding another finger to shove into her, out of her, covered with her sticky moistness. Continuing the delicious torment, he bore down on her nipple and tugged it into his mouth. She cried out, struggled to break free of his hold, but he held on. He wouldn't take her by force, but he sensed her struggles were not in earnest. Raking his tongue over her peaked bud, around the sides and back to nibble at its tip, he continued to plunge his fingers into her time and again, massaging the sensitive skin within.

"Please."

Whether her plea was to let her go or to continue making love to her, he didn't know. Determined to find out, he released her wrists and lifted off her. Her eyes, sparkling with desire, met his and he had his answer.

Daniel licked his lips, kissed her quickly on hers and feathered kisses along the slope of her neck. He kept going, following the swells and valleys of her body, along the soft mound of her stomach, teasing her, building his anticipation along with hers.

He was ready to experience his tongue on another part of her body. "Spread wider."

She obeyed him. Thrilled with her easy acquiescence, he slid his tongue in the crease between her leg and her crotch. She jumped, tensing as he nibbled and sucked his way to her womanly part. He took his time, moving slowly over the sensitive skin, licking, sucking, creeping closer.

She groaned, making a sound very similar to a growl. Daniel ran his hands up the insides of her legs, then pressed his thumbs at the creases. She jerked again, pleasing him, letting him know that she wasn't used to being touched so intimately. With a moan that started deep in his chest, he placed an arm under each leg, gripped her buttocks and brought her pussy to him.

She could never be too close. Not with the yearning he had. He ached to be inside her. To be a part of her. To have everything about her.

Daniel parted her sex lips and raked his tongue over the heightened nub. She gasped, yet instead of trying to wiggle away, she reached out for him. He devoured her, changing her sighs into soft mews of delight. He licked her harder and harder until shudders stormed through her body. She burst open again, quivering under his touch, tremors shaking her from head to toe. Her body, so slick, readied for him.

Pushing up, he placed his body over hers and sought her eyes, telling her this was her last chance to stop him. *If* he could stop.

What he saw made him take her legs and drape them around his waist. Guiding his shaft, he edged into her, again waiting for her to deny him. She didn't and the last bit of restraint vanished. She moaned, spreading her legs wider. He slipped into her welcoming heat, shoving as far inside her as he could. Her resulting moan encouraged him and he moved into her body, rocked her, pumping into her again and again. Together their bodies worked as one, joined together for one primal purpose.

He gripped her ass, increased his speed to go faster, deeper, longer. Placing a hand on her fuzzy patch, he opened the folds and tortured her swollen pussy. His gaze fell to her breast, bumping back and forth, until he latched on to her nipple.

For every move he made, she matched it. For every ounce of power he used, she equaled it.

Sensation after sensation assaulted him, making him feel as he hadn't felt since Torrie's death. This was something more. Something wilder, hotter, stronger.

The animal inside him roared to life, howled for the renewal of his manhood. The volcano grew hotter, boiling to the top until, at last, the end was near.

Slamming into her, Daniel groaned and unleashed the power of his release. He shook, wave after heat wave blazing from his toes to his head. The climatic surge called for the inner wolf's freedom, but he held on. To let the beast run wild, to sink his fangs into her, would mean accepting the female hunter as his mate. Instead, he held on, fighting to keep that last level of control. His release flushed outward, threatening to shatter his grip on that control and he turned his face away from her.

Needing to give his inner wolf a taste of freedom, he partially shifted, bringing out his fangs and claws. He dug his claws into the pillow next to him, tearing it to shreds.

Lauren grabbed him, held him to her so that her spasms met his. His body relaxed a little more with each subsequent wave. At last, he fell to the side, panting as his claws and teeth retracted, unthinking, uncaring what happened next.

Unlike previous sexual encounters, he'd had no thought of Torrie to distance him from the woman beside him. Instead, he rolled onto his side to place a kiss of thanks on her collarbone.

"I can't believe this. That was..." Daniel played with one of those wild curls, a soft smile lifting the corners of his mouth.

"What you had planned all along?"

Is that what she thought of him? Her slight smile, however, told him the truth. "I'm assuming you're kidding, right?"

She snuggled against him and skimmed a finger down the valley between his pecs. "I am. Still, I'm thinking that taking a hunter—a former hunter—to bed wasn't an easy thing for you to do."

She had a point. "Well, since someone in the pack probably heard us, I'm going to have some explaining to do. But, if you're telling the truth, it's not like you've actually killed one of us. Right?"

His good mood faded quickly with each second it took her to respond. He'd tried to accept her story but now, with her silence, the doubts crept back in. Moving to lie on his side, he squinted at her, and struggled to keep the hole in his gut from growing. "That's right, isn't it? Since you say you didn't kill Tyler, then you've never actually killed a shifter?"

Why wouldn't she look at him? Taking her chin, he forced her to face him. "You've never killed. Tell me I'm right."

Moisture filled her eyes along with the truth. Stunned, he pushed away from her, and flung his body out of the bed, needing time to gather his wits. He dressed with his back to her, then slowly faced her and found her, her knees snug to her chest, her head down. "You've killed."

"No."

The one word he desperately needed to hear was barely more than a whisper. "No?" Until then, he hadn't realized that his breathing had gone shallow. "Then you haven't?" He needed her to say it again, ached to hear her say the words.

"I meant I couldn't tell you that. But I've only shot one."

Only one? She said that as though killing one was better than killing several. That only one didn't count. Daniel snarled, the growl in his throat sifting through clenched fangs. "When? Tell me when and where you killed."

Why it mattered, he didn't know. But it did matter. An inner warning signal said it mattered a lot.

"It was a year ago. On one of my first hunts. I shot at the werewolf along with everyone else." She looked at him, torture dulling her eyes, slumping her body. "I didn't know any better then. I believed what my boyfriend had told me. That shifters are animals, evil creatures that we have to eradicate."

She'd killed a shifter a year ago? Torrie's murder happened a year ago. "When? What month did this happen? Where did this happen?"

His jaw hurt from grinding his teeth. He could barely move his neck from the tension taking up residence there, but he had to know.

"What does it matter when or where?" She reached out to him. "I'm not the same person I was back then, Daniel. I know better now. I understand—"

"Tell me when and where!" His shout startled her, frightened her, but he didn't care. He cared about nothing except her answers. "Was the shifter male or female?"

Hurt and scared, she nonetheless defiantly stuck out her chin. "The hunt was last fall. Here in the city. It was a female."

He gripped the back of a nearby wingback chair. "What happened to the body? Did one of your friends get rid of her?" He couldn't bring himself to ask if the body had been dumped in the woods. Especially if her answer confirmed his worst fear.

"No one wanted the body. It was too badly disfigured." She choked back a sob. "John, the leader of our group, took the body to the woods and left it there."

"Left *her* there. Quit calling her an 'it'. She wasn't an 'it'."

She winced, then nodded. "I'm sorry. You're right, of course. I didn't mean to imply any differently."

Daniel pushed the words past his coarse throat. "Tell me what she looked like."

His body shivered as though he'd walked over Torrie's grave, but he held on, hoping that he was wrong. He willed her to tell him what he wanted to hear. To tell him that it had been a different shifter. That she wasn't the hunter who'd killed Torrie.

"She was beautiful with brown fur. I remember she had a white paw." Lauren pulled the bedspread higher. "She was amazing and powerful, and I couldn't believe I'd destroyed her."

The horror struck Daniel, wiping strength from him. The world around him spun, taking him to another time, another day. He saw Torrie at his feet, cold and lifeless, her blood staining the grass. Pain ripped through him as it had that day and he groaned, unable to stop its flight. He closed his eyes, willing the image to leave him in peace, forcing the agony out of his body. At last, it did, leaving him shaken and breathless.

The woman he had taken to bed, the woman he liked, was the hunter who had killed his mate. Lauren had murdered his Torrie. The room closed in on Daniel to squeeze the air from him, stripping him of reason, leaving only his instincts. He reached out, his fury compelling him to kill her. She misinterpreted the gesture as reaching out to comfort her and his growl swept from his gut to strangle the air in his throat. He saw his hands opening before him, ready to encircle her neck, ready to press his thumbs to her throat, to choke the life from her.

"Daniel? Are you all right?"

His gaze met hers and held. Without meaning to, he searched her eyes and was stunned at what he found. A sorrow deeper than he'd thought possible floated just below the surface, tearing away his fury. No evil murderer resided behind those eyes. No brutal killer lurked in those velvet pools. What he found was Lauren, open, honest and concerned. Making an unrecognizable sound, he wrenched his hands away from her, then whirled and rushed from the room.

Lauren sat on the edge of the bed, trying to see through the closed door. Daniel had departed two days earlier, his features a work in agony and rage. For a moment, she'd thought he would turn that anger on her. Then, almost as suddenly as it had appeared, the anger was gone. He'd dashed out of the room before she'd had a chance to find out what had happened. Would he ever return? Since then, the only person she'd seen was the guard who'd brought her new clothes and food.

"Where are you, Daniel?"

She would've gone after him if the guard outside her room had allowed it. She wanted to explain further, to make him understand that the werewolf she'd helped slay was her first and only kill. He had to know that she had changed that night, that her goal was to help his people. Even if it meant putting her own life in jeopardy.

She touched her fingertips to her lips, remembering how they'd felt after he'd kissed her. Who would have believed that she'd have sex with a shifter? And she was fairly certain he hadn't planned on having sex either. But she was happy that they had. Lying on the bed, she closed her eyes and relived the experience.

Daniel had treated her like no other man ever had. He'd taken her to the brink, almost to the edge of force, yet still leaving her with the right to refuse him. His lovemaking had left her breathless yet full of vitality. His masculinity had given her shivers, making her feel like a damsel in distress and he the valiant knight who rescued her then claimed her for his own. His lovemaking was more than practiced sexual moves. He was powerful yet gentle, arousing her with his hands, his mouth, his tongue. She couldn't help but compare him to John and found John's horny escapades unemotional, almost impersonal. If she could choose between them, she would take Daniel without thinking twice about it.

Lauren shot up, swinging her legs to the floor. She'd choose Daniel, the werewolf alpha, over John, her boyfriend? She shook her head, wondering at her thoughts. Although she planned on breaking up with John, how could she choose a shifter over a human male? The idea was ridiculous. Especially when Daniel had left her so abruptly, so strangely. Sure, he wanted her body, but what about everything else she had to offer? Would he ever want her heart? Could she ever give her heart to him?

Daniel Cannon was everything she'd always hungered for in a man: sexy, courageous, confident and a natural leader. He was the type who made women's heads turn and men wish they were more like him. Yet she could sense another side to him, a softer side that was so rare. She heard it in the inflection of his tone when he asked her questions. That softer side was what she ached for in her life.

But he's a werewolf.

Maybe if she reminded herself enough, she would stop thinking of him in such attractive terms. She paced to the door, reached for the doorknob and steeled herself for whatever might happen next. Gripping the handle, she wiggled the knob and, to no surprise, found the door locked. She was the pack's prisoner. Yet instead of alarm creeping up her spine, a nervous excitement took its place. She wasn't simply the pack's prisoner. She was *his* prisoner. And although she wouldn't have admitted it out loud, she couldn't help but get excited at the prospect. What would being Daniel's prisoner be like? Would it mean crazy wild sex? Consensual and otherwise? *God, I hope so.*

Shocked at her brazenness, Lauren wiggled the knob again. She had to try to escape. If only to save herself from her own wanton thoughts, thoughts that would place her in more peril than she was already in. Once he was finished with her sexually, what would he do to her? Suddenly, she didn't want to stick around and find out.

"If only they hadn't taken my cell phone away," she murmured.

The door opening sent her scurrying to the opposite side of the room. Tucker, the tall white-haired god of the pack, closed the door behind him and winked. "Hey, darlin'. I thought I'd better check on you. To make sure everyone's treatin' you right."

She inhaled, suddenly aware that sex, especially nonconsensual sex, could happen with shifters other than Daniel. In fact, she was at the mercy of the entire pack. Drawing herself as tall as she could, she plastered on a brave face and sent him an unspoken warning not to try anything. "I demand you let me go."

His laughter echoed around the room. "You demand, huh? Wow, that's a good one."

She tried not to let him see how flustered she was. Her meanest face hadn't fazed him. "That's right. Let me go now and we'll call it a truce."

"Darlin', shifters don't make truces with hunters." He moved closer, eating up the distance before she knew he'd started walking.

Lauren placed her back against the wall and bit the inside of her cheek to keep from screaming. Tucker brought his face, emotionless yet with amber eyes flashing, within an inch of hers.

"They won't stop until they find me, you know. And when they do, they'll, they'll…" What would John and the others do? Fight an entire army of shifters? Hell, she doubted John would even look for her. He probably thought she'd given up on the hunt and gone home.

"Are you talking about your hunter friends, darlin'? And your boyfriend, the leader? Either way, we've taken care of that." He rested his hands beside her head, trapping her.

What had they done? Had they found John and the others and killed them?

Tucker brought out his claws, his eyes growing a darker gold. Growling, he ran a claw down her cheek, pressing hard enough for her to feel the sharpness of his nail, but not hard enough to break the skin. "Don't worry, darlin'. You're safe with me." His gaze slid down, then back up, pausing on the rise and fall of her chest.

"Daniel won't like it if you hurt me." Lauren wasn't sure why she'd blurted it out, but she had to hope Tucker believed her. His eyes widened, then narrowed, unnerving her.

"Is that right? So you and Daniel are what? Buddies now?" His gaze landed on her chest. "Bosom buddies maybe?"

She didn't respond, letting him interpret her silence any way he wanted. Besides, how could she answer when she didn't know what Daniel thought of her?

"Hmm. That's interesting. I'm gonna have to speak to Daniel about you, aren't I?"

Tucker pushed away and strode to the door, leaving her shaking and breathless. She stumbled to the bed, falling on it before her knees gave out.

"What the hell am I going to do?"

"Daniel. We need to talk."

Tucker's appearance at the door to his study was expected. Still, he wasn't ready for the discussion he knew was ahead. Daniel held up one finger, motioning Tucker to remain silent until he'd finished his phone conversation. This was one conversation that came before anything else.

"Lance, your Uncle Jason is right. You can't throw a bee's nest at your sister and expect not to get into trouble. Even if the bees were gone." He hoped his son couldn't hear the smile in his tone. "I don't care what Tracey did to provoke you." He listened a little longer, letting the young boy vent his frustration. "Okay, Lance, I've heard enough. I realize it's hard, but I know you can handle whatever your uncle decides. I'm proud of you." He laughed at his son's response. "No, not because you hurled the nest at Tracey, but because you're going to take your punishment like a real alpha. Goodbye, son, and give your sister a kiss for me."

"Like he's really going to kiss his sister?" Tucker chuckled. "If I know Lance, he'll probably punch her on the nose and tell her you told him to do it."

"You're very likely right." Daniel slumped into his office chair, the good mood he'd gotten from talking to his children gone. He glowered at the papers strewn over his desk. He'd spent endless hours hidden in his den, trying to work before the call. But the only thing he'd managed to do was think about Lauren. She was like a drug that had instantly trapped him in an addiction and he couldn't shake the aching need to touch her, to taste her, to take her. "Go away. I'm busy."

"Can't."

Daniel snarled at his right-hand man. "Then this better be good."

"Don't you think it's about time you decided what you're going to do with her?"

"I don't have time for this." Daniel returned his attention to the file folder, although he knew that wouldn't dissuade Tucker from entering. Sure enough, Tucker wound up flattening his hands on his desk to position his face a foot from Daniel's.

"So you're not worried that we're going to have the human authorities looking for her? Two days is long enough, man."

Two days? The time away from her had seemed like an eternity.

"Did you leave a message at her office like I told you to?" At Tucker's nod, he waved the man off. "Then we have no problem. As far as anyone's concerned, she's out of town, taking care of a family emergency."

"How long do you think that excuse will hold? Especially when it wasn't Lauren who left the message? Besides, this wasn't the plan. We were supposed to mess a hunter up to put them on the alert that we're on the offensive. Not take one of them captive. Especially one of the hunters who killed Tyler. I know we don't normally resort to revenge, but I'm not sure we can let his death go. The pack is up in arms about it."

"Your job is to make sure she's safe."

"And I'm doing that. But holding her prisoner is too much trouble and could lead to major complications." Tucker flopped into a chair. "Something more is going on here. Something you're not telling me."

Daniel kept his head down, pretending to work. "You're imagining things."

"Then why not do what we planned? Let's rough her up a little, then turn her loose to hobble on home and lick her wounds. Maybe even let the pack think we did worse to her. She'll tell all her hunter friends about her narrow escape from the evil werewolves and they'll know we strike first now."

He could almost feel Tucker's questioning scowl burning a hole in the top of his head. "Trust me, Tucker. We'll get around to that soon enough. For now, she stays where she is."

"Holy shit, Daniel, do you have a soft spot for the little dentist?"

Daniel fought the flame inching up his neck and into his face. "Don't be stupid. She's a hunter."

"Yeah, but she's also a woman. An attractive, sexy woman. Of course, you'd know just how sexy since you were the one playing tongue-tag with her in the dental chair. Is this more than simply finishing what you started with her?"

Daniel gave up trying to ignore him and leaned back. "I am aware of her sexuality. But that doesn't mean I can't keep my mind on business even if I decide to have some fun with her." He averted his gaze from his friend's, fearing he'd see the lie.

"So you're saying you can keep your head about you? All while keeping your dick inside her?"

The animal within him roared, fangs sprouting and wolf ears lying down. His vision changed, the amber in his eyes coloring the world. "Watch it, man."

Tucker held up his hands, palms out. "Hey, don't go getting riled up. I don't care if you want to tap that. But do it and get it over with. As long as it's just sex, it's okay by me. But we will have to let her go at some point. Very soon, in fact." His scrutiny grew more intense. "You want her for sex and nothing more? Right, Daniel?"

That answered one of his nagging questions. The others hadn't heard them having sex that first day. Or at least word hadn't spread. "What else?"

"I mean, I'm only asking because you Cannon brothers like taking human mates."

"Human, yes. Hunter, no."

"What about Jason's mate? She was a hunter."

"Not that it's any of your business, but her adopted father was a hunter. She never wanted to hunt and, in fact, she already had shifter blood in her." Not to mention the fact that she'd never killed any shifters. If only Lauren hadn't already killed. "Besides, I already found my mate, remember?"

"Sure, Daniel, sure." Tucker's tone was low and soft, the challenge in his tone gone. "But you know Torrie wouldn't want you to be alone for the rest of your life. And there's the council's recommendation to consider, too."

Recommendation, his ass. Command was more like it. Daniel struggled to make his inner wolf heed his warning to back off. But Tucker wasn't helping. "Keep Torrie out of this." Twisting his mouth, he wrestled the transformation into submission. "And stay out of my personal life."

Tucker shot him a confused look. "Hey, man, where's all the hate coming from? I'm on your side, remember?"

Daniel saw the hurt on his friend's face and regretted his words. Tucker had proven his loyalty and friendship many times over, becoming more than a friend. Hell, he was as close to Daniel as Daniel's brothers were.

"I know. And I'm not mad." Maybe he should use Tucker as a sounding board for the crazy ideas he had about Lauren. Like keeping her for a long time. Like getting to know her. Not just sexually, but for real. "Come on, Tucker. I can't work any longer. Let's get a drink."

"Or several?" Tucker's wide grin wiped the hurt from his expression.

Daniel laughed. "Definitely several." Together, they moved down the hallway.

A scream ripped into him and sent him running. He recognized the voice.

"Lauren."

Fear clutched his heart, propelling him into action.

Chapter Six

Daniel dashed toward the room where Lauren was held captive, sliding around the corners of the halls until, at last, he came to her open doorway.

"Holy shit."

Tucker's exclamation echoed in Daniel's ears, saying aloud what he was thinking. Bracus, one of the pack's guards, was on top of a struggling Lauren. In much the same way as Daniel had done, Bracus secured her arms over her head. Everything else, however, was different. Bracus had his legs between hers, his huge body, larger than most werewolves, crushed against her lower half, forcing her pelvis against his groin. He growled and bent his head to bite at her nipple through her shirt. Lauren, pinned to the bed, thrust her body every way she could. Her wild eyes met Daniel's, the raw plea for help shining through her tears.

Daniel couldn't think, couldn't breathe. Instead, he released the beast inside and changed, his clothes tearing away from his body with the rapid contortions. The bones of his jaws elongated and fangs burst through his gums. Claws sprouted from his fingertips as fingernails fell off. Clothes ripped away as human muscle gave way to animal strength and bones broke then reformed. Lowering to all four paws, he crouched, then leapt into the air. He struck Bracus on the back, digging his claws into flesh, pulling him to the floor.

Bracus roared his surprise and scrambled from under Daniel. Daniel, however, caught him, clamping down on his ankle, breaking it with a resounding *snap*. The larger man yelled in pain and rolled onto his back into a submissive posture. But Daniel didn't care. Blinded with rage, he jumped on top of the man who didn't shift, could only lay shaking, belly exposed and waiting for death.

"Daniel!"

Tucker's shout did nothing to stop him. He wanted Bracus dead. Dead for disobeying his command to leave the hunter alone. Dead for daring to come near her. Dead for touching her as he had touched her.

Daniel bellowed, opened his jaws wide and pushed the man's chin up to expose more of his throat. Saliva dripped from his fangs onto the whimpering man and he wrenched his mouth wide, ready to sink his fangs deep into his jugular.

"No! Stop, Daniel!"

Her tone, so forceful yet pleading, stopped him, commanding he twist his head around to stare at her. She sat, sheet drawn to her chin, her hair wild, her eyes glistening. Keeping the man's head under his paw, he snarled at her, unable to believe what she'd said. "What?" Daniel croaked out another question. "Why not?"

She shook her head, the plea in her eyes eating at him, but not answering his question.

Tucker stood at the end of the bed, his brow furrowed, claws extended, but not fully transformed. "Answer him, Lauren. Bracus has disobeyed a direct command which has dire consequences. Daniel's letting you make the call. Not that I get why."

Lauren wiped away the tear streaks on her cheeks. "I want you to let him go. I don't want anyone hurt."

Tucker's face dropped. "Damn, darlin', I was so hoping you'd say rip out his throat. Things have gotten boring around here."

Her horror at the idea had Tucker laughing again and Daniel tilting his head. With a swish of his tail, he stepped off the frightened man. He stretched, his facial features growing wider, shorter, with fangs withdrawing. Flesh flowed along his skin, replacing fur, and paws cracked as knuckles returned. Hands and feet replaced claws while fingers grew longer with nails. His body changed, a liquid skeleton molding into a different form, returning to human. Daniel watched the awe on Lauren's face, her eyes locked on him, taking in every nuance of his transformation. He hoped her wonderment wouldn't turn into fear. Or worse, disgust.

Returned to human form, Daniel came to her side, careful to cover the bare areas where his torn clothes gave him no coverage. "He didn't follow my order to leave you unharmed. For that alone he should receive a severe punishment. But for what he was about to do to you..." He glanced at her body, checked for any signs of injuries, and noted the bruises on her wrists. Had he left those bruises, or had Bracus? "Tell me you're okay." He couldn't bring himself to ask her which of them had caused the bruising.

She tugged the sheet higher. "I'm fine."

Tucker lifted Bracus off the floor. "What do you want me to do with this reject?"

Daniel arched an eyebrow at her. "Well?"

"My answer is the same. Don't do anything to him because of me."

"Are you sure?" The hunter confused him. She could shoot shifters, but she didn't want one punished for attacking her. "But you know what he would've done to you, don't you?"

Lauren nodded, keeping her eyes on Daniel as though she were avoiding Bracus. "I do. But he didn't." She reached out and placed her hand on top of his. "Thanks to you."

The heat from her palm rushed into him, sending mixed messages of warmth, caring and desire. She was a contradiction of enemy, friend and something he couldn't quite comprehend. All of which made her both frustrating and intriguing.

"Okay. Whatever you want." He lifted his head to find Tucker gazing at him, his brow furrowed, his attention darting between them. At last, his gaze settled on their joined hands. Daniel jerked his hand away from hers, cleared his throat, then gave the order. "Tucker, take that skuzzy mutt out of here. I'll decide what to do with him later."

"Sure thing." Tucker clutched the shifter's sleeve. His knowing gaze dug into Daniel. "Aren't you coming?"

"In a minute." Daniel shook off Tucker's inquisitive look, but knew he'd have to explain later. "Lock the door on your way out, Tucker. I'm going to question the hunter."

Tucker chuckled. "Sure thing, boss. You definitely need to *question* her."

"I don't get you."

"Sometimes I don't get me either." Lauren resisted the impulse to take his hand, hoping he'd make the first move. Yet she couldn't help but be pleased that he cared enough to want to understand her.

"Why wouldn't you want an attacker, especially a werewolf, punished?" He narrowed his eyes, his examination making her squirm. "Or is it because he's one of mine? And one of your captors?"

"What does that mean?" He didn't have to say anything. She interpreted his answer by the haughty lift of one eyebrow. "Are you serious? Do you think I instigated the whole thing? That I lured him into the room so I could seduce him and win him to my side?"

"Sounds like a plausible plan to me. You get him hung up on you, then you talk him into setting you free." He crossed his arms, daring her to deny his accusation.

"Right. Mister, you've got a big problem if one of your men can be *talked* into betraying you with sex." Her tone dripped sarcasm and she added the air quotes for good measure. Did he really think she was that underhanded? That deceitful? She paused. Wait a sec. Did he really think she was that *sexy*?

"A beautiful woman can turn a man's head in more ways than one."

She let his description of her play in her head awhile longer. So he really did think she was that attractive. After all, he'd called her beautiful. And no man had called her beautiful in a long time. Too long. In fact, she couldn't remember the last time John had complimented her. But wait. Did he think...

"Do you think that's what I was doing when I... When we did what we did?" She couldn't believe what he was implying, hoping he'd deny her allegation before she had to say the words. But he only continued to stare at her, suspicion written all over his face. "Are you thinking I had sex with you so you'd let me go?"

"Well, it does seem odd that you've already had a wrestling match with two of us."

She'd bolted out of bed and thrown the vase before she realized she'd picked it up. He caught it in midair, gingerly setting it down on a nearby table.

"Hey, watch it. That and most of the other pieces in this room are expensive. Like the finer stores say, 'You break it, you buy it'."

"If I had hit you, it would've been worth the price ten times over."

He studied her again, the amber growing stronger in his brown eyes. She returned his silent attack, determined to give as good as she got. He drew her in, pulling her deep into those golden-russet orbs, diving past the pupils and into his very soul. Yet instead of seeing hate, she saw something more. Something akin to confusion. She peered harder, wanting to fall into those depths, and was startled to find something even more amazing and familiar: sorrow. At once, her irritation vanished, squelched by the desire to understand what caused his pain. She knew it was more than mere physical pain. His ache came from a place of sheer agony that only heartbreak could cause. The kind of gut-wrenching sorrow caused by great loss. The kind of sorrow that came from guilt.

She whispered, afraid a louder tone of voice would hurt him again. "What happened to make you so angry?"

He blinked, opened his mouth to speak, closed it again, then took a breath. "You know. Hunters and their damn guns killing my people. Why else do you think we brought you here?"

"I understand that's why I'm here. That you meant to hurt a hunter but then took me prisoner instead. Although why you're keeping me safe from the others, I don't understand." She waited, but he remained silent. "But that's not what I'm talking about." She took a step toward him, wanting to touch him, to make the pain go away. Maybe if she could fill the hole in his heart, she could ease a little of her own weighty guilt. "Something happened to you. Something horrible. Something you want to blame hunters for."

"Hunters *are* to blame. Just like your group is to blame for Tyler's death. And maybe Mysta's too if she doesn't come around soon." He mirrored her moves, staying just out of her touch.

She took a steadying breath. "No. That's not it. This sorrow I see inside you—" she fisted her hand to her chest, "—is older than that. Worse than losing your friend." She reached out, urging him to take her hand. "Tell me."

His face was inches from hers in a split second, his hand hooked around her neck. "Look, Doctor Freud, I don't know what kind of game you're playing, but stop trying to analyze me. You're a dentist, remember? Not a shrink."

She swallowed her fear and watched his eyes take on more amber. If he shifted, who knew what he might do. "Please. You're hurting me."

A flash of regret was there and gone in the next instant. He backed off, pacing to the opposite side of the room. "I need information. I need to know exactly what happened."

Gone was the barely controlled anger. And gone was her connection to him. He was all business.

"I didn't shoot at Mysta and I've already told you about Tyler. I shot into the air. Just like when I shot over your head."

He paced around the room, circling her like a predator toying with his prey. "I'm not talking about them. I want to know about the other time. I want to know about the she-wolf you murdered a year ago."

Murdered? He couldn't have hurt her more if he'd physically struck her. "Why is that one so important?" She wiped away a tear.

"Because that's the one you admit you actually shot."

A chill ran through her. Hadn't she already told him about that awful day? Why did he care so much when it happened so many months ago? "I don't like talking about it. In fact, I wish that day had never happened. If I could change things, bring her back, I would."

"You'd sacrifice yourself for her?"

"I would."

"Tell me how it happened. What she did. What you did."

She turned away from him, trying to smother her sob. "We found her just inside the city. She was so beautiful, so wild. I envied the freedom she had."

Daniel's tone was cool. How could he have grown cold so fast? "I don't care about your observations. I want facts. Details."

"I was new to the hunter group so John told me to take the first shot. I did exactly what he told me because I trusted him. When he told me to shoot, I pulled the trigger. God, I was so stupid, so naive."

She turned toward him. His eyes were closed, his body rigid.

"What happened next?"

"Other shots came after mine. She jumped into the air, her body twisting as though she tried to dodge the bullets. Oh, God, I can still hear that horrible screeching sound she made."

Opening his eyes, he glared at her, and she fought to keep from cowering under his harsh scowl. "How many times did you shoot her?"

"Just once. Before I could think about what I'd done, she lay on the ground." Another sob wracked through her, shaking her shoulders. "I rushed over to her and knelt down beside her." She reached out to plead his forgiveness. "Once I saw her, once I looked into her eyes, I knew I'd made a terrible mistake. I could see the human side of her pleading for my help. Then when she spoke to me, I knew I'd done an unspeakable thing."

He clenched his fists and ground the words out. "But you didn't help her, did you?"

Lauren bowed her head. "I wanted to. But, I don't know, I think I must've been in shock. She wasn't anything like I expected."

"What did you expect? An insane monster, an unthinking killing machine? Do you think werewolves are the devil's spawn?"

"I don't now, but I did. John and the other hunters always talked about how vile and inhuman shifters were."

She lifted her eyes to his and ran a tongue over her lip. His gaze held hers, then dropped to her lips, and he growled. For a moment, she'd seen how much he wanted to kiss her. But then why the growl?

"But I know better now, Daniel. Hell, that was the night when I realized everything they'd told me was wrong. Whoever that she-wolf was, she's the one who changed me."

Conflicting emotions swept over his face, confusing her until, at last, his expression hardened again. "But you didn't help her."

"No. I didn't have time. She died a few minutes later."

"And if she hadn't died? If you'd had time, what would you have done?"

A flicker of anger swept over her face. "What you're thinking is correct. I probably wouldn't have done anything. I wouldn't have known what to do." She glared at him, as angry at herself as she was at his probing questions. "I went home that night and spent the rest of the weekend thinking about her. I thought about what I could've done to help her if I'd realized that John and the rest had fed me a bunch of bullshit. What I figured out was that, although it was too late for her, I could help other shifters in the future." She stuck out her chin, challenging him to call her a liar. "And I have tried to help."

He paced to the door as though to leave, then confronted her again. If only he'd tell her what he was thinking. Instead, he studied her, his brows dipped between his eyes.

"I know what I did, Daniel, and, if I could, I would take it back. I wish I hadn't listened to John, but I did. Yes, I killed, but I've changed. I'm not a killer."

"Torrie was the werewolf you killed." He shook his head, as though trying to rid his mind of an unbearable thought. "She was the one you helped kill."

"Torrie?" She inhaled, realizing that he'd known the wolf she'd shot. "What was her last name?"

He swallowed, a tenderness replacing the harshness in his face. "Cannon. Her name was Torrie Cannon."

The shock hit her and she clasped a hand to her mouth. "Oh, no. Please, Daniel, tell me she wasn't your sister."

"She wasn't." Yet before the relief could wash through her, he told her, "Torrie was my mate."

Her face paled and she buckled. If he hadn't caught her, she would've slumped to the floor. He took her by the arm and led her to the bed. At first, the world swam around her and she thought she might faint. She darted her gaze around the room, avoiding his until he caught and held hers.

"I didn't know, Daniel. How could I have known?"

"Would it have made a difference?" He wrapped an arm around her, hugging her, making her feel better. But how could he comfort the villain who'd taken his adored Torrie from him?

"If I'd known her name before the hunt, then, yes, it might have. If I'd know about shifters before that night, it definitely would have." She clutched his shirt. "You have to believe me. Knowing her name would've made all the difference in the world. I never thought about shifters having names, much less being someone's wife."

"Torrie was my mate. But it's the same thing as being my wife."

Lauren let go of him. How could he still want to touch her? "Please forgive me, Daniel. I was ignorant and…" She leaned away from him. "No, that's no excuse. I did what I did no matter what the reason and I deserve any punishment you want to give me."

Daniel stared across the room as though seeing to another time and place. "Torrie was sweet, willing to forgive, and I have to wonder what she would think of you. I know she would've believed you. But could even Torrie forgive the hunter who'd killed her?" He leaned farther away from her, breaking her heart more than she'd thought possible. "I can't… I don't know what to think right now. I'll think about your punishment and let you know."

She bowed her head, ready to acquiesce to whatever he decided. "Whatever you decide, please try to forgive me. Can you do that, Daniel? If not now, in the future?"

He rose, standing beside the bed, then, without a word, strode from the room.

Lauren paced from one side of the room to the other. She'd killed Daniel's mate. What had been the worst day of her life, the day she'd taken a life, had suddenly grown even more appalling. A bang against the outside wall jolted her, sending her scurrying to the far corner.

Was Daniel coming back? Had he decided her fate? Yet another day had passed with no word from him. Was the longer he took to make a decision be a good sign or a bad one? Now that he knew she was the one responsible for his mate's death, he was bound to hate her. Although she would accept any consequence Daniel wanted to dole out, she couldn't help but wish for a reprieve.

She took a deep breath, assuming the guards had hit the door by accident. Or did they purposely keep bumping against the walls to frighten her? Was that the first of many mind games they had planned? Or did she dare hope that Daniel could forgive her and convince the rest of the pack to set her free?

"Oh, sure, Lauren. No problem. Daniel will just forget about his dead mate, then pat you on the head and turn you loose. Girl, you are such an idiot." If she'd given up hunting after the first hunt, after killing Torrie, she wouldn't have ended up in this mess. But could she have turned her back and walked away without at least trying to help other werewolves? The answer came quickly enough: no way. Not even if she'd known how her decision would change her life, ending up a captive of the pack.

If only Daniel would come and talk to her again, give her a chance to explain. She hadn't seen him since he'd rushed out of the room. Had he left her at the mercy of the other werewolves? If so, would they keep her safe? The alternative crept in, chilling her. Had he left the house, thus giving them time to do whatever they wished to her?

The noise outside her door grew louder and with each bump she jumped a little higher. Her stomach churned, queasy from the food she'd eaten. Why didn't they get it over with? Not for the first time since she'd last seen Daniel, she silently urged the shifters on the other side of the door to come and get her. Anything was better than suffering this endless wait.

Even so, when she saw the knob start to turn, she swiftly missed her solitary existence. She squashed a nervous giggle.

Tucker threw open the door and grinned at her. "Hi, darlin', how ya doing? Hey, watch it, man."

Daniel brushed past the massive white-haired man and, without thinking, she rushed toward him and jumped into his arms. "Daniel!" She wrapped her arms around his neck, hugging him as hard as she could. His aroma, a mix of forest, wildness and masculinity wafted over her. "I'm so glad it's you."

"Damn, Daniel. I didn't realize you and the little hunter were such good friends."

Lauren untied her arms from around Daniel's neck and slid to the floor. Peering around him, she smiled shyly at Tucker. "I'm just really happy to see him."

"I didn't expect to get that kind of a welcome."

"I didn't expect to give you that kind of a welcome." His indefinable expression left her wondering and his lack of warmth unsettled her. Was he here to seal her fate? Was that why he seemed so...different? "Why haven't you come to see me?"

Not that she couldn't guess why, but she wanted him to confirm her suspicions. If he came to tell her what he planned to do to her, then let him get on with it.

"Tucker, send the others away and take a position outside her door."

Tucker paused for a moment, then answered with a curt nod and stepped outside. With a voice commanding and forceful like Daniel's, he ordered the guards away. Daniel closed the door, then faced her. Lauren blew out the breath she hadn't realized she'd held in check. *Oh, my God. He's going to tell me. Please, God, don't let it be too painful.*

"I stayed away because I had a lot of decisions to make. But the more I thought about what you told me, the more questions I had."

Maybe she shouldn't have brought it up, but the words were out before she could stop them. "You mean about Torrie? About my part in her...demise?"

He laughed, but his laugh held no humor. And yet, she didn't sense any anger, either. "Demise? Don't you mean her murder? Demise sounds too...nice. Too clean. Like she died in her sleep."

"I'm sorry, Daniel. I wish I could change things and bring her back to you, but I can't. If I'd known how shifters really were, I'd have never gotten involved with hunters in the first place. Please. I hope you believe me when I tell you how sorry I am. If not now, maybe you can later. After...you know."

He quirked his head at her, the familiar gesture bringing a light to her chilled heart. "After what?"

Irritation made an unexpected visit, threatening to make her say foolish things. She struggled to keep her temper in check. "Please don't toy with me. In fact, just do it now and get it done." Lifting her chin in a brave gesture she didn't feel, she quipped, "The least you can do is to make it quick."

"Make it quick?"

Why was he playing dumb? To make her suffer more? If so, he'd miscalculated. Instead of drawing out the inevitable wait, he was pissing her off. However, she had to play nice. What choice did she have? "Yeah. I know I don't have the right to ask for any favors, but I'd appreciate it if you'd handle the deed yourself. Get it over with as fast as humanly, or should I say, as fast as shifterly possible."

"I don't think that's a real word."

His guffaw made her feel worse, but she wasn't about to let him put her down. Not even in death. "Gee, I can't tell you how happy I am that my death is providing amusement for you."

"Your death?" He gaped at her. "Oh, that's what you're talking about. No, Lauren, I'm not going to kill you."

"You're not? Then what? Are you planning on torturing me? Maybe holding me captive forever? Turning me into a sex slave?"

He chuckled again, then finally noticed her irritation. "Sorry. I hadn't thought of any of those things. Although the sex slave idea is interesting."

Daniel's sex slave? Yeah, it was definitely an interesting—and appealing—idea.

"So if you're not doing any of that, are you letting me go?" Had he forgiven her? Would he really turn her loose? She didn't want to, but she allowed a brief spark of hope to thrive.

His smile died. "No. But I still haven't decided what to do with you. Like I said, I have more questions."

"More questions? How much more can I tell you?" Her heart plummeted to the floor and then, almost as quickly, lifted again at the idea of spending more time with Daniel. "Never mind. Fire away." She blanched. "Oops. I'm sorry. Poor choice of words."

He waved off her apology. "How did you become a hunter?"

She scoffed at the memory. "How else? By being stupid. I met John in a bar and, like anyone who'd spent her life studying and working, I thought he was dashing and dangerous. Then when he started talking about shifter hunting, I couldn't believe this other world existed. I mean, compared to the other men I'd gone out with, he was Indiana Jones and Han Solo all rolled into one. Then once I accepted that werewolves actually existed, the hunting part seemed adventurous, even glamorous."

"I guess people can convince themselves of anything if they want to." Daniel moved to gaze out the window. "You started going on hunts?"

"Not right away. John had to spend a month lecturing me about shifters, how awful they were, how hunters were doing God's work in wiping them out. We spent every night together, talking about werewolves and how to kill them." She willed him to turn around so she could see his face, see if what she told him made any difference.

"In other words, you were indoctrinated first."

His tone was flat and unemotional. She wanted to touch him, but was afraid to. "More like brainwashed, now that I look back on it."

"Then you went on a hunt."

He'd fed her the next line to her tale. "That's right. After a couple of lessons teaching me how to fire a rifle, John said I was ready for a hunt."

He whirled to face her, scaring her again. "And that was when you killed Torrie."

She nodded, her speech failing her. Could he understand how stupid and trusting she'd been? Did he realize she knew better now? That, had she known, she wouldn't have killed his mate?

He shook his head, the movement so tired and so sad. "It's strange. I should hate you. In fact, I should've already ordered your death or killed you myself. But I can't." His face closed up, confusion etched in the lines of his face. "The problem is that I can't help thinking that Torrie would have forgiven you."

"She would have?" Tears formed, threatening to fall. Instead, Lauren thrust out her chin, defying the tears to disobey her. "Torrie must've been a very special woman."

He cleared his throat, emotion flitting across his features. "She was. Which makes my decision that much harder. I keep thinking about what Torrie would have done." He laughed that mirthless laugh again. "This has caused me to rethink everything. Your punishment. Taking the pack on the offensive. Even what I believe about hunters."

"I'm sorry." What else could she say? If she could bring Torrie back, she would. How else could she bring him peace?

"Do you realize how long I've dreamed of avenging her death? How long I've daydreamed about killing the hunter who took my mate from me?" He raked a hand through his hair and groaned. "I never expected her killer to be someone like you. In many ways, you remind me of her. Like you, she was kind. She was always going out of her way to help someone in trouble even if that put her in danger. Always wanting to believe the best of people, to right the wrongs she saw in the world." He laughed a little lighter this time. "And like you, I sometimes had a hard time understanding her."

"I remind you of her?" She wished she could have known Torrie. Could she be as forgiving? "I'm honored that you think so." The thoughtful look he gave her warmed her to her core. Unexpected wetness flowed between her legs.

"Torrie looked a lot like you, too. In human form, of course."

"She did?" She was intrigued by his late wife and found herself wanting to be like her.

"Yeah. She was your height, your weight." His gaze slid over her, taking in every inch. "But more than that. Hell, if one of my men had attacked her, she would've forgiven him right then and there, just like you did. She also had spunk like you." A cloud darkened his face. "That's part of the reason she was in the city. A friend of hers needed her help and I had too much work to do to go with her. I warned her not to go alone."

Lauren reached for him and was thrilled when he let her take his hand. "But she went anyway?"

His eyes filled with pain and his voice grew hoarse. "Why didn't she listen to me? If she'd only waited a few hours, I'd have gone with her. I'd have protected her."

"You blame yourself for letting her go." He didn't have to confirm it. She could see it in the way he ground his teeth, the way his shoulders dropped.

"I could have saved her."

"Or died with her."

He pulled away and strode to the other side of the room. "I would have preferred death than life without her."

The swift slash of envy almost knocked her over. Would she ever know such a wondrous love? Would she ever find anyone who would lay down their life for hers? Someone who she would give her life for? Torrie hadn't lived a long life, but she'd had a rich one, filled with an amazing man who'd treasured her.

"Daniel, from what you've told me about Torrie, I don't think she'd want you searching for revenge. She sounds like the kind of woman who would've wanted the best for you, and who would've hoped you could enjoy all the happiness you could find."

"Torrie wanted the best for everyone. She refused to harm hunters even when they threatened her." A cloud darkened his features. "Which, of course, meant she was an easy target."

Guilt washed over Lauren. She'd taken Torrie from him by murdering a kind soul who had deserved to live a full life. If she hadn't joined the hunters, hadn't listened to John's lies, Torrie Cannon would be alive and Daniel wouldn't be filled with regret and pain. "Daniel, it's okay. Do what you need to do. If it takes my death to make you start living again, then kill me. I deserve it."

"Like I said, you've got spunk, too. You're a bit foolish maybe, but spunky."

She couldn't help it. The way he grinned at her made her smile.

The hardness of his face left and his eyes grew soft. "I don't want you harmed. Not by me or anyone else. You're a brave woman, Lauren Kade."

"Pff. Don't let me fool you. I'm whining and crying on the inside like crazy." Did she dare risk asking? "Daniel, do you believe me? Do you forgive me?"

"Yes, no. I don't know." The humor fled him as quickly as it had come. The alpha leader was back. "We'll find out soon enough if you're telling the truth. We'll see if Mysta confirms your story when she wakes up. If she wakes up." He sat on the edge of the bed. "I've gotta say, Lauren. With Mysta not awake yet and Tyler missing, I'd say you're doing a bang-up job of helping us werewolves. Maybe we'd be better off if you stopped trying to help us."

"Hey, I'm doing the best I can. I've saved quite a few werewolves over the past year and you weren't even aware of my help. But if John ever found out… Well, I'd rather not go there. Have you heard from Tyler?"

Daniel rubbed the back of his neck. "No. I sent a couple of men to scout the area where you left him, but they couldn't find anything. Of course, that doesn't mean much. Anything could have happened to him."

"Maybe he was able to get away but couldn't make it back to the pack. If he's injured, he might still be out there, hurt and alone."

"I'll send another search party out to cover a bigger area and see what they come up with."

She sat beside him, daring to let her arm brush his. A sizzle, reminding her of their lovemaking, fired through her. She licked her lips, wanting to entice him to kiss her. "I think you're starting to believe me, aren't you? Come on. 'Fess up." But she didn't give him time to argue. "Think about it. I had plenty of time to kill Mysta if I'd wanted to. Why would I let her live if I was a cold-blooded killer?"

He frowned, considered her reasoning.

"Do you remember my gun lying on the ground? Think about it, Daniel. What hunter would place her gun on the ground after cornering a wounded animal? A very stupid one, right? And, aside from letting John brainwash me, you know I'm no dummy."

"I don't know what to make of you." He spoke the truth, the clarity of it ringing in her ears. "You're a different kind of hunter, all right."

Lauren blinked, then smiled. "Gee, thanks. I like you, too."

He laughed for real this time, loud and bold. Damn, how she loved the sound of his laugh. If only she could make him laugh more often.

"I didn't say I liked you."

"Fine. On that point, we'll agree to disagree." She moved closer to him, sensing sensual tension between them. "But I think you do. Or at least you like me enough to do you-know-what." She glanced at the bed.

"Sex doesn't mean I like you. In fact, I don't like most of the women I take to bed."

Had she misinterpreted his signals? No, she didn't, wouldn't believe that. "Again. Gee, thanks. But I still think you like me." If nothing else, she intrigued him. Could his interest grow into something more?

"Why do you think that?"

"Why else would you bring me here? You could have hurt me in the alley, on the way here, or earlier. But you didn't. Why didn't you, Daniel?" She rested her head against his arm. "Because, Mr. Cannon, you like me. Whether you know it or not. Whether you admit it or not."

"You're right."

"Ah-hah!"

"Now hang on. You're right that I could've hurt you at any time. In fact, that was the plan. But plans change for a lot of reasons."

"What was the reason this plan changed?"

"There are two reasons. First, I don't like hurting women. Even female hunters."

"Good to know. And the second reason?"

Daniel trapped an auburn hair curled in front of her face and brushed it back. "I had to have you."

"Oh." A blush flowed into her cheeks, warming them. But it was the way he looked at her that sent liquid fire to the cleft between her thighs.

"I wanted you and now I want to believe you." He skimmed his thumb over her lips.

"And I want you to believe me." She peeked her tongue out to lightly touch his skin. "Believe me because it's true." Her eyes sought his. "Can you tell me you do, Daniel?"

"I don't know."

He disappointed her, a twinge in her gut telling her that it hurt. But why? She barely knew the man. He was her captor, the shifter who'd kidnapped her. Yet he was so much more. In Daniel, she saw the qualities she'd always wanted in a man. But he was filled with contradictions. At once treating her like the prisoner she was, then holding her, comforting her, taking care of her.

The sound of someone speaking to Tucker reminded her that Daniel had others to answer to, others to protect.

"No way will the pack accept that a hunter would help shifters."

Their eyes met and joined forces. Lauren leaned forward, parted her lips and closed her eyes. *Please, Daniel. Kiss me. Make love to me again. If you don't believe my words, then believe my touch.* When he didn't answer her plea, she opened her eyes to search his face.

He tilted his head at her in that endearing way he had and narrowed his eyes. She held her breath, afraid to hope that he'd heard her thoughts. With a groan, he leaned in and grazed his lips over hers. The slight touch magnified her senses, doubling them so that every nerve came alive. She pushed against him, wanting him closer than was physically possible. He answered her, enveloping her in his arms, crushing her breasts to his chest.

"Do you want this, Lauren?"

"Mmm-umm." She tickled her tongue against his lips, then slipped her tongue inside his mouth to eagerly enjoy his taste.

Daniel clasped the back of her head, holding her to him, his kiss growing harder, more possessive. Their tongues intertwined, playfully drinking the juices from each other. She wanted to stay this way forever, man and woman, hunter and shifter.

Daniel broke free and took a long look at her. She swallowed and waited. Would he stop? If he did, what could she do to keep him kissing her?

He dropped his gaze, taking in the rise and fall of her breasts, then brought his attention back to her face. "I don't ask."

"I'm sorry?"

"I don't ask. Women have always done whatever I told them to do. But you're..."

"I'm what?" The one who'd taken Torrie from him? Or could he mean something better? Maybe he would say she was too beautiful, too alluring, too much woman for him. At least his rejection wouldn't hurt as much.

"You're different."

She hadn't expected that. Different? Was that better? "Okay."

Daniel rubbed the frown off her forehead. "Different as in special."

"Oh, I'm special now?" She made air quotes around the word. "What do you mean by special?"

"Special is good. You're not like the other women I've known since..."

She fingered the button on his shirt. "Since Torrie?"

"Yeah."

"Are you saying this is more than a good time? More than a captive and captor fling?" She prayed he'd say the answer she desperately wanted to hear but was afraid to hope for.

He searched her, his mouth set. "I don't know what or how this is different. Not yet. I just know that you're not like all the rest."

Lauren could see his uncertainty, feel the way he held his body apart from her. Lifting her lips toward his, she closed her eyes and passed her tongue over them, tempting him to kiss her again. He crushed his mouth to hers, taking her tightly by the arms.

She mewed at the taste of him, the unfamiliar taste of wolf mixed with man, and yielded to him. The kiss deepened, growing at once hotter and sweeter. Again their tongues played the game of exploration, rolling over and under. She had to have him, no matter what happened afterward. Standing, she locked her hands behind his neck. She smiled, moving her core against the bulge in his jeans. "You don't have to ask me either, Daniel."

"I don't?" He buried his face in the hollow between her breasts.

"No, you don't. Because I'm telling you. Take me."

He lifted his head, his face flushed by her skin. Giving a quick howl, he nipped her neck, then skimmed his teeth over her skin down to the nipple hidden under her shirt. She rocked against him, delighting in the growth between her legs, and fumbled to get his jeans open. He copied her, tearing the buttons off hers as she yanked off his shirt. Her shirt was next as he ripped the material away.

"Hurry, Daniel. I need you."

He growled, at her or at himself, she didn't know. She helped him scoot his jeans to his ankles while tugging her own off. Soon, nothing stood between their naked bodies. Mimicking his growl, she dragged his lips to hers. The kiss was as wonderful as before, but Daniel was after more.

Taking her underneath her arms, he broke the kiss, then slid his hands down her back and over her hips to cup her buttocks. Lifting her, he moved her bottom back and forth, rubbing against his cock.

"Do me, Daniel. Now."

Taking hold of him, Lauren guided him, kissing him as he nuzzled her neck. His shaft slipped inside her and her walls gripped him, welcoming him. She leaned her head back, closing her eyes to concentrate on the feel of him encased by her. He slid back and forth, taking his length almost to the last part of her, then pushing inside again. Together, they rocked, enjoying the sexual dance.

"Oh, Daniel." No other man had ever made her feel as womanly, as sexy, as alive as he had. She laced her fingers around his neck and dipped her head for another kiss. Her breasts brushed his chest, eased away, then brushed it again, tingling her nipples. Taking his hair, she tugged his head, forcing him to look at her. Brilliant amber eyes blazed at her and, for one sweet moment, she saw both beast and man within them.

"Daniel?"

He panted his reply. "Yes?"

In that moment, she knew what she wanted from him, what she needed from him. Suddenly the stories about a werewolf biting a victim to change them into a shifter became enticing, sexy. Her gaze locked onto his fangs tipping over his lower lip, teasing her. She arched her neck, exposing her throat to him, offering herself in the most intimate way she could. He tensed, growing still.

"Lauren." The sound was soft, loving, neither a question nor a statement but something in between. He clutched her, his body tightening more, then groaned his release as he buried his face in her neck.

Why didn't he bite her? Lauren's climax followed, jolting the question from her.

"Daniel?"

Who said that?

Strong hands lifted her off of him, tossing her to the bed. Daniel leaned his body in front of hers, blocking the view. A smirking Tucker stood at the door.

"What the hell do you want, Tucker?"

Lauren scrunched behind Daniel, making sure his large body would hide hers. With her luck, her butt would stick out anyway. The humor in Tucker's voice, however, told her she was too late.

"Mysta's awake and asking for you."

Chapter Seven

"It's about time you came around." Daniel eased into the chair next to Mysta's bed, then enclosed her hand in both of his. "That bullet must've done some real damage to keep you out of it for so long."

Lauren sidled away from Tucker, slipping closer to the window. Unlike the room where she was held hostage, this window was large and without bars. Sunlight spilled through the lace curtains to slice a path across the bed. Traditional furniture decorated the space and a neutral color highlighted the paintings on the walls. But it was Daniel's obvious affection for the injured werewolf that stabbed her heart. Were the two together? Was Mysta his next mate? The thought angered and confused her. Yet why should she care?

The lovely woman, the human counterpart of the beautiful werewolf she'd tried to help in the alley, smirked at Daniel. "Fuck off, bub. I'm doing the best I can. Besides, I figure I deserve a rest after everything I've gone through."

So much for the mouth matching the sweet exterior. A chuckle slipped from Lauren's mouth and all eyes fixed on her. "Oops. Sorry."

Mysta tilted her head at Lauren. "You look familiar." She sniffed, then shook her head. "And your scent is familiar, but you're no shifter. How do I know you?" Her demeanor changed, instantly on guard. "In fact, you smell like the hunter in the alley—" She silently questioned Daniel.

"Yeah." Daniel shot Lauren a warning to stay silent. "This is the human who had you cornered. Later, after the hunt."

With Daniel's help, Mysta struggled to a sitting position and zoned in on Lauren. "Yeah, now I remember. Didn't I tell you to fuck off?"

"I don't remember you using those exact words. Although you weren't exactly friendly considering I was trying to—"

"What do you remember, Mysta?" Daniel cut Lauren off and leaned toward the injured shifter.

"I remember getting shot and it hurting like hell."

He laughed, throwing his head back. "Yeah, it usually does." He grew solemn, yet eager to hear more. "I need to know what you remember about her. It's important."

Mysta studied Lauren, her brow furrowing with the effort. "She was with the hunters, but I don't think she ever shot at me. She found me after I collapsed."

A small rush of relief filled Lauren. Maybe, just maybe, Mysta would remember everything and prove her innocence. She inched closer, giving Mysta a better look at her.

Mysta rested against her pillow. "You said you wanted to help me. Said you'd call my people or take me to a doctor. Not that I believed you."

Daniel placed his hand on her arm, the gesture both endearing and demanding. "Are you sure that's what she said? Did you think it was a trap?"

Mysta shook her head, slowly, indecisively. "I'm sure that's what she said, but I knew I couldn't trust a hunter. Although, she did put her gun on the ground..." She bit her lip, then came to a decision. "But who knew what other weapon she had? She could have had another gun on her body. I mean, what kind of hunter puts down her gun when she's got a wounded shifter in her sights?"

"That's what I figured." Tucker squelched Lauren's enthusiasm.

Mysta groaned, her face growing pale. "I'm sorry, Daniel. That's as much as I can do right now. I need more rest. Maybe you could come back later?"

Daniel placed a quick peck on her forehead and patted her shoulder. "Don't worry about it. We got what we came for."

Did that mean he believed her? Or did he believe the worst like Tucker? Lauren started to follow Daniel out of the room.

"Daniel?" Her tone betrayed her uneasiness, but Lauren stood tall, fighting not to let anyone see how nervous she was.

"Just hold up, little hunter."

She bumped against the big galoot of a werewolf blocking her way, determined not to let him intimidate her. "He has to know I'm telling the truth. You know I am, don't you, Mysta? Will you tell him when he comes back?"

"Daniel can make up his own mind." Taking her arm, Tucker escorted her into the hallway and toward her room. Once there, he waved the guard aside and opened the door, motioning her inside. "Until then, you'll stick inside your room and keep your mouth shut. If you know what's good for you."

"But—" She barely had the word out before the door slammed shut. "Now that was just plain rude."

Lauren was telling him the truth. After hearing Mysta's side, Daniel believed her. The more he spoke with Lauren the less he could imagine her as a killer. And if she was telling the truth about Mysta, then more than likely she was telling the truth about Torrie.

Could he get past her involvement in Torrie's death knowing that John had misled her, had trained her to hate shifters before she knew the facts? Wasn't she a victim of John's hatred, too? After all, once she'd recognized that a human still existed in its werewolf's body, she'd realized her mistake and had changed. He poured a drink of vodka and swished the clear liquid around the glass, studying the drink as though it held all his answers.

Could he forgive Lauren for killing Torrie? He swallowed, letting the sting of the alcohol course down his throat. He had no doubt that Torrie would have. And now, knowing what had driven her to kill Torrie, he could see how Lauren was as much a victim as Torrie. Daniel closed his eyes and sighed. But what about Tyler? His gut told him she was telling him the truth about the missing shifter. If only they could find Tyler.

He had to set her free. Problem was, he wasn't sure if Tucker or his pack mates would agree.

"Hey, man, don't you know you shouldn't drink alone?"

Tucker ambled in, his demeanor laid back, but Daniel wasn't fooled. Tucker wanted to talk. Daniel poured his friend a drink and got ready for whatever came next.

"I don't know what's going on between you and that female hunter, but don't let it cloud your judgment." Tucker slugged back the vodka. "We depend on you to make the right decisions for the good of the pack."

Daniel poured them another drink. Maybe he could drown the turmoil in his gut if he chugged a few more. "Are you questioning my loyalty to the pack?"

He gave Tucker a few moments to make his decision. If he decided to challenge Daniel, then big trouble was ahead.

Tucker, however, took a diplomatic route. "Come on, man. Can you blame me? You know how tricky hunters can be. And she seems smarter than most."

"But you think she's playing me? Why?"

Tucker stepped away, putting distance between them, a sure sign that what he needed to say wouldn't sit well with Daniel. "It's been a year since Torrie's death. In that time, you haven't let anyone, especially any female, get close to you. Then this little hunter—"

"Stop referring to her as 'little hunter'. She has a name. Use it." His hand tightened around the glass. "Get to the point, Tucker."

"Fine." Tucker dropped his glass on a nearby table. "We took Lauren hostage days ago. Which would be okay if she was just some nobody. But people like the employees at her dental office are probably starting to wonder about her. We've got to either come up with a better cover story or let the chips fall as they may. Or better yet, let's do what we planned, then dump her and let her walk home. I don't like messing up a woman any more than you do, but a few bruises won't kill her."

"If you touch her, you'll pay a price." The glass in Daniel's hand shattered, shards cutting into the flesh. Without a sound, he picked the glass out of his hand, then wrapped it with a nearby hand towel. The pain in his palm didn't come close to the ache in his heart.

"Damn it, man. That's what I'm talking about, Daniel. You're losing control of the situation. Why do you care if she gets hurt?"

"I don't."

"Like hell you don't. You almost tore my head off just now. I think you're getting too close to her, Daniel. You have to remember she's a hunter."

"I know she's a hunter. You don't have to remind me," he grumbled, hating what Tucker said but knowing his right-hand man had hit the problem on the head. "I'm holding her so I can interrogate her some more."

"Bullshit."

Fangs erupted, claws extended as the two shifters confronted each other. Daniel, all alpha, dared his best friend to land the first blow. But Tucker backed off, bowing to Daniel's authority.

"Chill, man, and remember who you're talking to. Other than your brothers, who knows you as well as I do?"

Tucker had never used their lifelong relationship in an argument before. Daniel's anger defused a little, making him ashamed of his actions. "No one. That's why you need to trust me on this. The more time I spend with her, the more I learn. For the pack's safety."

"Okay, Daniel, if that's what you say is happening, then that's what's happening. But the men are starting to talk."

"I don't give a damn what they say."

"Shit. That alone scares the hell out of me." Tucker downed his drink. "How long are you going to keep her here?"

"For as long as I want her." He caught his mistake a second before Tucker did. "For as long as I need to."

How had he gotten so close to Lauren in such a short time? When he'd first met her, he couldn't stand her, had wanted her as far from him as she could get. But now? Now he didn't know what to think or feel. If only she weren't a hunter. If only she hadn't helped take his mate from him.

Tucker's tone was resigned. "Fine. Then what do we do to cover our tracks? And are you still planning on hurting her when you're finally through *interrogating* her?"

"Let me handle it." He instinctively trusted Lauren. But what if he was wrong? Would trusting her put the pack in danger? "I'll have Lauren put them off."

"And how's she going to do that?" Tucker crossed his arms and met Daniel's gaze, the nonverbal equivalent of a wolf challenging the pack's leader.

Daniel shoved away the primal urge to strike the insubordinate werewolf. Only Tucker could get away with the gesture. "I'll ask her to call them."

Tucker's surprise almost made him laugh. "Are you serious? Let me get this straight. You're going to hand her a phone and say 'pretty please' and expect her to make the call without any problems? What if she shouts something out during the call or gives them clues about where she is?"

"She won't do either of those things."

"What else would she do? Invite her buddy Bobbie on a double-date with us?" Tucker grinned. "Not that I wouldn't mind giving Bobbie a little date action. Followed up with me checking out her teeth with my tongue."

Leave it to Tucker to take things in a different direction. "Okay, not an image I want to hold on to. No. Trust me. I can handle Lauren."

His friend's eyes narrowed into sly slits. "Oh, I get it. You've been diddling with the dentist to get on her good side. Giving her your own version of a bedside manner, huh? Hell, why didn't you say so in the first place?"

"Nice, Tucker. Diddle? Seriously, you need to improve your vocabulary."

"Hey, can I help it if I read classy mags?"

Daniel scoffed at his friend, whirled around and strode toward Lauren's room with Tucker on his heels. Although Tucker had soured his disposition, he couldn't help but notice that he grew more excited with each step closer to her. His mood grew lighter, while his shaft grew longer, thicker. He could see her waiting on her bed, reading one of the many books he'd given her or laughing at some ridiculous sitcom on the flat-screen he'd brought in for her entertainment. She'd break away from the books or the screen the moment he walked in, her face lighting up for him, sending the warmth of her smile into the coldest recesses of his heart.

The visits to see Lauren had become his favorite part of his routine. Even when they didn't have sex, he came away from the visit feeling more alive than he had in a long time. He'd been happy for the first time since Torrie had died, and whenever he thought of letting her go, that dark cloud that had followed him for the past year reappeared, darker than before.

Daniel waved the guard to step aside, motioned for Tucker to stay outside in the hall, then swung the door wide. Instead of finding her sitting on the bed waiting for him, he saw a lump the size of her body hidden under the sheets and comforter. She was asleep? A slow grin tipped the corners of his mouth upward as he quietly closed the door behind him. Sneaking over to the bed, he fisted a bunch of comforter and yanked.

"Wake up!" Sheet and comforter flew away from him, and he jumped, landing on top of pillows—and nothing else. He reached around the bed, a silly move when he could easily see she wasn't there. "Lauren?"

When she didn't answer, he frowned and rolled onto his feet, then ducked to glance under the bed. Where the hell was she?

Had someone taken her? Had Bracus come back for another try? Growling at a possible betrayal, he glanced around the room, checking for any sign of a struggle. But no such sign existed. If Lauren had gone, she had left willingly. "Lauren?"

"Um, Daniel? Is that you?"

"Yeah, it's me." He followed the sound.

"I could use some help here."

"Lauren?" Daniel knocked on the bathroom door. Relief flooded him along with embarrassment. He'd let his emotions take over, but now he was back in control.

"Daniel?"

"Yep. Still me. What's wrong?" He rested his weight against the door, partially shifting to use his werewolf's sensitive hearing. Had she fled into the bathroom, seeking refuge from danger? The hairs on the back of his neck stood at attention. "Lauren, come out of there. Now."

"I can't."

"What do you mean you can't? Just open the door. Pronto."

"Are you the only one out there?"

Why should she care? Did she think he'd need reinforcements to knock down a flimsy little bathroom door? Like hell, he would. Even without changing all the way, he could rip it off its hinges with one hand. "What's going on? Answer me, Lauren."

"Uh, I'm, uh... Tell me you're alone, okay? I'm in a slightly compromised position."

"Fine. Yes, it's just me. Are you alone in there?" He winced at the needy tone in his voice. But all he wanted right now was to know she was okay.

"Of course I'm alone. Do you think I invited the guard to watch me use the facilities? Sheesh. I'm not some kind of pervert."

He smiled, reassured by her joke. "I know you're not. But you're also not telling me what's going on."

"Could you please stop playing Twenty Questions? Come in here and help me. I'm...stuck."

"Stuck? Stuck where?" Did she fall into the toilet and get stuck? Did that really happened to people? Granted, she had a generous bottom, but he doubted it would be large enough to get her trapped by the porcelain throne. He clamped a hand over his mouth, stifling the chuckle that almost slipped out.

"Daniel, I swear to God if you're laughing at me, I'll...I'll... Well, I don't know what I'll do, but I'll think of something very unpleasant."

"Is she stuck in the toilet?"

"What's going on in here, man?"

Daniel shushed Tucker and Luca, the guard, motioning them to stay quiet as they moved from the bedroom door to stand behind him.

"I am not stuck in the toilet. Damn it, Daniel, who the hell gets stuck in the toilet? Will you please come in and help me. *Please*?"

Daniel shot the two shifters a stern look—which was hard to do while trying not to laugh—then backed up and got ready to kick down the door. Tucker, however, placed a hand on his shoulder, then gave him an all-purpose key that opened every door in the mansion. "Okay, I'm coming in. Are you ready?"

"Daniel!"

Daniel turned the lock and opened the door.

"Holy shit!"

"Wow."

"Daniel? Daniel, are you in yet?" Lauren squirmed in the opening of the small bathroom window, her top half hanging outside into a central courtyard and her backside hinged against the sides of the window. "Daniel?"

"Damn, how did she do that, man? Talk about a moon over the mountains."

"Who cares? Just enjoy the view."

Lauren gasped, closed her eyes, and prayed to die. At least if she died, she wouldn't have to face the humiliation of having them pry her big butt out of the window. One of the voices belonged to Tucker, but the other was unfamiliar. Was Daniel still there? "Daniel?"

"Yeah, Lauren. I'm here."

"Could you please make the gawkers go away and leave me with at least one ounce of dignity? Then come back and help me, okay?"

"Yeah, I could do that."

She breathed a sigh of relief and puffed a strand of her hair out of her face. Thank goodness Daniel was the one who'd found her.

"I could. But I'm thinking I like what you've done to the place. The bathroom definitely needed a woman's, um, touch."

Her appreciation for him evaporated in a split second. "Are you frickin' kidding me?"

"Now, now, Lauren, don't go getting your panties in a bunch. Oh, wait, they already are. They're bunched up at the window."

If she made it out of this damn window in one piece, she would rethink her position on killing shifters. Or at least one shifter in particular. "Dan-iel. This is so not funny. Get. Me. Out. Of. Here."

"Daniel, do you want me to get some bars installed in the window? You know, to prevent little hunters from getting their butts stuck?"

"Naw, we've never needed them before, Tucker. The werewolves who've used this room knew they wouldn't fit."

She groaned. Not only did she have a big butt, but she was too stupid to see that the window was too small. "Great. The humiliation just keeps on coming. Thanks loads, guys. Especially you, Daniel."

"Well, now that you mentioned loads…"

"Wide loads, that is."

"Tucker, if I ever get out of this window, I swear I'm going to skin your hide, one strand of fur at a time." Threats while stuck in a window were ridiculous, but she had to say something.

"Okay, men, I think we've had enough fun at the lady's expense. I'll take it from here."

Thank goodness he was doing what she asked. Finally. The pain coming from resting her body weight on the bottom of the window frame grew worse, the wood cutting deeper into her skin. Why she'd ever thought she could get through the tiny window she'd never know. She'd never given any thought to escaping. Not since Daniel had started visiting her every day.

But when she'd heard a couple of unfamiliar shifters talking about "taking her out and leaving her for dead", she'd decided it was time to take her fate back into her own hands. Still, better planning would've helped. Now she was as helpless as a girl with a wide load could get.

The two other shifters grumbled, then left the room, their laughing comments echoing back to her. Lauren tried wiggling again, then gave up. What had possessed her to try getting through the bathroom window? "I am so not watching any more cop shows."

"Is that where you got this idea? Because all the criminals elude the police by squeezing through small bathroom windows?"

At least he recognized that the window was small and maybe wouldn't realize how big her butt was. "Uh, could you please help me? This isn't the most comfortable position I've ever been in."

"Oh, I don't know. But I bet it's right at the top of the list as far as the most interesting positions go. Excluding the positions I've put you in, of course."

Someone giggled in front of her and, dreading what she'd find, she lifted her head. A crowd of shifters, male and female, formed a loose half-circle in front of her. Amused titters greeted her, the crescendo of giggles growing into outright laughter. "Great. Now I'm putting on a show for the rest of the pack. Oh!" She jerked, scraping the wood into her side. "Damn, Daniel, you could've warmed up your hands first. Or at least warned me."

A hand moved from the top of her hip to pat her bottom. "Sorry. This is my first hunter-in-a-window removal job. I'll be sure to heat the paws up next time."

Since when had he turned into a comedian? "Just get me out of here." She hated hearing the whine in her tone and dropped her head again, preferring to stare at the flowers below her than to watch people make fun of her.

Daniel ran his hands over her hips, her legs, checking every inch attached to the window. She sucked in her gut every time his fingertips skimmed her stomach and vowed to finally use her new treadmill. Right after she removed the clothing off it.

"Okay, Lauren, I think I know the best way to free you. On the count of three, I want you to hold your stomach in while I pull. Do you understand?"

"Yes, but please hurry." The gut-stabbing dent into her belly had grown more intense, her desire to get out of the hole more urgent.

"Good. Here we go. One. Two. Three!"

Lauren closed her eyes, clenched her stomach muscles and pushed on the wall. Daniel's strong hands gripped her legs and, with one tug, he pulled her out. She slid through the opening, wood tearing the front of her shirt, but she didn't care.

"I'm free!" She twirled around, lost her balance and fell against her rescuer. "Thank you, thank you, thank you."

Daniel's warm eyes sparkled at her and he wrapped his arms around her, holding her close. "Just call me your wolf in shining armor, baby."

Lauren grinned at him, enjoying the feel of his hands on her aching body. "Sounds good to me." Without thinking, she reached up, cupped his face in her hands and brought his mouth to hers.

Lauren shuddered, loving the way his hands molded to the shape of her back. At first easy, his kiss grew harder, more forceful. Her hands lay against his chest, but she didn't push away, couldn't find the will to do so. Instead, she leaned her body into his, tempting him, torturing her. He groaned, taking possession of her with his mouth, his tongue. She moaned in return, offering him everything he wanted and more.

Daniel broke the kiss, then flicked his tongue at the corner of her mouth. Skimming his lips along her cheek, he found her earlobe and nibbled, his warm breath tingling her skin. The way he held her, controlled her, made her feel reckless and more alive than she'd ever felt.

He picked her up and placed her on the chilly bathroom countertop. Her head bumped against the mirror, but she didn't care. Instead, lifting her bottom, she helped him yank off her jeans and toss them to the floor. Her shirt followed and she panted, trying to rid him of his clothes. Seconds later, she wrapped her legs around his naked torso.

He bent over her, his movement showing his muscled chest to perfection and shoved her breasts together to take both nipples in his mouth. She wrapped her arms around his wide shoulders, playing her fingers along the hard, smooth surface. She tightened her legs around him, tugging him against her. Her heels brushed against the swell of his buttocks and she moaned at the yearning to fondle them. She twisted her fingers in his black hair, holding him, holding on. "Daniel."

He nipped her breast, warning her to stay silent. Cupping her breasts, he looked into her eyes, the twitch in his jaw the only sign that he was aroused. Well, almost the only sign. She gasped at the glow of amber flecks inside his eyes and wondered how close his inner animal was to the surface. He pushed against her and rubbed his manhood against her already slickened pussy.

"You shouldn't have tried to escape." His voice, deep and rich, cascaded embers of lust through her.

"I know. But—"

"No buts about it."

"Could we please not mention the word 'but' ever again?"

"Deal." Reaching across her, his arm brushing against a nipple, he took a towel from the rack and twisted it.

"Are you planning on popping me?" She giggled, her nerves kicking in.

"Not exactly." With a lecherous grin, Daniel took one wrist and tied the towel around it. Then he crossed her arms in front of her, placing them under her breasts. Running the towel behind her, he tied the free end to her other wrist. "I guess I'll have to teach you not to try to run."

"You will?" Her whisper barely made it out of her mouth and, although she was both afraid and excited, she was ready to play along.

"This is your punishment."

She halfheartedly struggled, the towel acting like a straightjacket. "What if I swear not to try to escape again?"

"Don't bother. I won't believe you. Now take your consequence like a good, er, bad girl."

He slid his tongue over the curve of her breasts and his rough beard scratched a trail below the hot path. He placed his hand over her mons and pressed his cock firmly against her. His desire matched hers and she bent back, pushing against him. He slid his thumb between her folds, found her hot center and rubbed.

Lauren panted, frustrated by the binding that prevented her from touching him, yet loving every second of the fantasy. Her soft cry brought his head up again, a look of pure lust coloring his features. Arching her back, she made him take her nipple, and he gently bit the sensitive bud. She tightened her legs around him, trying to bring him into her, but he resisted.

"Not so fast. I want to take my time with you."

She mewed, irritated at her lack of persuasion. "Can't we move to the bed?"

"Not yet. I want you here where I saw your pretty little ass hanging in the window."

Pretty little ass? Was the man blind? Lauren started to ask him, but that was before he lowered his head and put it between her legs. She inhaled, stunned and pleased. Keeping one hand on her breast, he grazed her aching nub with his fingertips and she jumped.

"You're a sensitive one, aren't you? And so beautiful, too."

She was unsure if it was Daniel's hot breath on her pussy or his words that sent her first orgasm crashing through her. Embarrassed, she shielded her gaze from his and silently hoped he'd make her come again and again.

Daniel moved a finger between her folds and into her core, playfully teasing her with his light touch. She pulled at the towel around her arms, wanting to push his finger deeper inside her. "Is this my punishment? A little teasing? Why not punish me more by taking me?" She thrust her hips forward, trying to force him to do what she wanted.

"Easy, baby." Daniel shook his head and his hands stayed busy. "No, sweet one, I'm calling the shots." He pushed his finger inside her, rubbing against her hot button of desire with his thumb in between swipes of his tongue. Flashes of heat rushed through her. His low chuckle added to the sensation and another rush of wetness flooded out.

Giving up on keeping her cool, she begged him, "Please, Daniel. I want you. I need you to fuck me." His amber eyes sparkled above his upper lip flattened against her skin, and, when he stopped to grin at her, the tips of his fangs peeked out. She should've been frightened, tied up and held by a werewolf, but she wasn't. Instead, she was hot and eager to succumb to him.

"Do you want more?"

"Yes."

He plunged another finger inside her cave, his thumb continuing to massage her throbbing clit when he wasn't sucking on it. He tweaked her breast, then did the same to the other one.

Lauren glanced down at the purplish mark he'd left and imagined a different kind of mark, a permanent mark on her neck. Why she wanted that sign of his possession on her, she didn't know. She didn't have the ability to concentrate, to think. Instinct alone guided her.

A third finger joined the attack on her as Daniel slid up her body to suck her nipples again. She ached for him, content with his physical touch for now. "God, that feels good."

"Do you want something more? Something different?" He rocked against her, trapping his hand between her cleft and his cock.

"Yes, please. I want more and different." She growled and earned a smile from him. "Daniel, come on. Make me come again."

"Have you forgotten who's in charge?" But his laughter lightened his tone as he did what she wanted, stroking her harder, faster.

She closed her eyes, letting yet another release wash over her. How many times could he make her come? How much longer before he put his shaft where his fingers were?

Daniel continued to finger-fuck her, taking her higher than she thought possible. Her body stiffened, her center tightened in response, the pulse of her blood pounded a faster rhythm. Blackness came, not from closing her eyes, but from the roar of the tornado building inside her. If he didn't take her soon, she'd get lost in the vortex and never surface. She shuddered, her orgasm wracking her body, clearing her mind to feel nothing but the sex.

Suddenly, he left her, the air chilling her nipple. But she forgot about that when his mouth latched onto her pussy again, replacing his fingers with his tongue and lips. He gripped her legs, and she wrapped them over his shoulders.

"Oh, shit." She gasped, tried to steady herself and could only hold on for the ride. He plunged his tongue inside her, then nipped at her nub, and did the same again, time after time. She looked down, loving the sight of his head between her legs, and wished she could reach out to touch him. "Damn it, Daniel, turn me loose. I need my hands."

Daniel's answer was to suck on her, ridding her of her ability to speak. His tongue stroked her, dove into her, imitating what his shaft would do to her—soon, if she could only convince him. The familiar powerful swirl began again, readying her for yet another release. This time, however, as she felt her body building toward another one, he stopped.

Daniel stared at her with lust, wonder and another emotion she couldn't interpret. His amber eyes were wild and clouded with confusion. He unnerved her, frightened her, thrilled her. "Are you okay, Daniel?" She grew anxious when he didn't answer her. "Daniel?" she whispered again.

He blinked, frowned and seemed as if he'd only now heard her. "Yeah. I'm good." The mask of emotions was swept away with his grin. "But I'm going to get better." Sliding his hands under her arms, he slung her onto his shoulder and strode from the room.

Daniel ripped the top sheet off, dumped her onto the bed, then tore the sheet into long shreds. Lauren tried to catch her breath, her mind reeling with ideas of what he'd do with the strips of fabric. She didn't have to wait long to find out.

"I'm going to tie you up, Lauren, so tell me now if you don't want me to do that. And while you're tied up, I'm going to do whatever I want. Hell, I'm going to do to you what you need to have done to you, what you deserve to have done to you."

What could she say to that? Instead, she nodded and swallowed.

"At any time, sweet one, I want you to know you can stop me. Just pick a safe word, a word you can say and I'll stop." He raked her body with his gaze, warming her more than any roaring fire could have. "What's your word?"

"Cauliflower."

"Cauliflower?" He paused shredding the sheet. "Why cauliflower?"

"Because I hate vegetables, especially cauliflower."

"Yeah?"

"Yeah. Since I hate cauliflower, I won't say the word, especially while doing something I love." She grinned at his confusion. "And I know I'm going to love this."

He laughed. "I can definitely remember that word because I hate the stuff, too."

She expected him to tie her up, but she didn't expect him to pounce on top of her, straddling her. His shaft rested on her belly and he leaned over her, the gleam in his eye growing more heated as he slid his gaze over her. With an ease that spoke of practice—more practice than she wanted to think about—he removed the towel to loop one wrist then the other with a strip of sheet. After testing the knots, he then tied each strip to one of the bedposts, spreading her arms wide above her head.

He paused to survey his work, then skimmed his palms from her shoulders along her arms down to her elbows. What should've tickled her had the opposite effect, sensitizing her nerve-endings in an erotic explosion of senses. Encouraging sounds flowed from her, sensual sounds she was unable to restrain. He continued his hands' exploration, moving from her elbows to her wrists, his body stretched over hers.

"I've never had a woman like you."

"Like me?" Did he mean he'd never had a hunter?

"Someone who makes me think of doing naughty things to her, all while wanting to know every part of her, all about her."

She spoke in between short exhales and inhales. "But I bet you've had lots of women. Hundreds."

His light kiss on her lips left her more breathless than before.

"I'm talking about..."

Lauren froze, mesmerized by his face filled with indecision. "Go on, Daniel. What were you going to say?"

The vulnerability she saw in his expression vanished in an instant. A wicked grin and a glint in his eye took its place. "Forget that. Let's get back to the fun."

She almost cried out, her need to hear what he'd meant breaking her in half. Yet in the next moment, he stole all comprehension from her as he slid his body down hers. He kept going, pausing only to nip or lick this hollow or that, until she had no choice but to lift her head and grit out her words. "Daniel, stop teasing me. I need you to—"

"Spread your legs."

Frustrated, she dared to challenge him. "And if I don't?"

Daniel's smile alarmed her and yet sent chills of a delicious kind down her spine. "Then you leave me no choice but to do this."

Roughly taking one ankle, he wrapped a strip of cloth around it, tugged the knot tight and secured the other end to the bedpost.

She yelped, kicked out her other leg as he tried to grab it, but it was no use. With arms and one leg already tied, moving was too difficult and escape was impossible. Not that she really wanted to escape. She could've stayed tied to his bed forever. Using little effort to catch her ankle, he tied her other leg as he'd done with the first one. Nonetheless, she kept putting up a fight, straining at her bindings. Her breasts jiggled with the effort, bouncing enticingly and catching his attention. Groaning, he moved on top of her again.

Taking her breasts in his hands, he buried his head between them, then licked across one to the other. Like a peasant worshiping at an idol, he stared at her nipples, caressing each one with reverence and complete abandon. He was rough, squeezing her, kneading her, moaning against her. Her heart pounded in her chest, blood pounded in her ears, and her mind grew fuzzy. Her body cried for him to take her, to slam inside her, to make her his. She closed her eyes and cried his name.

Two fingers entered Lauren, pushing deep inside, rubbing the tender walls of her clenching vagina. She screamed again, a call of pure ecstasy, and bucked underneath him. His hot breath scorched her ear, then traveled along her neck to a spot at the end of her collarbone. Nipping her, he whispered soft words of yearning. She echoed his words, giving to him whatever she could.

"Open your eyes."

Lauren did as he ordered to find him straddling her again, his magnificent cock held in his hand, only inches from her face. Free to do so, she lifted her head and swiped her tongue over the tip. Daniel jerked, inhaling his delight, and held her treat away from her.

"Look who's the sensitive one now." She couldn't keep the smug expression off her face.

He chuckled, teasing her by holding his cock just out of reach of her tongue.

"Give it to me. I want to suck your skin off."

He watched her through hooded eyes, unmoving, his face unreadable. Would he give her what she wanted? What she was sure he needed? She moaned, bringing the sound from the bottom of her throat, and received the reaction she'd wanted. He leaned forward, offering her his shaft.

"Suck me off, woman."

She licked her lips, eager to do as he wanted. Covering his tip with her mouth, she dragged him in. He inhaled slowly, then closed his eyes and leaned his head back. He rocked back and forth with his hips and she pulled on him, taking in his precome, delighting at the texture of his skin against her cheeks and tongue. She yanked at her bindings and thought about using the safe word. Not to stop him, but to gain the use of her hands again. Oh, how she wanted to feel his hot rod in her palm and stroke him until he cried out his release. Yet as much as she longed to touch him with her hands, she loved the power she had using her tongue.

"You can't break free. And I don't think you really want to." He chuckled, the sound morphing into a moan as she wrapped her tongue around him.

Daring him to laugh at her again, she skimmed her teeth along his length and watched his abdomen muscles tighten. She pulled on him, harder than before. His cock swelled, twitching from her attention until, at last, he pulled out of her mouth and jumped off the bed.

"Daniel?" Would he leave her? *Could* he leave her?

Instead, he turned to face her again, fangs inching out. His amber eyes glowed with an eerie sexual tension. Taking one of the strips holding her leg, he tore the material, freeing one leg.

"Are you finished playing already?"

Growling, Daniel bent the free leg toward her chest and fell between her legs. He pulled apart her folds and latched onto her, sucking, licking, poking her with his tongue. She cried out, then fought to catch her breath. Bucking, she closed her eyes and let the fire from her core burn upward, outward. No man had ever taken her in such a wild way, opening her to him, tearing her apart with his tongue, his teeth. Stars twinkled behind her eyes, changing into meteors of conscious desire. Again she cried his name. And again she climaxed, once, then twice more.

He released her and her body rebelled, shaking at the loss. Panting, she wanted to beg him to take her, but couldn't find enough air to speak. If he didn't fuck her soon, she'd explode or go insane.

Daniel, his face filled with desire, his body rippling as though he was trying to hold back a volcano, asked in a voice so low she almost didn't hear him, "Do you want to use your safe word?"

She smiled, her eyes on his prize. "What safe word?"

He positioned his body between her legs, placing his cock at the opening of her cave and held it there. "I can't promise to take it slowly."

"Daniel?"

"Yeah?"

"Will you shut the hell up and fuck me?"

Pushing her leg up again, he slammed into her, driving her toward the headboard. His body tightened, every muscle, every sinew putting its power behind his thrusts. She mewed with each pounding, yanking on the ties that held her and lifting her head to watch. Daniel watched, too, keeping his gaze glued to her, his tongue licking the sweat that ran onto his lips. Each time he shoved into her, she felt him touch the back of her.

Taking hold of the material circling her wrists, she held on, forcing her body to meet push with push. Together, they used each other, riding on the other's body, drawing from the other's power. She came twice again, clenching her walls around him. He stiffened, the power within him growing to an eruption. At last, he howled, his release undulating through him.

He fell over her, holding his body up with one hand on either side of her. A drop of sweat fell from his forehead to her cheek and he gently wiped it away. One hand, however, was not enough to keep him upright and he fell to her side. Several minutes passed as they lay together, listening to each other's breathing. She lay next to him, the tips of his fingers touching hers, and she smiled, happier than she could remember being in a long time.

Daniel removed the bindings, his brown eyes meeting hers. She worked her wrists, massaging the soreness away. "Are you all right? I didn't tie you too tightly?"

She smiled at him and jerked her leg, tugging at the bedpost. "No, I'm fine. But could you untie my leg, too?"

"Do I have to?" He wiggled his eyebrows at her. "Although, now that I know you're into this kind of thing, I should've asked about putting a gag on you. Anytime I can get a woman to keep quiet— Ow!"

"Watch it. A man's nipples aren't as sensitive as a woman's, but I can still do some serious damage. Now untie me."

"Yes, ma'am." Daniel undid the knots around her ankles, whipping the material off and tossing it to the floor. The humor faded from his face and he bent over to place a sweet kiss on her lips. Sighing, he rolled to her side, bringing her into an embrace. "I don't know what's happening here, Lauren. I don't understand what we're doing."

"I don't know, either, but, honestly, I don't care." She could stay wrapped in his arms until she died, safe and protected from hunters and werewolves alike.

"The pack is starting to ask questions."

She had wondered if their trysts would cause trouble within the pack. Although she'd heard the guards talking about Daniel and his visits to her, she'd hoped they trusted their leader. "Are you in any danger?"

"No. But they want to understand what's going on. And since I'm not sure either, I can't tell them."

She craned her neck to look at him. "Seriously, Daniel, if our being together is causing you problems, then maybe..." She couldn't bring herself to say the words.

"Maybe we should stop having sex?"

Was that all their time meant to him? Just sex? "You could let me go, you know."

"True. But I'm not ready to do that."

Did he mean he wasn't ready to let her go? Or did he still not trust her? She'd given him information about the hunters—nothing that would get anyone hurt—but her openness hadn't assured him of her trustworthiness yet.

"Why not?" She sat up cross-legged beside him. "Why can't you let me go? Mysta confirmed my story, so why don't you believe me? Is it because of Tyler?"

He stared at her, diving into her to search for his answer. After several minutes, he answered. "Actually, I do believe you. And I trust you."

"Then turn me loose."

"No."

Chapter Eight

"You have to get me out of here, Daniel. After what I heard, I don't feel safe." Lauren hugged her knees to her chest, watching him retrieve their clothes from the bathroom. He tossed hers on the bed, then dressed.

Concern instantly transformed him. "What are you talking about? What did you hear?"

"I heard some men outside talking about getting rid of me. I don't know if they were serious, but I don't like the idea of hanging around to find out."

"Who were they? Did you get names? Did you recognize them?" Daniel paced the floor next to the bed. "Could you recognize the voices if you heard them again?"

"I don't have a clue. I happened to catch part of their discussion before they walked past the window. But I heard enough to know I need to get out of here."

His growl rippled through the air. "If anyone even thinks about hurting you, I'll skin them alive."

The vehemence in his tone both frightened and delighted her. Would he get so upset if he didn't have feelings for her? Or was his upset caused by his men's disloyalty?

"That's why you need to let me go, Daniel, as soon as possible."

He shook his head. "No. What I need to do is prove that you're trustworthy, that you're not a threat to them."

"I thought you said you trusted me." Lauren glared at him, hurt mixing with anger.

"I do trust you, but if there was a way of proving it… Not for my sake. For yours. For the pack's." Daniel reached out to her, but she slipped her hand away. "If I had a way for you to prove that I can trust you, would you do it, Lauren?"

She narrowed her eyes at him. "What do you have in mind?"

He fished his cell phone out of his pocket. "Call anyone else who may be wondering where you are. Tell them you're away visiting a sick relative. Tell them whatever you need to put their minds at ease."

He wanted her to help him keep her as his captive? Was he really making her his sex slave? Was she nothing more to him? "Shouldn't you threaten me? Isn't that how real kidnappers do it?" She feigned a frightened expression, held her hands up to ward him off and cried, "Please, Mister Bad Guy, don't hurt me. I'll make the call."

"Cute. Anyway, if I did threaten you, I don't think you'd believe me."

He was right about that. Daniel had gone from terrifying werewolf to something else. What that something else was, she wasn't sure. But she knew he wouldn't hurt her. "Fine. I'll do it." She took his phone, started to dial. "I know you won't hurt me, but I want you to believe you can trust me, okay? That's the only reason I'm doing this. See? I'm dialing."

Bobbie picked up on the second ring. "Hello?"

Lauren smiled into the phone. Wasn't a smile supposed to make your voice sound brighter? "Hey, Bobbie, it's me."

Bobbie's excited chatter kept up for several minutes before Lauren finally had to stop her. Gathering her resolve—which was easier when she stared into Daniel's sparkling eyes—she lied to her best friend. "Listen, Bobbie, I'm sorry I haven't called before now, but something came up."

She went on with the lie, adding embellishment to the story about a sick aunt, and promised to return as soon as she could.

"Yeah, well, I thought it was weird when Tucker called earlier."

"Tucker called?" Daniel nodded, urging her to go along. "Oh, right. I forgot that I'd asked him to call."

"I didn't mind. I mean, I'd rather have spoken to you, but I certainly didn't mind talking to him. So, you've gotten to know him?"

Bobbie's underlying question was clear. "Not that way. Tucker's a friend of a friend."

"Good. I mean…"

"It's okay, Bobbie. I know what you mean. Could you give John a call, too? Not that he's actually worried." She'd yet to break up with him, but hadn't she already done so in her heart? He probably thought she'd left the hunt on her own—which would've been fine with him and the other hunters—and taken some time for herself. Still, a girl liked to think she'd be missed. "Has he called?"

Lauren listened to Bobbie's attempt to make excuses for her so-called boyfriend, then interrupted her. "Hey, it's no biggie. But give him a ring anyway, okay?" She thanked her friend and ended the call. Handing the phone to Daniel, she fought to keep her irritation at John's lack of consideration from hardening her tone. "There. All done. Are we good now?"

"Yeah, we are. And I do trust you or I would never have given you the phone. But the pack is another matter."

"You got that right, boss dog."

Lauren shrieked and dove under the covers, scrunching her pillow on top of her for extra protection. "For Pete's sake, does he always have to barge in unannounced?"

"Tucker, have you ever heard of knocking?"

She listened to Tucker's footsteps as he came to the side of the bed and wished she'd taken the time to get dressed. If he lifted the comforter and the pillow, she'd pass away from embarrassment.

"I didn't think I needed to knock to come into a prisoner's room."

"Think again," said Daniel.

"Oh, I'm thinking, man. And the whole pack is giving this thing between you and Miss Hunter a lot of thought, too."

"Have you heard any threats toward Lauren?"

She dared to peek out from under the covers. Daniel stood toe-to-toe with Tucker, his arms crossed, his body relaxed yet ready for action. Tucker didn't back down, but he didn't answer the question either.

"It's time to stop the fun and get down to business. And that means no more monkey business. Come on, Daniel, make a decision. What are we going to do with her? Other than what you're doing *to* her, that is."

Her mortification shot sky-high again. She wished she could argue Tucker's innuendos, but she wasn't in a position—much less a stage of dress—to protest.

"Tucker, you're pressing your luck." Daniel's tone was low, filled with suppressed anger. "I'll let you know when I've made my decision."

"Can't you tell me how you're leaning, man? Tell me and I'll pass the news along to the rest of the pack." Tucker shot her a look that made her wish she wasn't in the room. "Because, yeah, there's been some talk."

Daniel tensed, his body growing rigid in mere seconds. "If you know who's doing the talking, tell them they'll have to deal with me if anything happens to Lauren."

Tucker's surprise had him glancing between them. "Can I tell them that you'll make a decision soon?"

"You'll be the first to know."

Lauren gaped at him. Tucker would know first? What about her? And what happened to trusting her?

Another shifter burst into the room, sending Lauren diving under the covers again.

"Daniel, they found him."

Lauren had to see. Tucking the sheet around her, she crossed her arms over her chest. But she needn't have worried about gawkers. Their eyes were on the guard.

"They found Tyler?" Daniel gripped the guard's arms. "Is he alive? Where is he?"

"He's alive and at Luna's home in the city. Fortunately, the bullet went straight through his leg. He crawled off and stayed hidden until he could heal enough to make it to safety."

"Did he say anything else?"

The guard shot Lauren a knowing look. "Yeah. Luna said he's talking about how a female hunter saved him. He said she used blanks and pretended to shoot him."

Lauren slumped, relief flooding through her. But even the relief didn't feel as good as Daniel's smile when he turned toward her. She was sure he'd decided to believe her before Tyler's return, but now he had proof.

Lauren was wide awake, wondering what Daniel's decision would be, when she heard the creak of the door. She bolted upright and threw off the covers. Was it Daniel? Her heart pounded, excited at the prospect of a late-night booty call. Although she'd never been the kind of girl that liked men calling last minute—especially for sex—she couldn't resist Daniel. He was like a pure chocolate and she was the chocoholic. She waited, peering into the darkness.

"Daniel?" she whispered.

Should she turn on the lamp? Or did the darkness play into his fun?

When no answer came, she took a deep breath to steel her nerves and tiptoed toward the door. If he wanted to play with her, then she'd go along with the plan. Her toe bumped into a hard object, making her squeak. Whatever it was rolled away from her. Following the sound on the hardwood floor, she went down on hands and knees, and ran her hands over the cool surface.

"Damn it, Daniel. Can't we turn on the lights?"

At last her fingertips touched a metallic object with a paper tied around it. Unable to stand the game any longer, she made her way to a nearby table and switched on the table lamp. The object, as she'd expected, was a flashlight and attached to the flashlight was a note. She shone the light around the room, expecting to see a grinning Daniel, but only emptiness waited. Disappointed, she read the note.

My dear Lauren,

She smiled. He'd never called her anything remotely that loving before.

Please remain calm.

She reread the line, trying her best to do as he'd asked and failing. The beating of her heart took on a different rhythm, a fearful rhythm. How did she know the note was from Daniel and not another shifter?

You're in danger and you must leave tonight. Some members of the pack still want to harm you. I've distracted the guard. Use the map below to find your way out of the mansion. Once you're free, do not return to your home. Follow the main road outside, taking care to avoid cars. Find a safe refuge. I'll find you once it's safe.

Signed,

Cauliflower

He'd used her safe word, confirming that he'd written the note. She bit her lip and reread it. The danger was great enough that Daniel was afraid for her. But why? Now that Mysta and Tyler had confirmed that she'd helped them, why was she still in danger? She frowned, knowing the answer. In the pack's eyes, she was still a hunter and they wanted to hurt her. But why couldn't Daniel lead her to safety? Could she escape on her own?

Gathering her courage, she dressed, opened the door without making a noise, then slipped out. Sconces cast a yellow glow so she shut off the flashlight and, being as quiet as she could, hurried down the hallway.

Three turns later, Lauren squinted into the dim light and froze, listening to the voices coming toward her. Stifling a giggle, she darted into a dark corner and tried to become one with the wall. Two shifters she didn't recognize strolled past her, discussing the latest person voted off a popular reality show. She started to let out the breath she'd held in check, then abruptly stopped, caught between breaths. The larger of the two shifters, a black man that towered over the other one, stooped to tie his shoe.

At that moment, the map she clung to dropped to the floor and floated within inches of his heel. If he glanced behind him, he'd see the paper and her escape would fail. Lauren closed her eyes and thought about Daniel, hoping that would squelch her almost overwhelming need to giggle. She kept her eyes shut until, at last, the shifters moved on, their voices trailing behind them. Releasing her pent-up anxiety, she stayed in the dark corner a few moments, giving her wobbly legs time to regain strength. At last, she scooped up the note and moved on.

Luck stayed with Lauren the rest of the way. She tried to hurry while taking care not to rush headlong into danger. How big was this place? If she made a wrong turn, she could wind up in the middle of the mansion instead of finding an exit. Suddenly, moonlight drifted through a side door and she almost squealed with happiness. She reached the door, turned the lock as quietly as she could and stepped into the night air.

Although the fresh air tempted her to stop and enjoy the slight breeze, she kept moving, sprinting down the driveway, certain that at any moment, a werewolf would see her. Lights from an approaching car had her taking refuge behind a row of parked cars and she counted the seconds until it had finally passed.

The main street beckoned, and she rushed down the green expanse of the manicured lawn and through the ornate gates cracked opened just wide enough for her to slip her body through. She took one last look at the mansion and whispered, "Come and find me, Daniel. I'll be waiting." Giving a muted shout of victory, she dashed down the road.

Once Lauren was sure no one followed her, she slowed her pace and walked for several miles, heading to a nearby neighborhood, a few bright lights drawing her like a magnet. If she could get to a phone, she could call for help. A taxi sounded like heaven and Lauren wished Daniel had given her a cell phone. Disheveled and dead tired, she trudged into the newly built housing development, hiding in the darkness whenever a car came by.

"Once this is over, I'm going to sit down and never stand up again. Ouch!" She slipped off her boot and dumped out the offending pebble. She scanned the houses, searching for one that still had lights on inside. She was about to walk up the driveway to one house when she saw the mailbox of the house next door. A *Support Your City's Zoo* sticker was plastered to the side. "Thank God."

Tala Wilde, veterinarian and consultant for the zoo, had done a television spot from her home and Lauren was certain this was the place. Ordering her feet to keep moving, Lauren stumbled onto the front porch and pressed the doorbell. "Hello! Can someone please open the door? Tala?"

The door swung open, revealing Tala in sleep shorts and a tank top. "Yes?"

Not giving the woman a chance to reject her, Lauren fell into her arms and, with Tala's help, shuffled to the sofa. She slipped onto the suede material and soaked in its warmth and comfort. "Oh, my God, I can't believe how good it feels to sit down. I am so not in shape for what I just went through."

Tala sat on the ottoman in front of her, her face clouded with concern. "Are you okay? Who are you? What's going on? And why are you ringing my doorbell at two in the morning? Is there an emergency?"

"Yes, it is. I-I'm sorry to barge in like this, but you were the nearest person I could find to help me. I remember seeing you on television and I remembered your house. I'll answer all your questions, but could I please have something to drink first? I'm worn out, bruised and blistered."

"Of course you can." Tala darted into the kitchen that opened up to the living room, filled a glass with water and hurried back. "Here you go. How about we start with your name?"

"I'm Lauren Kade." Lauren took a long drink, then placed the cool glass against her forehead. "Ah, now that's how I spell relief."

"Do you feel well enough to tell me what's going on? Should I call the police?" Tala sat next to her and clasped her hand in hers. "You look like you've gone through hell and back. And brought a little bit of hell back with you."

Lauren giggled, relieved that she could finally tell someone what had happened, and amazed that Lauren had let her into her home. "Thank you for letting me in. I mean, I'm a stranger and all."

Tala shook her head. "Yes, but you're obviously someone in need."

Tala's eyes flashed, a glint of amber highlighting them—just like Daniel's did. But Tala couldn't be a werewolf. Could she? More likely, Lauren was just imagining the change in color. And who could blame her after being held captives by shifters? Lauren paused, then dismissed her suspicions. Now that she was already inside, she had no choice but to trust her. "It's a long story and not one you're likely to believe." She laughed louder, imagining how ludicrous people would find her story. "I'll get straight to the punch line." She squeezed her new friend's hand. "I was kidnapped."

"Kidnapped?" Tala's eyes grew wide. "Are you serious?"

"Don't I look like I'm serious? I escaped tonight and walked all the way here." She downed the rest of her water. "But that's not even the wildest part of my story."

"You're kidding. What else?"

"Hold on to your shorts because you are not going to buy this, but I swear it's true." Lauren paused, reconsidered telling a tale no one would believe, then plunged ahead. "I was kidnapped by werewolves." Lauren waited for one of two reactions. Either she would react in shock or, more likely, laugh in her face. But Tala did neither one. "Did you hear what I said? I was kidnapped by werewolves."

Tala nodded, then slipped into the kitchen to refill her drink. "I don't mean to sound doubtful and you've obviously been through something awful, but why do you think they were werewolves?"

"Oh, I don't know. Maybe because I saw them change from men into wolves. Big, hairy, wolves that can talk." Had she said too much? Maybe she should've left out the part about talking werewolves.

"Let me make sure I understand you. You think you were taken not by ordinary, run-of-the-mill kidnappers, but by werewolves? And not just any werewolves, but talking werewolves?"

Lauren could see it now. Tala must think she was a wacko. In fact, she'd be lucky if she didn't call the mental hospital. "I know it sounds like I've inhaled way too much nitrous oxide—I'm a dentist—but I'm telling the truth. So help me God."

"O-kay. Let's say I believe you. Why would werewolves—and there's more than one, right?" She continued at Lauren's nod. "Why would they take you? Did they have a problem with their dental care? I can see how that could cause problems, what with their big teeth."

"Tala, please. I'm serious."

Tala's smile faded, her expression grave. "I'm sorry. I shouldn't make fun of you, but you can understand how difficult this is, can't you?"

"Sure. I understand your hesitancy." Lauren took the leap of faith in her new friend. After all, she was asking her to make a big leap, too, by believing her. "Look, Tala, I have a secret. A secret that can explain why they chose me."

"O-kay. What's your secret? And are you sure you want to tell me?"

Tala's tone was the type doctors used with mentally confused patients, but who could blame her for her skepticism? "Yes, I want to tell you. I'd like someone to know this besides the people who are involved in it."

Tala leaned forward, her face a blend of pity and concern. "You're not going to tell me you're part of some kind of weird cult, are you?"

Was the hunter group a cult? Not in the strictest sense of the word, but it did have similarities. "Yes and no. My boyfriend is part of a hunting group."

"Are you talking about hunting animals? With guns? And I'm assuming out in the countryside, right? Not that I condone such things, of course. I prefer a more humane ways of dealing with animals."

"My group hunts in the mountains sometimes, but most of our hunts are in the city."

"That's kind of dangerous, isn't it? I mean, an innocent person could get shot."

"We're careful not to let that happen." She let out a sigh. This wasn't getting any easier. "What we hunt is the hard part."

Why didn't Tala seem more surprised? She didn't seem concerned in the least about what Lauren had told her.

"You hunt werewolves. Is that right?"

She was ashamed and unsettled by Tala's easy guess, but she had to admit the truth. "That's right. Or at least I used to. And that's why the werewolves took me."

Tala grew quiet, unnerving her even more. When she finally spoke again, it was Lauren's turn to be shocked. "I believe you."

"You do?" But how? Hell, she wouldn't have believed her story had she not lived it. "Why? I mean, telling you that werewolves exist was hard enough, but to say they're talking werewolves? Well, that's just stacking lunacy on top of craziness. But you really believe me?"

"Absolutely, I do. I'm sorry. I didn't mean to give you a hard time, but I had to be sure you believed what you were saying. I've seen a lot of strange things."

"Because of your work as a vet and a consultant for the zoo?"

"Because of that as well as other reasons."

"Other reasons?" Suddenly, Lauren didn't like the way the conversation was headed. Or the way Tala was looking at her. Like Tala was sizing her up. She rose and edged toward the door. "Uh, you know what? It's really late. How about I call a cab and wait for it outside so you can get back to sleep? Can I borrow the money to pay for it? I'll pay you back tomorrow. I swear."

"Who's our guest, Tala?"

Lauren twisted in the direction of the voice and Tala's smile. A large man with long black hair and sparkling, dark eyes pulled Tala into his arms and kissed her. The kiss, lingering long enough to make Lauren uncomfortable and even a bit aroused, finally broke apart.

"Devlin, this is Lauren Kade. Lauren, this is my husband, Devlin."

Hard dark eyes clamped onto her, stiffening her body. Lauren hoped her unsteady legs would hold her. Panic started to strangle her breath again and she thought about running but doubted her legs would carry her very far. "This is your husband?" Why did he look so familiar?

Should she try to make a break for the door? Yet she doubted she could make it past either Tala or her large husband.

She stood as straight as she could and studied the solemn-faced man, all while trying to quiet the alarm bells clanging in her mind. Their eyes locked onto her, glinting flecks of amber. How had she managed to jump out of the skillet and into the fire? "Tala? Is your husband... Are you a werewolf?"

"Uh-huh. I'm Devlin's mate and proud of it."

Had she run back into the pack? Lauren closed her eyes and wished she was in Daniel's safe arms. *Daniel, please help me.*

"Lauren, calm down. Everything's okay. Devlin won't let anyone hurt you. Will you, honey?"

"Not as long as you're not out to hurt us." The amber flecks shown in his eyes, taking over more of the cool brown and warning of the animal lurking below the surface.

"Not me." She looked longingly past him toward the door. "I love werewolves." She inwardly winced at her pitiful attempt to placate them. And judging from Tala's and Devlin's expressions, they weren't buying it. In fact, they seemed to be playing with her the way a cat plays with the mouse he's about to eat.

"By the way, Lauren, I use my maiden name for business, but my married name is Tala Cannon. Devlin is an alpha in the Cannon pack."

Lauren took off running as though her legs had planned on escaping all along and had forgotten to tell her mind. But she didn't get far. Devlin's strong arm wrapped around her, picking her up and plunking her down on the couch. "Stay."

She obeyed him, too afraid to do anything else. "You're a Cannon? Oh, shit. That's the group that kidnapped me."

"It is?" Devlin took the armchair next to the sofa and Tala sat on the arm. "Why did they do that?" His narrowed eyes zoned in on her, warning her of the raw power he controlled.

"Don't you know? I mean, you're an alpha. You're Daniel's brother, aren't you?" Mentioning Daniel's name calmed her. If Devlin was anything like his brother, maybe she could rest easy.

"I've been out of the state for a while. And yes, Daniel's one of my brothers. But the pack has never kidnapped anyone. Exactly who took you?"

"Daniel, Tucker and the others took me. They caught me when I got separated from the rest of my group."

"Which group is that?"

Lauren didn't want to tell him. Once he found out she was a hunter, who knew what he'd do. She looked at Tala and sent her a silent plea although she knew it useless

"Honey, Lauren is a hunter. Or used to be." Tala held up her hand to calm his flash of anger. "Now hold up. Don't react too hastily. Remember that Sydney grew up with hunters, so don't jump to conclusions. Let's hear what she has to say first." Tala gestured for her to hurry up and explained, "Sydney is mated to the other Cannon brother, Jason."

Encouraged by Tala's readiness to listen, Lauren told them everything from the first day she met John to the way Daniel had helped her escape the mansion. By the time she'd finished, she hoped she'd gained a little of their trust. At least enough to keep her safe until they contacted Daniel.

"What the hell is going on?"

Lauren flew off the sofa to find a very sexy, but none-too-happy Daniel striding into the room. She barreled into him, relief swamping through her. She was safe now that he was here.

Daniel held her at arms' length. "Lauren, why the hell did you come here? I helped you escape and, instead of running to freedom and a human friend, you come to a shifter's home? You're just lucky I came to talk to my brother."

Okay, maybe she wasn't safe after all. The emotion of the past few days, the fear and anger, welled up inside her to reach a boiling point.

"Back off, buster." Daniel actually took a step back, almost making her smile. "I did go to a human's home. Or at least I thought she was human. How was I to know she'd mated a werewolf? It's not like they had a welcome mat saying 'Werewolves Welcomed', ya know?"

"She's right, Daniel. She just stumbled onto us." Tala slipped her arm around her husband.

Lauren pointed at Tala, emphasizing her point. "Yeah, that's right. I had no idea that I'd gone from one house of shifters straight into another one. But at least this one has fewer werewolves to contend with. Plus, I don't think they plan on locking me up." Worry replaced her irritation, lessening her strength. "You don't, do you?"

Devlin raised his hand, silencing the others. "If I have a say in this matter—and as an alpha I do—then I think locking her in the mansion and throwing away the key is a damn good idea."

Chapter Nine

"Oh, my God." Lauren struggled to pull in the next breath. Was she born under an unlucky star? Or was her crappy luck her own fault? Not that it mattered now. She was knee-deep in trouble.

"Hang on. I didn't set her free only to have you take her right back." Daniel took her by the arm, helping her to make it back to the sofa. "We made a mistake in kidnapping her." He closed his eyes and heaved a big sigh. "*I* made a mistake in kidnapping her."

"Why did you take her in the first place?" Devlin crossed his arms, a silent defiant gesture.

"My plan was to go on the offensive. Instead of always running from the hunters and reacting to what they put in motion, I wanted to hit them first for once."

"Like a preemptive strike?"

"That's it exactly. I wanted the hunters to feel what it was like to be the hunted. Haven't we all had the same idea at one time or another?"

A few moments of silence passed as the shifters reflected on Daniel's words. Lauren had to admit, if Daniel's idea was to make hunters know how shifters felt, he'd certainly made his point with her.

"I get that. I do." Devlin relaxed. "Bro, I understand where you're coming from. Torrie's death, then what happened to Mysta and Tyler made you want revenge, but changing a policy we've held for years was not your decision to make. You should've gone to the council first. Or at least presented it to Jason and me."

"Yeah, I know. I realized my mistake the second we found our hunter." He glanced at her. "But by then, it was too late."

Lauren wanted to touch him, to tell him he was forgiven. Instead, she resisted the urge and looked to Devlin. "So does this mean you're not going to throw me to the wolves again?" She shot them a tentative grin.

Devlin's laugh sounded a lot like Daniel's and the fear stiffening her spine disappeared. Did that mean she was safe at last?

"No. We won't send you back."

"Even though you wanted to lock me up and throw away the key?" Hell! Why couldn't she keep her yap shut for once? Devlin's laugh eased her fear again. If she could bottle the Cannon brothers' laugh, she'd make a fortune.

"You should never have been taken in the first place. But, Daniel, why the escape? Why not tell the pack that you made a mistake?"

Daniel took his time to answer, his uneasiness obvious in the rigid way he sat, his gaze aimed at his brother. "I could have when she first came. But I kept her, using the time to—" he cleared his throat and glanced at her, "—interrogate her for hunter information. I was stuck and, by that time, the pack wouldn't accept letting her go."

The admission of how he'd led the pack on was difficult for Daniel to admit, but she loved the flutters in her stomach. He'd never interrogated her except to ask how she'd gotten involved with the hunters. Not once had he asked her to reveal any sensitive information about John and the others. Instead, he'd asked her questions about her life, her family, her dreams. That had to mean only one thing. Daniel did care for her. Although they'd come together for strange, even sinister reasons, he'd saved her because he'd grown to care for her. But where could this lead? He was shifter and she was human, a hunter in the eyes of his pack.

"I think we have three choices."

Lauren couldn't help but catch the hopeful tone in Tala's voice. "Really? What are they?"

"First, we could take you back to the pack and try to convince them to forget the initial plan. If Devlin backs you, they just might go along."

"Even if they do, most of them will want to continue going on the defensive. Including Tucker." Daniel kept his gaze on his sister-in-law. "Next choice."

Tala didn't appear fazed by his discounting her first idea. "Or we could get her home and let her friends, her fellow hunters, protect her."

Daniel let out a caustic guffaw. "Right. Because they protected her so well the first time. Again, next choice."

Devlin reached out to take Tala's hand. Lauren noted how tenderly he touched her, encouraging her with his eyes as well. Could she and Daniel ever find that easy understanding? "I can see one other choice. She's still safe and alive because of Daniel. So, I think the best thing to do is for Daniel to make sure she stays safe."

"None of those are great choices." Devlin tracked his fingers through his hair, a gesture that reminded her of Daniel. "But if anyone can do it, Daniel can. We'll tell the pack that he's using her, gaining her trust by staying with her in the city. But only to get leads on future hunts, not to harm her or any other hunter. We're going back to the old way. No harming hunters except to stay safe. To do otherwise would cause a war that would last years and cost many lives on both sides. And I'm not prepared to do that." He studied his brother. "Is this what you want to do? Do you want to keep her safe?"

Daniel didn't hesitate. "Yes." Lauren's elation, however, was short-lived. "But Lauren has to make a promise in return."

"What promise?"

Daniel took her hand, nodded at Devlin and Tala, and started for the door. "We'll talk about it at your place. Right now, I want to put more distance between us and the pack. They're already on the hunt for you."

Lauren glanced over her shoulder at Tala and Devlin, and couldn't help but wonder. She'd already jumped from the pan into fire. Was she now fueling the flames?

Daniel took Lauren home, watching and listening for any sign of the pack. Staying in the city wasn't new to him, but staying in a human's—hell, a hunter's—home was different, disconcerting. Especially when he couldn't trust his usual pack contacts. Until the other shifters accepted Lauren's release and their return to the pack's prior way of dealing with hunters, he had to be careful whom to trust.

He stretched, then squinted at the city lights sparkling in the growing darkness. Spending the whole day with Lauren was a joy he never wanted to give up. He turned away from the scene and studied her ample bottom that wiggled as she scrubbed the kitchen countertop, and felt his cock twitch. Soon, however, they'd have to face their problems.

"Lauren, we need to talk."

She made a face. "Uh-oh, this doesn't sound good. Are you breaking up with me already?"

He loved her sense of humor. In fact, she was the only one who'd made him laugh since Torrie. He didn't want to lose that so he tossed her joke back at her. "You wish."

"No, I don't."

Daniel's eyes met hers and drilled her to the core, suspicious. Could love have found him not once, but twice? Could he trust her? Could he trust himself?

"I really don't, Daniel."

With that simple declaration, making him believe, she stripped him of every thought, every intention—save one. Groaning, he yanked her to him and crushed his mouth on hers. She uttered a small cry and clung to him. He lifted her, his kiss deepening. Taking her with him, he laid her on the floor, then pulled her on top of him, enveloping her in his arms. She gripped his hair, clutching it in her fingers, hanging on as though keeping him from escaping. He tunneled his fingers through hers, letting it fall forward to frame her face.

"Lauren."

She kissed him again, shutting down what he wanted to say, so he said it with his mouth, with his hands. He kissed her harder, growing urgent, experiencing the myriad of tastes that was Lauren. Her breasts pressed against his chest, their bodies producing the friction to peak her nipples. He released her hair to run his hands along her back.

Lauren straddled him, the cleft between her legs lying hot against his growing shaft. She pushed her hands flat on his chest, letting him slide his hands to her bottom. The look she gave him stopped his heart and his mind.

"Is something wrong?"

She gave him that soft smile he'd come to love. "No. But about the other time... The time when you tied me up. If you want to do that again..."

Lauren couldn't have said any sweeter words. "Hell, yes, I do." A flicker of one of those indecipherable looks crossed her face. "But not this time." He rolled on top of her, took her face in his hands, intent on her understanding him, knowing him, wanting him. "That time was great, sexy as hell, and yeah, I do want to do that again. But right now, I want more than sex with you." He swallowed, suddenly fearful of her reaction. "I want to make love with you."

Her eyes moistened, then closed. He held his breath, every second lasting an hour. But when she opened her eyes, he knew without question, without words, that she wanted the same. Tugging her along with him, he led her into the bedroom.

Her bed was covered in a blue comforter with colored pillows creating a headboard against the yellow wall. A nightstand and dresser completed the room with a few select objects resting on their clean surfaces. Bright and airy, this room was a reflection of her: cheerful and thoughtful.

Daniel watched her turn down the bed she'd made only a few hours earlier, keeping the comforter folded straight. She smoothed the simple white sheets, preparing their bed. Didn't she realize how rumpled he intended to make the sheets? He smiled, turned her to face him and kissed her. He continued feathering her mouth, her eyes, her cheeks with kisses as he tugged the T-shirt over her head. She giggled and tugged his shirt off in return. Her braless breasts made him ache and he had to touch them. Running her hands along his arms, she laced her fingers behind his neck, lifting her breasts in welcome.

"Daniel."

He shushed her and unbuttoned her jeans, letting them fall to the floor in the same moment she freed him of his. Twisting one finger in her panties, he tugged, easily ridding her of them. She lowered her eyes, acting shyly. Lifting her chin, he studied her and let her do the same.

"You're beautiful."

She blushed, then giggled that wonderful sound she made.

"You can still use your safe word. If you want."

She shook her head, but didn't speak. Taking that to mean what he wanted, he kissed her again and lowered her onto the bed. She lay down and tried to cover her body with the bedspread.

"No, don't." He slid over her, holding his body away from hers. "I don't want you to ever feel like you should hide from me." Would she understand that he meant her thoughts as well as her body?

She swallowed and he couldn't resist licking the hollow at her neck. He breathed in deeply, taking in her scent and memorizing it. If he had to, he could find her anywhere by her scent alone.

"Make love to me, Daniel."

"Yes." He dipped lower, dragging his lips from the hollow of her neck, between her breasts, then over to one, then the other. He cupped her breast, loving the way it fit his palm, and nuzzled her other one. Teasing her with his tongue, he played with the nipple, flicking it, making it grow taut with his teeth.

Lauren arched her back, giving her breasts to him. She caressed his legs with hers, stealing the strength to hold his body away from hers. He lowered his torso, putting his shaft next to her warm mons. Wrapping her legs around his waist, she captured him and brought him to her.

Daniel crushed against her and, fearful of hurting her, rolled, placing her on top. She nibbled soft kisses over his chest, murmuring words he couldn't hear but understood. Closing his eyes, he couldn't help but wonder how he'd come to find this woman. And with the wonder came the fear. How would he keep her? Would she want to stay? Or would she go back to her human life and forget him? Forcing the unwanted thoughts away, he lifted her, placing her pussy on top of him.

She tossed her hair, her breasts jiggling along with her movement, and he took them in his hands, wanting the weight of them.

"I need you, Daniel. I can't wait much longer."

He'd planned on taking longer, much longer, but her desire flowed into him. Her body trembled, an earthquake that rumbled into his.

His incisors erupted, ready for the marking. The wolf within roared its demands, telling him to throw her on her stomach and ram into her from behind. He suppressed a greedy growl and told his wolf to back off, keeping the animal inside. *Not yet*, he thought. *She isn't mine yet*, he told his wolf. She wasn't his—theirs—unless he forced it and he wouldn't risk forcing her. Watching the emotions—lust, ecstasy, anticipation—on her face, he saw an almost ethereal glow spread over her. She was beautiful, inside and out.

Lauren rocked up and down, backward, forward, her eyes closed. She placed her hands on his pecs for balance, her nails digging into his skin and jolting him out of his trance. Moaning, he gripped her hips to move her in the right direction. His cock, full and near completion, pumped into her, and her vaginal walls surrounded him to hold him as securely as chains would have. He was the captive now and she the keeper.

The avalanche that preceded his release swept through him, expected yet surprising in its intensity. Lauren tensed along with him and leaned back, placing her palms on either side of his legs. Her brow furrowed with concentration and he had a sudden urge to lick the furrow away. She deserved everything he could give her, including peace, at whatever cost to him. In the seconds before they climaxed, he made his decision.

Snarling, he pounded into her, bucking her like a rider on a bronc. She yelled out, her juices flowing down to his curly patch. He matched her yell with a shout and threw back his head, his shoulders and arms shaking in the release. Crying as though she were in pain, she fell on top of him.

He smoothed her hair, inhaling the sweet smell that was Lauren. She was nothing that he'd thought she was, yet so much more. Snuggling her close, he closed his eyes, peaceful and content for the first time in many months.

"Daniel?"

"Hmm?"

"You said we needed to talk. Please tell me you're not breaking up with me. Especially not after having mind-blowing sex with me."

He chuckled, moved her to the side so he could see her face and nuzzled into her neck. Was this the same joke? Or did she really fear his leaving? Her sweet scent aroused him again and, for a second, he opened his mouth, ready to sink his fangs into her. If he had his way, he'd claim her for his mate. The thought sent a warm happiness through him.

She was right, however—they did need to talk and he couldn't delay it any longer. Growling, he lifted himself onto his elbow and ran a finger from one side of her chin to the other.

"No, I'm not breaking up with you." Funny, how they'd fallen into being a couple without ever discussing it. "But this is serious. Lauren, you have to stop hunting."

Her eyebrows dove toward her warm brown eyes. "I thought we had this straight. I'm not a hunter."

"I know you're not. At least not any longer. But you have to stop going on hunts and trying to fool the other hunters."

Her confusion warped into annoyance in record time. "You know why I go on the hunts. I have to try to help. After what happened to Torrie, then Mysta and Tyler, what else can I do?"

The fact that Lauren wanted to help his people, even after all the danger involved, made him vow to hold her in his arms and protect her with the last beat of his heart. Protecting her, however, meant getting her to stop risking her life.

"We'll find another way for you to help. But you can't go on. Either the werewolves will get you or the hunters will figure things out. I'm not sure which is worse and I don't want to find out."

She huffed, pouting her lips, but he could tell she wasn't serious. "Can't we talk about this later? After you run out and get us something yummy?"

He ran a finger over her mouth, loving the way her soft lips felt. "Okay. But you'll be careful while I'm gone?"

Her eyes softened. "Of course. Besides, nothing's going to happen before you get back."

"Good." The knot in his stomach unwound a little. He nuzzled her ear, then licked her collarbone.

Her answering lick came as a surprise, throwing him off-balance. "How about a gallon of my favorite ice cream? And I want a shower to freshen up a bit while you run down to the market and grab us some mint chocolate chip. I want to make myself pretty."

"You're already pretty." He returned her lick with one of his own. If he had his way, he'd lick her all over her body.

Lauren laughed and wiggled out of his arms. "Go on. If you hurry, I might still be in the shower when you return."

He grinned and grabbed for his clothes. "Don't shower too quickly. I want to wash you. Every inch of you."

"Then get moving, wolfman."

Lauren hurried out of the shower and grabbed the phone. "Hello?"

"Where the hell have you been, Lauren?"

The familiar voice sent a chill through her and she pulled the towel tighter around her. "John?"

"Well? What do you have to say for yourself?"

No "I've been worried about you" from this jerk. Lauren bit back the retort. Still there was no need to get him any more riled up than he already sounded.

"I thought Bobbie called you and told you about my sick aunt. What was I supposed to do, John? Ignore my family when they needed me?"

"You're supposed to keep your boyfriend informed of your whereabouts. You disappeared from the hunt and I didn't know what had happened to you."

"Oh, come on, John. Admit it. You figured I'd gotten fed up lagging behind everyone else and went home. You were probably happy that I left the hunt early and stopped slowing you down." The silence on the other end confirmed her suspicions. "See? I knew it."

"Okay, yeah, I was. But then when you didn't answer my call the next day, I had to wonder. Your lack of consideration threw off my entire week."

She couldn't believe her ears. She vanishes without a trace and he doesn't call to check on her until the next day? And then does nothing else when she didn't respond? If John were standing in front of her right now... Or better yet, in front of Daniel. She smiled, thinking of Daniel and ice cream. Oh, what a sexy combination!

"I'm sorry. I really am. But I'm back, so would you please calm down? I promise I'll make it up to you." Not on his life. The next time she saw John she'd break up with him. Maybe she should go ahead and break up with him over the phone?

"Damn straight you will. I'm not just a patient who gets messages from the receptionist."

"Bobbie is my friend, not merely my employee. But can we talk about this later?"

"Not that I should do you any favors, but since you did manage a kill the last time we went out, I figured you'd want to know about tonight's hunt. In fact, we're about to get going."

"What? Now? I don't know. In fact, John, I've been thinking—"

"Look, Lauren, I know it's short notice but it is what it is. We've got a line on a female. A *pregnant* female. Think about it. We can wipe out two at once." He chuckled and she heard the excitement in his tone.

Lauren bit her lip. Hoping to please Daniel, she'd decided not to go on another hunt, but how could she let John hurt another werewolf? Especially a pregnant female? She imagined the werewolf, her belly swollen with child, lying on the ground, her blood and the child's life force spilling from her body. She shook her head. She'd had to watch as the hunters killed other werewolves, but she'd be damned if she'd do nothing to prevent this tragedy.

"Lauren, are you there? Are you coming or not?"

"Sure. Count me in. I'm ready for some action. Are we meeting at Luigi's?"

"Yeah, the usual. But you've got to get here in the next few minutes if you want in. Otherwise, we leave without you."

Daniel would understand once he knew about the female and her baby. She had to tell him, but he'd left his cell phone behind. Still, if she left him a note, maybe he could warn the female. Or get the pack to help? But where should she tell them to find her?

Crooking the phone between her shoulder and ear, she quickly scribbled a note to Daniel, urging him to hurry to the hunters' usual meeting place behind Luigi's Italian Restaurant. Maybe she could stall the group, giving Daniel time to catch up with them. If not, she'd have to come up with a way to save the shifter herself.

If only there was a way to leave a trail for Daniel to follow. Her gaze fell on the horrible-smelling perfume her grandmother had given her for her birthday. Daniel had sniffed it earlier in the day, declaring it the worst thing he'd ever smelled. Unscrewing the bottle, she liberally applied the perfume to her body and grimaced at the stench. If Daniel couldn't follow her now, then he needed his nose fixed.

"Lauren, don't even think about up and disappearing again. That kind of shit has to stop."

"Okay, I've got it. I'll see you as soon as I can." She clicked off the phone and took a moment to reconsider her decision. Daniel would understand, right? Once the hunt was over and she'd saved another life—two lives—she was sure he'd forgive her for leaving without him.

Chapter Ten

Dressing as quickly as she could, Lauren grabbed her rifle bag and rushed downstairs. The few minutes it took her to get to her parking space dragged into an eternity.

Lauren jumped out of her car and hurried to the back parking lot of Luigi's. John and the others huddled in the dimming light, speaking in lowered tones. Deciding she couldn't turn back now, she held her head up, thrust out her chin and plastered on a smile.

"Hey, guys." Ignoring the fact that no one—not even John—returned her greeting, she unzipped her bag and hefted her gun into her left hand. Thank goodness Daniel had returned her rifle with the blanks still in it. Could she use the same trick a second time? "Ready to go shootin' for shifters?" Her voice sounded tinny to her ear. "Sounds like a game show, doesn't it? Get it? Shootin' for Shifters?"

The glum looks that darted between the men and John told the whole story. The men didn't want her along. But did that mean she was busted? "Remember last time? I got him good, didn't I?"

John didn't hide his irritation. "Yeah, sure we do. Although some of the guys aren't too happy that you left the carcass there." A few grumbled their agreement. "Lauren, are you sure you're up for this? I mean, nobody's going to mind if you sit this one out." He scrunched up his nose in revulsion. "Crap, girl, you reek. You're wearing that shit your grandma gave you, aren't you?"

"Don't you like it?"

"Hell, no. And don't wear it again. You're liable to scare even a skanky-smelling werewolf away." Mumbles and nodding heads surrounded her like voice-activated bobbleheads.

"Of course I'm up for it. After sitting around on the sofa with my sick aunt and watching soap operas and game shows, I'm ready for some excitement." She knew she shouldn't risk it, but she couldn't resist. Anything to buy time. "Don't you want me to hunt with you, fellas?" Feigning a sad expression, she bet that the good nature of most of the hunters would win out and they'd remain silent. Judging by their sudden interest in the pavement, she'd pegged them correctly. "I think I'll take that as a yes."

John, however, wasn't giving up that easily. Taking her aside, he whispered, "Like I said before, you've got to know that you haven't done a very good job keeping up with the group."

Lauren hated to play girly games, but she would if she had to. "I know and I'm so sorry, John. I didn't realize I was such a burden." She thought about Torrie and worked up a tear. He hated to see women cry. Not that he felt bad for them. Instead, it made him nervous, and he hated feeling nervous. "Could you give me another chance? Pretty please?"

"Well, okay." He leaned in closer. "But try to stay up with us. No more falling behind to tie your shoes, got it?"

"Got it." She bit back a retort. *One day he's gonna get it, if I have my way.* "But hey, guys?"

The hunters turned toward her, frowns and scowls on their faces. They couldn't have voiced their dislike of her any better with words.

"How about I treat everyone to a beer first? Or maybe even dinner?"

"What the hell are you talking about?" John gaped at her as though she'd lost her mind. "We don't have time to socialize. We've got a shifter to kill."

Lauren grabbed his arm, keeping him with her. "It's just that we never got to celebrate my kill. So I just thought we could take a few minutes to heft a beer or two."

"Think again." John shook off her arm. Giving the signal to follow him, John sprinted down the adjacent alley with Lauren and the rest on his heels. She moved into the middle of the group to take a position where she could go either faster or slower, left or right, whichever way she needed to cause a diversion. They ran, stopping to rest after a mile, then started again. Lauren kept glancing around her, hoping to see a shadow that signaled Daniel's arrival, but she saw nothing. The others, confident in their superiority, moved on, careless of their surroundings. Like so many times before, John was the one who spotted something and slowed them to a stop.

Lauren peered into the dimly lit alley in front of them, searching for a werewolf. Yet as hard as she tried, she couldn't see anything. "John, wh—"

John whirled on her, his finger to his lips. Jerking his head to indicate an area next to a Dumpster, he motioned for the others to crouch beside him. Lauren still couldn't see anything and she bet none of the other hunters could either. Nonetheless, they followed John's example and hunkered down. This wouldn't be the first time John had located a shifter when no one else could. The man had a finding-a-shifter knack.

Again Lauren searched the area. *Please, don't let it be the pregnant female.* Again she glanced behind her, hoping to see a dark werewolf on their trail. *Daniel, where are you?*

John gave another signal, telling them to stay close. As a group, they inched forward a few feet, then stopped when John went down on one knee. Lauren squinted and saw nothing, her pulse beating in her ears. How could she save the shifter if she couldn't see it?

The rifle was on John's shoulder and the shot off before she realized what had happened. A large werewolf leapt into the air, snarling, and came down hard. He backed into the darkness, his escape blocked on either side of him by walls. The only way out was through the hunters. Lauren's heart pounded, both in rage and shock. Damn, she hadn't had time to do anything to help the shifter. Now the only option left was her blank bullets.

"Well, it's not the female we're hunting, but I'm not complaining. I'm fairly sure I hit him." The smug grin on John's face made her want to upchuck. "Let's go finish him off."

The group hurried closer to the limping werewolf and formed a semicircle around him.

"Keep him penned up, men." John grinned at the others. "I want to take my time and enjoy this."

"Just take your time to aim better, okay? You didn't kill with the first shot, John. Maybe you're losing your touch."

John scowled at the hunter. "Maybe. But I'm also the one who found him. I didn't see you tracking anything, Walter."

The others laughed at the friendly barbs the two men exchanged. Lauren, for once, couldn't fake it. Did the shifter look familiar? Had she seen him at the mansion? Was this a friend of Daniel's?

Jumping in front of the group, she lifted her rifle and sent the werewolf a pleading look. "Get ready to *fall down* and die, you vile beast." She hoped the shifter caught the added emphasis she'd put on the words. If he didn't play along, then they were both in trouble.

"Hey! What d'ya think you're doing? This is my kill."

She stepped closer to the shifter, putting distance between her and the hunters. She looked down the scope, taking aim. "Come on, John. If this is my last hunt—" she checked the hunters' expressions and knew she'd hit a nerve, "—then let me go out with a bang." Mouthing the words "play dead" to the werewolf, she said a silent prayer and pulled the trigger.

For a moment, she didn't think the werewolf had understood. Then, almost in slow motion, the shifter fell to the ground, growled and lay still.

"Woo-hoo! She did it again."

"It's about time she learned how to shoot. Now if only she could hit a moving target."

John tugged her around to face him. "Since this is your last hunt—" he paused to let his declaration set in, "—I'll let that go. But don't ever pull anything like that again, got it?"

She puffed out a blast of pent-up air. "Got it." Raising her rifle into the air, she shouted, "Okay, everyone, back to Luigi's for a celebration on me."

The men hooted and started to follow her. John, however, had other ideas. He moved to stand above the shifter before Lauren could stop him.

"John, come on. Forget the carcass. You know I don't want it and it's my say-so what to do with it. Let's go party. Please?" She ran her hand down his back, dragging her nails. Getting close to his ear, she whispered, "Then we can have our own party after that."

John backed up quickly, almost knocking her over. "What the hell? It's still breathing." The hunters rejoined them, crowding her close to a fuming John. "Either you missed or..." He grabbed her gun, pointed the rifle at a box several feet away and pulled the trigger.

Lauren started backing up, preparing to run, but the hunters closed in on her. John stared at the gun, then turned to face them. "The gun had no retort and that box didn't move. She's shooting blanks." He tossed her rifle to the ground. "We've been had." John's face closed in, his frown morphing into a face of fury. "You used blanks the last time, didn't you? You didn't kill that shifter either, did you?"

Hands clutched her and forced her forward. The werewolf jumped to its feet and began pacing, once more a trapped animal. Angry words and calls of "traitor" assaulted her, but she barely heard them, instead concentrating on the furious man in front of her. She was cornered just like the werewolf.

"John, please let him go."

The men laughed, taking it as a joke. John, however, wasn't fooled. "Are you crazy? Why the hell would I do that?"

Could she make him see that shifters weren't the evil creatures he thought they were? Maybe if this shifter changed back into human form, he could show them how human he really was. "Get him to change back."

"Again. Why the hell would I do that? He's an animal no matter what form he's in."

The werewolf stopped pacing, his amber eyes narrowing. A low rumble of a snarl vibrated the air around them.

"In fact, I don't know why I'm even talking about this."

Lauren's stomach dropped as John whirled around and unloaded his clip into the shifter. The werewolf jerked and fell to the ground, blood gushing from a now unrecognizable head.

"No!" Enraged, Lauren fought against the men holding her, but it was no use. All she could do was scream and cry until she had no energy left. Her knees gave out and she remained upright only because the men held her. "You don't understand them, John." She glanced around, taking in each of the hunters. "None of you do. They're not that different from us."

"Are you kidding me? They change into beasts and kill innocent people."

Taking a deep breath, she pushed on, keeping her gaze from the dead werewolf. "Have you ever seen them kill anyone? Because I haven't." Turning to look at each hunter, she asked, "Have you?" When no one could say they had, she gained the encouragement to continue. "That's right. No one has. Why? Because the werewolves have a policy to not hurt anyone unless they have no other choice. They never initiate an attack. In fact, they avoid fighting unless they're trying to protect themselves."

John gawked at her, fury flaming his face. "And you know this how?" He confronted her, placing his face inches from hers. "You're not a shifter. I know you're not."

"You're right. I'm not." Lauren wanted to look away but held her ground. She had nothing to lose. "I'm not a shifter, but I know one. In fact, I know several. And they're not the devil's spawn you think they are."

The men released her, stepping away from her as though she'd contracted a contagious disease. John did the same, disgust mixing with the anger. "You're lying."

She glanced at the werewolf, bereft at her failure to save him. "Sorry, bucko. I'm not lying. I've lied about liking hunting, yes, but I'm not lying about the shifters."

Where she'd disliked John's vehement reaction before, she now shivered at his sudden coldness. He'd transformed from an angry boyfriend into a calculating enemy. "You're not merely their fan, are you, Lauren? Hell, you're on their side."

"I'm on everyone's side." She hoped they could see the pleading in her eyes. "Can't we all just get along?" For a moment, no one spoke, all of them placing the familiar saying.

Oh shit. I can't believe I said that. She giggled, her nerves, her grief taking over. "Seriously, though, maybe if shifters and hunters sat down and talked it out—"

"I don't sit down with beasts. I shoot them."

Why couldn't he see? "Look at him, John. Couldn't you see the humanity in his eyes? Couldn't you feel his fear?"

Confused, John glanced at the dead werewolf and shook his head. "You're not making any sense."

"Yes, I am. If you would've tried, you could have seen past his appearance to the human inside. But now it's too late." She moaned, the emotions of the terrible day she'd killed Torrie boiling to the surface to mix with her grief for the murdered shifter. "I saw the humanity, the pain, the anguish and that's what made me understand. If I could take back what I did, if I could keep from killing her, I would."

"Killing who?" John's eyes lit up. "You mean the one shifter you managed to shoot and actually hit?"

An ache born of regret ripped through her. "Yes, the one shifter I killed. If I'd only understood—" His roaring laugh stopped her, drilling his cruelty into her.

"You dumb bitch."

Stunned, Lauren opened her mouth to speak, but nothing came out. John's incredulous expression hurt her more than his words ever could have.

"You little idiot, you didn't kill it."

"What?" Lauren wasn't sure he'd heard her whisper, but it didn't matter.

"Listen up, you dumb twit. You didn't kill it. Hell, you never even came close to killing it." John scoffed, his derision overtaking him. "I guess it's your turn not to understand. Don't you get it? I let you take the first shot that day, but your bullet grazed the animal. Shit, I was shocked that you managed to get the gun to your shoulder."

"Are you sure? But how do you know?" She'd seen the werewolf, seen Torrie react to getting shot.

"You're still a newbie, aren't you? Even after everything I've tried to teach you." He snorted. "Shit, you're hopeless. You couldn't kill an elephant standing two feet in front of you, much less a shifter several yards away."

"But why? Why would you let me think I'd shot her?" Lauren didn't know whether to feel angry at John or happy that she hadn't murdered Torrie.

"Come on, Lauren, get a clue. I let you get the first shot off so you'd get all excited. Excited, then hot and bothered in bed later."

Anger took the lead. She wanted to shoot him but instead forced her question through gritted teeth. "Answer me. How do you know I didn't kill her? How do you know it wasn't my bullet that killed her?"

He snickered. "I marked our bullets, remember? Yours with an L and mine with a J? You thought it was romantic like any dumb broad would. But it was just another ploy to get your panties off. I couldn't believe you'd actually hit the beast, so I had the boys dig the bullets out of the carcass." His leer widened. "None of them was your bullet. I found yours, with a trace of shifter blood on it, lodged in a tree behind the beast."

Daniel peered over the edge of the building. Good thing he'd turned back to the apartment to ask Lauren if she wanted anything else from the market. At first he'd been angry after reading her note, but he'd had time to cool off and think. Of course Lauren would try to help a pregnant werewolf. Wouldn't he have done the same thing? He'd changed on the run, slipping in and out of back alleys. Although he'd arrived at the restaurant after the hunters had already left, the stench of Lauren's perfume gave him a tentative trail to follow. Hearing the shots, however, led him directly to her. He snarled, his gaze fixed on the dead werewolf, one of the youngest members of his pack. If only he'd gotten here faster. Crouching, he focused on John.

Lauren didn't kill Torrie. The sentence ran through Daniel's mind, over and over, trying to get it to stick. *She shot at her. But it wasn't Lauren who'd taken his mate.* He was unprepared for the emotion that assaulted him. Knowing that Lauren wasn't responsible for his mate's death let loose a flood of relief that almost knocked him off his feet.

Fury, unrestrained and raw, ripped through him, demolishing the relief and charging him with a power that had to find a release. He was blinded with one overwhelming need: to kill the hunter who'd taken his mate from him and was threatening Lauren. Transformed, Daniel snarled, then launched his body from the top of the building. He flew through the air, his snarl growing into a mighty bellow, and landed on John's back.

"Urgh." John hit the ground face first, dropping his rifle, his arms flailing outward. Daniel tore into his clothes, raking his back into long slits of red. John screamed and struggled to rise, but the large werewolf kept him pinned and vulnerable.

"Daniel. No!"

But the beast was in control now, holding a tight rein on the human consciousness inside him. Daniel could hear her pleas to release the hunter, but he couldn't, wouldn't let him go. Growling, he warned the other hunters to stay back.

"Someone shoot it!"

"No, wait. We might hit John."

The hunters were in total disarray, mindless bodies waiting for an order from their head, their leader. One by one, they approached Daniel but scurried away when he lashed out, his razor-like claws raking empty air in warning.

"Daniel, please let him go."

Instead, Daniel sank his fangs into John's shoulder and shook him. John screamed, the sound almost animalistic. Daniel released the hunter and prepared to take the bite that would end his life. He would avenge Torrie's death, fulfilling the promise he'd made to her lifeless body, and protect Lauren.

"Daniel, please."

Lauren's whisper caught his attention where her shouts had failed. She knelt beside them, her hands clasped in front of her.

"You're better than he is. Please stop. Please let him go."

Daniel licked the blood from his lips and shook his head. John's cries grew softer and Daniel listened to them, delighting in the pitiful noises the hunter made. She couldn't ask this of him. Not after what this hunter had done to Torrie. Not after how he'd treated her.

"Don't, Daniel. Prove that even in your animal form, you're still better than he is. Better than all of us."

His answered rumbled inside his chest. John's blood tasted sweet and he wanted more.

"Would Torrie want you to kill him?"

Lauren's question surprised him and his snarl died in his throat. Of course his mate would want this. She would. He was sure of it. Yet memories of Torrie challenged him. Torrie's sweet face. Torrie cornering a hunter, then letting him go. Torrie talking to Daniel. Torrie wishing for peace between hunters and shifters.

"Would Torrie want you to become a killer like John?" Lauren reached out, hesitated, then touched John's arm. John groaned and latched on to her arm, his fingers digging into her.

Daniel growled, warning him, warning her. If the hunter hurt her, he'd die a swift and painful death.

"What would Torrie do, Daniel?"

Lauren wouldn't stop, instead searching deep inside him, past the beast and into the man. He hoped the animal would win out, to cage the man within, without words, without conscience. But Lauren's voice kept dragging the man back. "You've punished him enough. Please, Daniel, you forgave me. You can forgive John, too."

The two were not the same. Daniel wanted to tell her that but couldn't. Lauren had gone on the hunt that had taken Torrie's life, but she hadn't realized what she was doing until it was too late. And once she had, she'd changed, vowing to help other shifters. John, on the other hand, thirsted for shifter blood and continued to kill.

"Let him go and we'll get out of here. Please, Daniel. If you won't do it for me, then do it for Torrie."

She was right. Torrie would want him to let John go. The thought struggled to take hold in Daniel, but his wolf fought against it, didn't want to see the truth of it. No, he wanted John to pay, to hurt the way Torrie had, the way he had, the way Lauren had. But he couldn't deny the honesty when he heard it. Both Torrie and Lauren would let John go. Howling his frustration, he jumped off the struggling hunter and stepped into Lauren's arms.

She embraced him, careless of the blood staining her clothes. "Thank you, Daniel. Thank you."

Daniel closed his eyes. Shoving the angry werewolf back inside was difficult, harder than ever before, but he shifted, his human form fighting its way to the surface. His chest heaved, his naked body covered with sweat, not from the physical exertion to change, but from the emotions tearing jagged wounds inside him.

"Daniel?"

He opened his eyes, found her searching him, tears glistening and ready to fall. "Are you all right, Lauren?"

She giggled and tossed her hair. "I should ask you the same thing."

"I'm fine. Or at least I will be once we get the hell out of here."

"Like hell you will." John grabbed for his rifle, snatching it off the ground seconds before Lauren reached for it.

Fear widened her eyes and a sinking feeling gripped him. They turned together, ready to face their enemies. John, battered and bloody, held a dirty rag to his bleeding shoulder and wobbled on his feet. Stone-faced, he pressed the muzzle of his gun against Daniel's head. "You're not going anywhere, shifter. Except straight to Hell."

Daniel growled, coiled and ready to spring, but froze as another hunter grabbed Lauren and dragged her several feet away. He snarled another warning, his fangs breaking the skin and sliding over his lower lip, the change just under the surface eager to take control again. "Let her go."

The scent of hatred flowed from John. "Shut up, you filthy beast." He lowered the rifle, shoving it against Daniel's ribcage.

The prod was painful, but watching them bind Lauren's hands hurt even more. The urge to tear John's head off hardened inside him, the werewolf inside calling for blood, but Daniel knew better than to risk charging the hunter. One shot and Lauren would lie dead at his feet.

John's evil leer made him want to vomit, yet instead, he managed a smile. "You don't want to hurt her. She's one of your own. She's human and a hunter." If he could get them to release Lauren, then he didn't care what they did to him. "Killing a shifter is one thing, but a human? That's murder, isn't it?" He scanned the other hunters, determined to appeal to what little sense of decency they had. "Do you want a human's blood on your hands? Is it worth life in prison?" Several of the hunters appeared nervous, glancing at one another and shifting back and forth on their feet. "You know what I'm saying is right. Hurt Lauren and you'll all be guilty of murder." He straightened, determined to die on his feet. "Come on. Let her go. If you'll do, I'll do whatever you want."

John's chuckle cut through him. "You'll do whatever I want anyway, beast." His face hardened as he turned to Lauren. "You screwed up big time, bitch. If you'd stayed in your place, I'd have trained you to be a good, dutiful woman. Hell, I was even thinking of marrying you." His sneer bled into his tone. "But you can forget that. Me marry a shifter-lover? No way in hell." John paused, looked at Lauren and then Daniel, and pieced it together. "Oh, my God. It's worse than I thought. You don't love him like you'd love a pet. You love him like he's a human man."

John clutched her hair and shook her. Lauren's cry sent Daniel into a rage, whipping the animal inside to a frenzy. He struggled not to change at the same time fighting the fury, the adrenaline that rushed through him so violently that he almost blacked out. The hunter kept his gun trained at him and, if he hadn't released Lauren soon after, Daniel would've charged him.

"Why, you dirty slut. You slept with that *thing*?"

"Don't blame the victim, man." Daniel plastered on a lecherous smile, hoping to make the hunter assume he'd raped her. Unfortunately, her innocence didn't mean anything to

John. His expression of disgust didn't change. "I took her sweet ass."

"Lying down with dogs is lying down with dogs. Any way it happens, you still end up with fleas." His scorn was directed at Lauren again. "I don't touch dirty animals, human or otherwise. Thank God you've acted like a bitch lately and kept me from wanting to fuck you."

"I'm surprised she'd ever let you near her." Daniel's stomach clenched at the idea of Lauren and John together.

Seeing a way to get to Daniel, John took his best shot. "Oh, I got to her, werewolf." His sneer grew wider. "I had her every way you can think of. Including doggy-style."

"You're a liar, you bastard."

Daniel grinned at Lauren's vehement denial. "The lady says differently, Johnny."

John gritted his teeth, grinding out his words. "She's no lady. Trust me. Her cunt's loose from screwing everything she can get, but her ass is still good and tight." He knelt closer to Daniel. "Tell me, dirtbag. How did you like my sloppy seconds?"

The hunter had finally crossed the line. Opening the cage and freeing his inner wolf, Daniel flew through the air, striking John in the chest. Lauren's shout to stop came too late. Instead, the only thing he could see or hear was the hunter beneath him. The shift came quickly, ripping through him faster than it ever had before. They hit the ground together, but Daniel stayed on top. Slamming John's head against the pavement, he dropped his jaw, ready to tear flesh and bone apart.

"Get him!"

"Don't shoot. You might hit John!"

The voices surrounded him and he sensed the others moving closer. But he didn't care. All that mattered was his need to taste the hunter's blood, hear the choking sounds as he took his final breaths. All that mattered was death.

A blow to the head rattled him and he twisted around to glare at the hunter holding his rifle by the barrel. He snarled, tried to shake the fuzziness away, but another blow to his head sent him rolling to the side. Daniel struck out, hoping to hit someone, something, but raked air instead. Another blow against his ear rocked him. His legs gave out and he collapsed, still clawing for John. Blackness swept through him, and he roared, fighting to stay conscious, fighting for a few more precious seconds. He had to kill John. For Lauren's safety. The blackness followed another sharp blow to his head and, at last, he lost the struggle.

Lauren screamed and lurched toward the fallen Daniel, but strong hands held her back. "Daniel! Please, Daniel, get up!"

Her throat cracked with the intensity of her shout, but she barely noticed. She had to help him. If she could save him, then whatever they did to her wouldn't matter.

John stumbled over to Daniel, grabbed his hair and lifted his head. "Yep, he's out." With a wicked laugh, he turned Daniel loose.

Daniel's head fell to the pavement, making a noise Lauren would never forget, but he still didn't move.

"Damn you, John. Damn all of you. He was right. What you do is nothing short of murder. You're not hunters. You're coldblooded killers." She struggled against the two men holding her, saliva forming in her lust to get her hands on John. He would pay. Someday, somehow, she would see that he paid.

John swaggered over to her, his cockiness overriding his pain. "Yeah, we're killers. We kill the scum of the world, the vermin that infests our city. If people knew about our sacrifice, the time, the money, hell, the dangers we face to keep them safe, they'd call us heroes, not murderers."

Lauren reared back, then sent a wad of spit flying at him. Her aim was true, hitting him directly below his left eye. She laughed full out and kept laughing until he struck her cheek. His blow made her sway unsteadily on her feet and she would have fallen if the men hadn't kept their grip on her. But she refused to let him wipe the smile off her face. "Go fuck yourself, John Rawlings."

He pinched her chin between fingers, shooting pain along her jaw line. "I'd rather fuck myself than fuck you again." Snorting, he jerked his hand away. "Max, Walter, Charlie, you men stay here and take care of this mangy mutt. Give him time to come to, then shoot him in the head. I want him to know what's going to happen to him."

"Don't you want to do the honors, John?" Walter kicked Daniel in the side.

Lauren held her breath, unsure whether to hope Daniel would move. If he did, then at least she'd know he was still alive. But that would mean his death would come that much faster. Instead, she prayed that he was alive but would remain unconscious awhile longer. Long enough for her to come up with a plan or for help to come. Had Daniel called the pack before he'd left?

"I'd like to." John licked his lips, making Lauren's skin crawl. "But I think I've already finished him off. The bullet to the head is easy and sort of, well, anticlimactic." He ran his hand along her shoulder, down her side to fondle her breast. "Besides, watching this bitch beg for mercy will be more fun."

Lauren wrenched away from him. "You want another spitball? How about a nice big fat one?" She made a show of gathering her saliva and got ready to spit.

John, however, wasn't taking any chances and backed away. "Damn. And I used to think you had class."

"I did. Until I started hanging with you."

He reared back to strike her again, but this time she twisted enough to dodge the blow. "Heh, heh, missed me."

John's face flamed to an angry red and he drew back to hit her again.

"John, hold up." Luke snagged John's arm. "I don't mind shooting werewolves, but when it comes to hitting women, I draw the line."

John yanked his hand away and looked like he was about to hit the young hunter. The low rumble from the others kept him in check and he grudgingly lowered his hand. "That's where you've got it wrong, my friend. She ceased being a woman when she started fucking werewolves."

"Still, I don't like it. What are you going to do with her?"

Lauren sensed that John wanted to do more than he was willing to say and she decided to use that to her advantage. "Yeah, Johnny, what are you going to do with me? I don't think these upstanding men will let you murder me like you're going to do to Daniel. So what can you do with me?" For a moment, with the hunters waiting to see what he would decide, she thought just maybe John would have to let her go.

"Like I said, Max, Charlie and Walter will stay here and exterminate this animal. The rest of us will take her someplace special." He chuckled, low and nasty. "I'll decide what to do with her after I've reminded her what it's like to be with a real man."

He was buying time to convince the others to do as he wanted. Could she get away in the meantime? The likelihood of escaping would decrease once he got her to his so-called special place.

"Let's go, men." John waved his hand and led the way back to their vehicles. "We'll swing by Doc Miller's first and get me patched up. I could use a handful of pills, too. Then we'll have ourselves some real fun."

Lauren struggled with the two men holding her, twisting around to get one last look at Daniel. She kept struggling through the dark alleys, making as much noise as she could. But no one was around to hear her.

Reaching the parking lot at Luigi's, Lauren looked around, desperately hoping to see any late-night diners, but only the hunters' vehicles remained. The darkness of the restaurant and surrounding businesses added to her despondent mood.

Norman slid into the back seat of John's Jeep, tugging her along with him. "Ow!" Lauren landed on her side.

"Sorry, but if you'd gotten in like we asked you to, then I wouldn't have pushed you." Bruce slid onto the seat beside her and slammed the door. "I don't like this any more than you do."

"Then put a stop to it." She lowered her voice and leaned in to the hunter. "You know what John has in mind. Do you really want to see me die?"

Bruce's color drained and he glanced past her to Norman. "John won't do that, will he, Norm? He's just upset right now, right? I mean, a man doesn't like to think of his woman fooling around on him, much less with one of those things. But that doesn't mean he's gonna really kill her, does it? Huh, Norm, huh?"

"Are you kidding me?" Lauren rested against the back of the seat so she could look at both hunters. "Come on, you two. I'm a witness to what he's done. A traitor in his eyes and he doesn't take betrayal well. He's going to shut me up for good and make it seem like I died in some freak accident. You know, like how a lot of people die by slipping in their showers? Let's face it. One blow to the head resembles another to the police, and accidents in the home happen all the time. Plus, John has friends on the police force so no one's going to question the grieving boyfriend's story."

The men squirmed in their seats, obviously unnerved. "Norm, you don't think she's right, do you? You don't think he'd hurt—"

"What are you two yapping about?" John, his face ashen with pain, entered the Jeep on the passenger side with a towel thrown over his bloodied back. Hooking his uninjured arm over the seat, he confronted them, suspicion oozing from him. "Don't listen to anything she has to say. She's a devil woman who can talk a man into anything. Just like she talked me into having sex with her."

Luke slid onto the driver's seat.

"Oh, please. Like I had to talk you into bed. You're a dirty dog, John, and you know it. Stop trying to make them think I'm something other than what I am. I'm the woman you plan on murdering." Lauren scowled, intent on meeting him eye for eye, when a blur to the right of the Jeep caught her attention. She glanced that way, then jerked her attention back to John. Had she seen a tail whipping around the corner? Keeping her composure, she forced herself not to look again. If the werewolf cavalry had arrived, she didn't want to reveal them to the hunters.

"Drive, Luke." John voice was shaky, yet cold as ice.

Lauren closed her eyes and sent a quick prayer skyward. With a little luck, the shifters would find Daniel and save him before it was too late. Slumping in her seat, she smiled, happy to know her lover had a chance.

"Where are you taking me? You said someplace special." She grinned, using the relief she felt for Daniel to make the grin sincere. "Oh, wow, John. Are you taking me to your favorite restaurant?" She tucked her head and whispered to the hunters beside her, yet loud enough for John's benefit. "He always takes me to the most expensive place he can afford. John, are we going to the Golden Arches again?"

Norm and Bruce broke into fits of laughter—until John glared them into silence. "Funny, Lauren, real funny. Why the hell do you think I took you to Mickey D's? I'll tell you why. Because you weren't worth spending any real money on."

Lauren quipped back, "Really? I thought it was because you like the kid's meal."

John grunted a laugh, this time going along with the other hunters' chuckles. "I'm glad you like to have a good time, pussy cheeks, because I'm taking you to the funnest place on Earth. And no, I don't mean Disneyland."

"Funnest isn't a word, you moron. And even if it were, no place is fun when you're there."

John looked like he wanted to jump over the seat and strangle her. "I may not have the education you have, Miss High-and-Mighty, but I do know one thing."

"Oh? What's that? That your boogers aren't the best tasting things around?" Lauren pushed back against the seat to avoid John's attempt to smack her.

"You better watch your mouth, bitch." He composed himself, wiping the grimace of pain off his face and bringing back the controlled John she liked even less. "Never mind. You'll see once we get there."

The Jeep sped by industrial buildings and factories, then past neatly organized neighborhoods into the outskirts of town. After a brief stop at a skuzzy-looking all-night medical clinic where John had his wounds disinfected and bandaged, they continued on into the countryside.

By the time they pulled into the deserted carnival, Lauren had already dismissed several escape plans. How could she trick four hunters and get away? She scanned the area around the dilapidated buildings and rides. Unfortunately, the area was deserted. If she screamed, would anyone hear her? And even if someone did hang out at Reject Land, would they ignore her cries and stay inside, safely out of trouble?

"Get out." John stood at the open door and waited for her to scoot out of the Jeep. If anyone had seen them, they would've thought he was a courteous boyfriend.

His glittering eyes were not those of a sane man, and Lauren wondered if it was insanity or the pain medication making him appear crazy. Was he so determined to hurt her that he'd do anything, take anything to keep going?

"Not a word, Lauren. You call for help and you die. Got it?" He struck his palm against his forehead. "Oh, wait. Not to worry. There's no one to hear you anyway. So go ahead. Scream, yell, whatever. Do your best. The coyotes won't mind."

What did she have to lose? Lauren leaned her head back and yelled. Her call of "help", however, changed into a combination screech and howl.

John clamped a hand over her mouth. "Damn it. Shut the hell up." When she did, he took his hand off her mouth. "Shit, Lauren. If I didn't know better, I'd swear you were already one of them."

She howled again, this time making it sound even more like a wolf call. Maybe if she got lucky, Daniel would be close enough to hear her.

"What the hell are you doing?"

She couldn't help it. She had to take another dig at him. "I know I wasn't the dumb one in our relationship, but come on, John. I assumed even you could figure that out." She scoffed and delighted in watching the vein in his forehead throb. The men chuckled along with her, but John put a stop to their laughter soon enough. "Okay, let me spell it out for you. That was a distress call." She bit the inside of her cheek to keep from giggling. But this time, the giggles were from enjoying the worried expression on his face and not her nerves. "I called the pack, John. So, if you know what's good for you, you'll let me go before they get here."

"No, you didn't."

She could see he was a lot less confident than he was trying to put on. "Oh, yes I did. And when they get hold of you, all of you—" she pointed at each hunter, "—you're going to regret it big-time. Why, John, is that sweat I see? Tsk, tsk. And here I thought you were the big, bad hunter."

"Watch what you say, skank. I'm in no mood for a snarky woman."

"Snarky? Did you learn a new word watching Nickelodeon?" John's hard shove couldn't wipe the zing of excitement she got from the look on his face. She giggled again. Still, she couldn't spend her time baiting him. Instead, she needed to concentrate on a way to escape. He grabbed her arm and pulled her past the entrance gates.

Her mind whirled with possibilities. Should she do the dead weight thing and make them carry her? At least it might slow them down in case the shifters were able to save Daniel and he was on the way to help her. *If* they could find her. Should she try to make a run for it? She knew she could outrun the other three, but John was faster. If he had to chase her, would that make him more determined to see her die?

"Up the steps."

She stalled for a moment and squinted at the fun house. In the daylight, the place would appear rundown and sad. But at night the dilapidated appearance worked with the darkness to cast eerie shadows. She shuddered, started to refuse to move and earned another shove. Gritting back a retort, she stomped up the stairs to the front door. If she'd made that much noise at her apartment, Mr. Gallagher from downstairs would've stuck his head out of his apartment to complain. If only Grumpy Gallagher were around! Again, she surveyed the area around her, hoping to find someone, anyone, and came up empty.

Fumbling with the rusty lock bought her a minute's delay but, at last, John broke the rusted metal apart and kicked the door wide.

"Lauren, is that you? Thank goodness."

Lauren and the hunters pivoted, ready to find a pack of werewolves on their heels. What she saw, however, dashed her hopes and made her heart clench.

Bobbie rushed through the entrance, past the merry-go-round and hurried over to them. "Good grief, Lauren, why didn't you let me know what was going on? I mean, one call? That's hardly keeping in touch. Thank goodness this is my day to visit my grandma or I wouldn't have passed by here and seen John's Jeep. When would I have heard from you again? And what the hell are you doing at this old carnival?" She stopped, her jaw dropping when she saw the hunters with their guns cradled in their arms. "Oh, I'm sorry. I didn't realize you'd gone on another hunt." Her brows scrunched together. "But wait. Didn't you say you were away visiting a sick relative? Did you come home early? If so, why didn't you call and let me know?" She crossed her arms. "This isn't like you to be so unprofessional. For Pete's sake, you have patients clamoring to get their teeth taken care of."

"Bobbie, run. Get out of here."

"Shut up!" John gripped Lauren's arm and twisted. She yelped and tried to yank him off, but couldn't.

Bobbie's surprise was matched by her indignation. "Don't you tell her to shut up, John Rawlings. Being her boyfriend doesn't give you the right to—"

John's rifle pointed at her head shocked Bobbie enough to shut her up. "Don't you two females ever quit flapping your yaps?"

"Lauren, what's going on?" Bobbie's voice trembled. Her gaze went from one hunter to the next, and the guns pointed at her. "You guys are scaring me."

"I said shut up." John slung Lauren into the fun house and waved the frightened Bobbie after her. "Come join your friend and keep quiet."

Moonlight filtered through the rotting wood, enough light to see the faded colors on the walls and the hallways exiting in each direction. Pictures of clowns covered the peeling wallpaper and cobwebs floated with the breeze.

"This is getting way too complicated." Luke positioned himself next to Norman and Bruce. "We never signed up for murder, man."

"Murder?" squeaked Bobbie and clung to Lauren.

"I told you. It's not murder. Lauren's as much a shifter as that animal she slept with." John nibbled at his thumb, a sign Lauren knew meant he was nervous. "This is another shifter extermination, plain and simple."

Bruce, however, wasn't buying it. "Naw, I don't think so. She hasn't changed. At least not as far as we know. I don't think you can catch shifter like you can the flu. You know, by getting too close, or kissing, or having—"

"He's right, John," said Norman. "She's human and killing her—them—is cold-blooded murder."

Lauren giggled. "Yeah, John. Your men know what's what so listen to them."

"They don't know squat. I say what goes. And I say when a woman sleeps with a shifter, she's his bitch through and through."

Bobbie leaned toward Lauren, her eyes sparkling with excitement and, for a moment, appeared to forget about the danger. "Oh, my God. Is it true? Are werewolves real? I thought you and John were just playing hunter, not actually hunting animals. And you actually know a werewolf? And you slept with him? Holy shit, Lauren, why didn't you tell me?"

Leave it to Bobbie to want the juicy details. "Daniel's a werewolf. And yes, we're lovers."

"Who's Daniel?"

It figured that Bobbie wouldn't remember Daniel. But Lauren knew who she would remember. "You remember. Tucker's friend. The tall, dark hunk of a guy Tucker brought into the office?"

Bobbie's excitement warped into high speed. "Oh, no you didn't!" She clapped and bounced on her tiptoes. "Oh, my God, you did, didn't you? And he's a real live werewolf? Wow, that's huge, Lauren." She gasped. "Does that mean Tucker's one, too?"

Now it was John's turn to laugh. "Too bad Daniel's not alive anymore. Is he, babe?"

Lauren's gut twisted. Was Daniel already dead? Or had his pack saved him? "If something happens to Daniel, John, I'm going to make you pay."

John's delighted demeanor swept away, evil overtaking his features. "No, babe, you've got it all wrong. You're the one who's going to pay."

Cocking his gun, he raised the barrel and aimed it at her.

Chapter Eleven

Daniel moaned and fought his way back to consciousness, back to Lauren. Voices floated around him, sifting through the fog surrounding his mind. He fought to remember, worked to get his thoughts clear and managed to bring forth bits of information. He remembered attacking John. If his head didn't hurt so much, he'd dance a jig. But then what happened? Why did he sense that something was wrong?

"You do it." The young voice continued, "Besides, you haven't had a kill in over a year. It's your turn, Charlie. Take it."

"Yeah, Chuckie, you'd better get it done before he changes out of wolf form." An older male joined the first man. "Shoot him in the head and let's get out of here. This place is giving me the creeps."

"Why do I have to kill him? I ain't never seen one turn human before. Makes me feel like I'm killing a real man. Besides, John's the one who wanted it done. Why didn't he do it?"

Hunters. Daniel lay still, waiting to hear more, gathering his strength. Why hadn't they already killed him? The brain fog slowly filtered away. He opened slitted eyes, sniffed and tried to sort through the myriad of smells. Yet the one scent he wanted to find wasn't there. Where was Lauren?

"I don't know, man. Maybe he was too mad about his girl. I mean that had to sting. His girl screwing around with werewolves? Talk about cutting him off at the balls." The man called Charlie moved closer and bent over Daniel. "Maybe he's already dead."

"Naw, he ain't. I heard him groan a minute ago."

The older hunter stood on the other side of him. If he knew where the third man, the younger man stood, he could ready his attack, taking out the two hunters closest to him first. Daniel wasn't certain he could disarm all three before one of them got off a shot, but he had to try. He couldn't simply lie there and wait to die. But where was Lauren? Was she nearby? He wouldn't want a stray bullet to hit her. And if she wasn't near, was she safe?

Daniel never heard sounds more wonderful than the ones easing into the night. Quiet movements at the sides of the alley, movements only his sensitive ears could hear. A dark form dashed from one side to another, unseen by the hunters. The relative quiet lasted a moment longer, then growls erupted from every side and with them, the cries of the three men. Wolves jumped out of the shadows, landing on the hunters, ripping their guns from their hands. Leaping to his feet, Daniel got ready to attack. But his attack never came. The pack had already surrounded the hunters, forcing them to the ground, their weapons lying on the pavement.

"Brother, how do you get into these messes?" said Devlin, his dark fur blackened with the blood of the hunters. He shook himself as though trying to rid his body of the blood, then changed into his human form.

"Beats the hell out of me." Daniel shifted to human, his injuries making the change more painful than usual. "How did you know where to find me?"

"Hell, Daniel, you know I'm not going to let anything happen to my brother. Tucker kind of figured something would go wrong while you were playing house with the little hunter, so I had him watch the place. You know, just in case."

"Why does everyone call Lauren 'little hunter'? Granted, she's not big, but you guys make her sound like a child."

"That's what you're thinking about? What we call Lauren? Not where she is or what we're going to do with these jokers?"

"Of course I'm worried about her. And, for the record, I'm glad you two checked up on us."

Tucker, his white fur splattered with blood, padded next to Devlin, then morphed, his growl changing to groans as limbs lengthened, and fangs and claws withdrew. He stretched to his full human height, his muscles rippling with each movement.

"Yeah, and it's a good thing we did, too. When I saw the little hunter, er, Lauren—" he grinned at Daniel, "—rush out of the apartment, I knew something was up. Then when you came dashing out of there, I stayed right on your heels. I called the pack together, got them to see what was what and, voila, here we are. Saving your sorry ass once again."

Daniel could've hugged both men, but he resisted. Especially since they were naked. "Like I said, for once I'm glad you butted your nose in where it didn't belong."

"Hey, just following orders, man. If you don't like it, talk to your bro."

Devlin signaled to a gray werewolf who changed, then raced into a nearby alley. He came back carrying clothing. Tucker took the clothing and gave Daniel a pair of jeans and a shirt. "Michael, you don't mind loaning Daniel your clothes, do you?" The young man started to argue, then shook his head. "Good boy."

Daniel pulled on the clothes quickly, pausing once to stomp on Charlie's hand. He yelped, dropped the cell phone he was trying to surreptitiously use and tucked his injured hand underneath him.

"Uh-uh-uh, bad hunter." Daniel scooped up the phone. "No texting while in class, kiddies. Men, confiscate their phones, then break their guns and toss them in the Dumpster."

The pack followed his directions, cracking cell phones with the butt of the guns, then breaking the weapons apart. The Dumpster rang with the noise of steel hitting the inside walls.

Daniel grabbed Charlie by the hair and lifted him off the ground. He had to admit he enjoyed how the hunter squealed and squirmed. "Charlie, old buddy, how about you tell me where they took Lauren."

If the guy were any more scared, his eyes would pop out of his head. "I-I d-don't know."

"Come on. Are you telling me you have no idea where good ol' John would take her? Do you hunters have a secret hideaway where you like to take prisoners? Maybe a special place to torture them?" His mood blackened at his thought, but he had to ask it. "Maybe somewhere John likes to teach girlfriends a lesson or two?"

If John hurt Lauren, he'd soon pay the price with a slow and excruciating exit from this world.

The horrified expression on the scared hunter's face reassured him. But not by much. If they pushed John too far, who knew what he was capable of? "No, sir. We don't have a meeting place like that."

Daniel got in his face and let his fangs grow. "Hmm, I think you're actually telling me the truth. But that still leaves us with the same problem. Where did he take her? Think and think hard."

"I'm not sure, but maybe he took her to his place?"

"Possibly. But that's too easy. I know John doesn't look very smart, but he does have a few brain cells. Especially when thinking up devious things to do." He snarled at Charlie to encourage him to talk. The terrified man writhed in his grip. "Let's try again. Where else would he take her? To his work place? Maybe to a doctor? I did get a few licks in."

Charlie shook his head but didn't offer any other help.

"Would you like me to give him an incentive to cooperate?" Tucker, fangs out and eyes blazing amber, stood to the side of them, his saliva-dripping incisors less than an inch from Charlie's ear. Charlie squeaked and struggled to get free.

"Calm down, hunter. No one's going to hurt you." Nonetheless, Daniel dropped his tone to a menacing level. "Unless, of course, you don't fork over the information I need."

"But I don't know anything."

"I'm betting you know more than you think you do." Fear oozed from the hunter and Daniel had to remind himself that he wasn't out to kill hunters. Unless he had no other choice to save Lauren. "Where does John like to go? Any special hangout places?" A glimmer passed through the hunter's eyes and Daniel knew he was on to something. "What, Charlie? What are you thinking?"

"I don't know if this means anything, but..."

"How about you let us decide what's important?" Devlin growled, giving the frightened hunter more reason to speak.

"John said he was going to take her to a fun place."

Devlin and Tucker were as clueless as he was. "What does that mean?"

"John likes to hang out at the old abandoned carnival. The one off the interstate."

"You think he took her to an actual fun house? Are you sure?" Daniel shook him again, just for good measure—and to hear him shriek. Normally, he didn't like treating anyone, even hunters, cruelly, but this man deserved it.

"Eek! Please, don't hurt me."

"I asked you if you're sure."

"No. But I can't think where else he'd take her."

Daniel didn't think the hunter would lie, not with so many sets of fangs ready to tear him apart. But if he was lying and the pack went to the wrong place, Lauren would pay the price. Making the decision he hoped he wouldn't regret, he dropped the hunter. Charlie landed in a heap at his feet. "Hunters, hand over your car keys. You won't be going anywhere for a while."

John dragged Lauren through the dizzying maze of hallways and slanted floors, into a small mirrored room. Tossing her roughly to the floor, he tied her hands and feet, pulling the knots as tightly as he could.

"Ow. Take it easy, you jerk." She fought against the restraints, her hands already starting to tingle from the lack of circulation. If she kicked him in the balls, would she have time to get away? Doubtful, but she figured the satisfaction would be worth the consequences.

"Shut up or I'll gag you. In fact, I might do it anyway." John grabbed one of the filthy rags scattered around the room and held it up. "Not exactly up to your usual clean standards, but prisoners can't be picky."

"Go to hell."

"Now, now, sweetie. Is that any way to talk to your boyfriend?"

"Where's Bobbie? I swear, John, if you do anything to hurt her, I really will turn hunter. Then I'll track you down and skin you alive."

He snickered. "Forever the bitch, huh, Lauren? Better readjust your thinking. After the boys and I get through with you, you'll wish you'd treated me better."

Lauren swallowed the bile that rose to her mouth and threw eye-daggers at him. If she got out of this mess, she'd make John beg for mercy.

"Are you comfy?" John cackled and pinched her nipple. "What? No more sweet words? Well, don't worry. I'll come back in a few and then we'll have a real good time. Until then, sit back and make yourself at home." Chuckling, he rose to leave.

"John?"

"Yeah?"

Did he look hopeful? Like he expected her to beg him not to leave? "You disgust me. You have since that first hunt. I pretended to be your girlfriend so I could keep going on hunts and messing them up for you."

The heat of his fury rushed to redden his face. "Why, you lying cunt."

She smiled her sweetest mean-girl smile. "Oh, and John?"

"What, bitch?"

The vein in the middle of his forehead throbbed, his rage building. "You suck as a hunter and you suck even more as a boyfriend. Consider us over." She grinned, pleased to have finally made the break.

He tried to say something but garbled his words in his anger, then gave up and exited through the nearest hallway.

Lauren stared at the mirrors surrounding her. Maybe if she could get free of the ropes, she could find her way back. But whoever had built this fun house had done a good job of creating one helluva confusing trap. Seeing her image, her mussed hair and streaked makeup only made her angrier.

"Bobbie!" Her voice echoed, bouncing off the mirrors to reverberate through the hallways. "Can you hear me? Are you okay? Bobbie?" She paused, hoping to hear her friend's call, but none came. "Damn that son of a bitch." Had he taken her friend to a different mirrored room? Or had he let the hunters have their way with her? Did she dare hope that he'd let her go? After all, Bobbie wasn't involved with either the hunters or the werewolves. Yet she knew John wouldn't release her friend. Not when she was a witness.

"Are you having fun, my sweet? This place has a great echo." John leaned against the doorway and dry-swallowed a handful of pills.

Lauren wished she were a shifter. If so, she'd sprout fangs and tear his heart out. Okay, maybe nothing that gross, but at the very least, she'd make the pain he had now feel like a mother's caress. "Where's Bobbie? I swear, John, I'll—"

"You'll what? Come on, Lauren, you've already threatened me once and look how well that worked out. Besides, what can you do? Sic your werewolf boyfriend on me?" Placing a finger to his lips, he feigned a thoughtful expression. "Oops. You already did and now he's dead."

Daniel couldn't be dead. If he were, she would feel it and she didn't. She clung to that small bit of hope. "Are you sure about that?"

The waver of his confidence was a good sight to see. Even if it didn't last long.

"Of course I'm sure. I left my best men to finish the job. Although a part of me does wish I'd shot him myself. I would've loved seeing his brains splattered all over, including all over you."

Was he that cruel? How had she ever found anything appealing in this murderer? "If he's dead, I'm going straight to the police."

His roar made the mirrors shake, but the laughter soon turned cold. "Don't be stupid, Lauren. You won't tell anyone. Would you like to know why?"

She didn't answer, refusing to play into his game. Not that it made any difference.

"No? Oh, come on, Lauren, babe. Tell me what you think is going to happen. What? Still not talking? Then I'll tell you." He squatted in front of her, took a strand of her hair and rubbed it between his fingers. "You're not going to the police because no one's going to believe you. Hunters killing a large wolf in the city limits? Get real. They'll think you're some weirdo claiming to see monsters. Besides, my men know how to clean up their messes." He let go of her hair and dropped his hand to her shoulder. "And secondly, babe, you won't be around to say anything to anyone."

Lauren's heart thundered against her chest. Was he serious? Had he decided to kill her even though the other hunters were against it? Was that why he'd taken her into this room? To murder her without witnesses? She tried to keep her voice level. "How are you going to explain my death to the other hunters?"

"Accidents happen all the time, don't they?" He gazed around the room. "Especially in old abandoned places like this. A misstep here, a fall there. You get the picture."

"Accidental deaths don't include rope marks on wrists and ankles, dumbass. Don't you think the coroner's going to notice subtle things like that?"

She'd caught him off-guard with the question. He blinked, unable to give her an answer. But he wasn't thrown for long. Instead, his evil mind took another turn. Dropping his gaze to her breasts, he slid his hand along her shoulder to the hollow of her neck, then walked his fingers lower. Lauren hunched her shoulders in a futile effort to keep him from touching her, but he merely scoffed at her pitiful attempt and slid his hand inside her shirt.

"Get your paws off me, damn you." Her breathing quickened, not in desire but in fear, lifting her chest under his hand.

"Come on, babe. Why not have a good time? You know, sort of a goodbye fuck." He cupped her breast, rubbing her nipple to attention. "See? You want it. All you sluts are the same. You say no but you mean fuck me." He licked his lips, sliding his tongue in agonizing slowness from one side to the other. "I bet you're already getting wet just thinking about my dick inside you. Or did you want to suck me off first?"

She tried not to smirk, but failed. "Yeah. Let me suck on it. Then I can listen to you scream when I bite it off."

John's leer froze on his face, then gradually grew into a grimace. He reared his arm back and closed his fist. Lauren lurched away from him, threw her body sideways, but she wasn't fast enough. He struck the side of her head and fire sprinted through her skull. She landed hard on her shoulder. A blackness flashed by, then John's blurry image solidified, reflected in the mirror across from her. She flipped over onto her back, kicking out with her bound feet. Her first kick missed him, but the next one struck him in the stomach, doubling him over. She kicked out again, but he'd had time to recover and knocked her legs away.

"Argh! You bitch!" John gripped the rope binding her legs, effectively stopping her attack. "Knock it off."

The blow on her chin left her dazed and she gasped for air. But that didn't stop her. She tried to yank her feet out of his grip and failed. And still she wasn't giving up. If nothing else, she would die fighting.

"I said to knock it off, bitch." John fell on top of her, pinning her to the dirty floor, his eyes wild and blazing. "We're going to do this the way you like it. Doggy-style." She struggled again, but she was no match for his drug-induced strength. He unbuttoned her jeans, using her struggles to help him pull her pants down. Her underwear came away with one tug. Flipping her over, he pushed her face against the floor and straddled her, holding her in place.

The image in the mirrors of John on top of her, her hair wild around her bruised face was too much for her. Closing her eyes, she listened to John unbuckle his jeans.

"You'd never do doggy-style with me no matter how much I asked. Why is that, bitch? Did you have to have a real dog to do it this way?"

"Go to hell."

"Yeah, no doubt I will. But it won't be because I got rid of vermin like you and your werewolf lover. In fact, maybe that'll buy me passage past the Pearly Gates."

"Daniel will tear you apart for this."

"Do you mean his ghost? I doubt he can hurt me when he's rotting in some sewer. In fact, I'll bet the rats are having a gourmet dinner with your Daniel as the main course."

He ran his hands along her bottom and spanked her. She cried out and tried to buck him off.

"No, no, babe. Save your energy for the good part. The part where I ram my dick inside your junk. I promise you're going to love it." His chuckle was pure evil. "Or, at least, you'll love that part. But the part that comes later? Not so much."

He leaned over her, grabbed her hair to jerk her head back and placed his mouth next to her ear. "Open your eyes, babe. You're gonna watch me fuck you."

Daniel studied the run-down building. "I'm open to suggestions. Anyone have a good idea on how we get into the fun house without endangering Lauren?" Devlin, Tucker and the remaining shifters who'd come along stayed silent. "No ideas? Great. Then I guess it's a commando mission."

"Wow, man. Listen to you get all military on us." Tucker grinned and dodged Daniel's halfhearted punch. "Seems to me the only question we have is whether we go in as humans or as werewolves. Personally, my vote is for fangs and claws."

Daniel noted the flimsy nature of the door but decided on an alternate way. "They'll expect us to come through the door. Which is why we're going in through the roof."

"The roof?"

"Yeah, Dev, the roof. We need the element of surprise. I don't want Lauren getting hurt."

"Roof it is then." Devlin shucked his clothes, motioning for the others to do the same. "We're going to need all our strength to break through. I suggest you get your tail moving."

Daniel didn't need his brother's encouragement. He sensed that time wasn't on their side. Lauren was in trouble and needed him fast. Having gotten rid of his clothes in record time, he morphed, closing his eyes to the ache the change always brought. Yet he didn't mind. He'd suffer any amount of pain to save Lauren. Hunkering down, he crawled forward, darting behind bushes, old rides and carnival booths to edge closer to the fun house.

"Ready?" Daniel glanced at his group and waited for anyone to voice a concern. "Remember. Keep Lauren safe no matter what else happens. And, unless you have no other choice, try not to kill them." He caught the telling glance Tucker sent him but ignored it. His friend would rather kill the hunters, but he didn't want any more deaths. "Let's do this."

The werewolves spread out around the perimeter of the fun house, leaving Daniel and Tucker at the front. Tucker growled softly, then bowed his head. "You first, boss dog."

"Dog, my ass." Daniel dipped his head in return, crouched and leapt to the roof. Thankfully, the sound he made landing wasn't as loud as he'd feared. The other werewolves spread out across the roof, all eyes on him, all eager for him to lead the charge. Lying down, he pressed his ear to the shingles, closed his eyes and listened. If he could hear Lauren or the hunters, then he'd know the best location to enter the building. He strained, calling on his acute werewolf hearing. Was that a woman's voice? Lauren's? He listened again, blocking out the other sounds, intent on hearing Lauren. But the sound he'd heard seconds earlier was gone. Still, it gave him a place to start. Pulling his mouth back to expose fangs, he growled and ripped the shingles off. The pack did the same, tearing through shingles and wood. In a matter of seconds, they shredded the roof, then dove through the holes they'd made.

Daniel dropped through the roof, landing on his paws, his head down. Snarling, he lifted his head and inhaled sharply. A startled John and a tear-streaked Lauren gaped at him. John, his dick in his hand, fell away from Lauren's exposed bottom, his horrified eyes locked on the black werewolf.

Fury, hotter and wilder than ever before, surged through Daniel. His vision blurred with the intensity, the saliva in his mouth flowing, his claws digging into the dirty linoleum floor. His earlier thoughts of not killing fled him. Instead, he was consumed with the need to taste John's blood on his tongue, to feel John's heart in his mouth. He howled, the vibrations rattling the glass walls around him.

John grappled with his jeans, pulling them up as he scrambled backward. Lauren, hands and feet tied, tried to tug on her jeans. She crawled away, her eyes wide and fixed onto Daniel.

Lauren had seen Daniel in his wolf form before, but this was different. Before, she'd always found the humanity behind those amber eyes, but not this time. Now he was all animal, all beast, all killer. She gathered her clothes around her, positioned her back against the nearest wall and held her arms in front of her chest, a pitiful shield against the unexpected. Looking at the ferocious werewolf, she wondered if he recognized her. If not, would he kill her along with John?

John. She had to help him. Not that he deserved her help. Not that she wanted to give it. But she had to save John for Daniel's sake. Daniel would regret killing him and she knew he couldn't handle any more guilt in his life.

The werewolf tensed, dropped his head even lower, his gleaming amber eyes shooting venom at John. His ears flattened against his head, his tail lowered, but not between his legs. Vicious-looking white fangs glistened with saliva and a growl rumbled deep in his chest. Daniel moved forward, one step at a time, as though taunting John, daring him to run. The hunter, however, couldn't find his legs, trying more than once to get to his feet. Instead, he brought his knees to his chest and sobbed silent tears.

"Daniel."

The werewolf ignored her, taking another two steps closer to his victim.

Lauren fought back a nervous giggle and gathered her courage. Swallowing, she called his name again, louder, with more force. "Daniel."

The werewolf stopped, then turned his head toward her. She searched his eyes, desperately wanting to find the man inside the animal, but couldn't. He was a predator and ready to take his prey.

"Daniel, please don't hurt him." She almost cried when she saw confusion in those angry amber eyes. Did he understand her? Taking encouragement from his pause, she reached out, extending her open hand to him. "Please, come to me."

For a moment, they studied each other, woman and animal. He had to understand her. If not, John wasn't the only one in trouble.

The beautiful wolf shook his head. Was he denying her? Or was it merely an instinctual movement? She tried again, this time inching forward to meet him halfway. He growled, chilling her to the bone, but she kept her tied hands out.

The werewolf blinked at her and Lauren got the impression, for a second, that she saw the amber in his eyes fade. Keeping low, he came to her and placed his muzzle in her palm. She released her pent-up breath and placed her cheek against his. Closing her eyes, she blocked out the noises around her, even the sound of John's footsteps as he ran from the room, and delighted in the touch of Daniel's fur next to her skin. "I was afraid you were going to bite me." She felt him change, knew he shifted, but kept her eyes closed until the shift was complete.

"I almost did." Daniel was naked and sexy as hell on hands and knees. His eyes, returned to normal and filled with humanity, sought hers.

"I'm glad you didn't."

He ran his hand along her arm, his expression hardening. "Get out. Hide in the surrounding woods. I'll find you when it's finished." Quickly, he untied her hands and feet.

She looked past him, then gave him a soft smile. "Why? I'm safe now. John's gone."

"I know. He ran off like the scared rat that he is, but he won't get far. If one of my pack doesn't get him, I will."

"No, please don't."

"I have to, Lauren. I can't let him get away with trying to…"

He couldn't say the words, but she could. "Rape me. He tried to rape me." In the instant the words were out, she regretted them. The flash of anger in him frightened her, but she held her ground. "He started to, but he didn't. Thanks to you. But I don't care. I just want to go home." She trapped a sob behind her hand. "Take me home, Daniel. Please."

Daniel took her hand and pressed her palm to his lips. "I promise I'll take you home, but first I have to end things. If I don't, John will try again. He murdered my wife and was going to hurt you. How can you ask me to show him mercy?"

"Don't you get it? I know what he did and I know what he would do if given the chance. But haven't enough people died? I'm so tired of people getting hurt." She wiped a tear away, a tear for Torrie and for herself.

"You didn't kill Torrie. He did. I heard him say so."

"I know and I'm glad I wasn't the one who killed her, but I tried to. And even when you thought I had, you found it within yourself to forgive me."

"That's different. He enjoyed killing her and didn't care who she was. Then he kept on killing. You didn't. You changed."

She had to make him see. If not for Torrie, she would never have known, never have understood that werewolves retain their human side even in wolf form. "I got lucky that day, Daniel. If I hadn't seen Torrie, seen the person she was inside the animal, I'd still be hunting shifters. I'd be just like John."

"Don't compare yourself to that scumbag." His voice dripped revulsion. "You're not the same in any way."

"Daniel, I'm asking you, begging you, for your sake, for our sake, don't kill him." She could see the struggle in his eyes, knew he wanted to give her what she wanted, but his need for vengeance was too strong.

"I'm sorry, Lauren. I can't do what you ask." After several seconds, with the sounds of a battle growing louder, Daniel morphed again, limbs shortening and bones cracking. Swishing his tail, he whirled around, sniffed the air and dashed into the left hall that led away from the screams and sounds of fighting.

Lauren stared after him as though doing so would somehow make him come back. The din continued around her, echoing through the building. She clamped her hands over her ears, wanting nothing more than silence for a few precious minutes. Suddenly, the noise grew quieter until she couldn't hear anything at all. The eerie quiet unnerved her.

Who had won the battle? The werewolves or the hunters? Was Daniel all right? Had the wounds he'd already suffered weakened him? She closed her eyes and whispered a prayer to keep him safe.

Lauren waited, holding back any sound that might cover up another, and listened. Had the others left her behind? Was Bobbie all right? Had Daniel found John? Should she go down the right hallway, the one that would lead to where she'd heard the noises? Or should she follow Daniel and hope she'd catch up to him? Summoning her courage, she chose a path.

Chapter Twelve

Lauren stumbled out of the mirrored room and into the left corridor, the same way Daniel had gone, but it wasn't long before she found herself in another small mirrored room with corridors leading in several directions. If she chose the wrong one, she'd never find Daniel. But how to choose? He could have gone in any direction.

A scream echoed to her right and, with nothing else to lead her, Lauren darted toward the sound. Maybe, just maybe, she'd find Daniel along with Bobbie. She feared for her friend's well-being, even for her life. Who knew what the hunters had done to Bobbie before the werewolves had arrived? Not that her friend was safe from the shifters, either. She didn't want to think about what the werewolves might do. A refrain of *hurry, hurry, hurry* pounded in her head.

The hallway slanted to one side, then the other. Bumps in the floor sent her falling, reaching out at the last second to stay upright. But she had to keep going, not slowing her pace any more than necessary. She turned several times, guessing at which way to go and praying she'd made the correct choice.

"What do you want us to do with them?"

At the sound of the voice, Lauren glanced up and saw a light. Someone was in a room a few feet ahead. But who was it? A hunter or a shifter? Deciding she was too far to go back, she hurried forward and tripped over another bump. "Arrgh!" Arms flailing, she fell forward into the light and landed face down.

"Well, what do we have here? Is this another playmate for us?"

Low chuckles sent shivers along her spine. Fearing the worst, Lauren pushed away from the floor and was greeted by the amber eyes of a large, gray werewolf. His demeanor was anything but friendly, but she plastered on a smile and greeted him anyway. "Uh, hi."

The wicked smile widened, but the eyes remained coldly golden. "Well, hi to you, too, sweet thang."

Lauren scrambled to her feet in the lobby next to the exit. Three hunters, bloody and beaten, sat against one wall, their arms and knees hugged to their chests, their heads barely lifted to gaze at her. Werewolves, a few in human form and the others in their wolf state, studied her. Taking a chance, she stuck out her hand. "I'm Lauren Kade. And you would be..."

"Name's McCain. McCain of the Cannon Pack." The gray wolf chuckled, then shifted to stand front and center, and very naked, close to her. Too close.

Lauren couldn't resist checking out his impressive manhood. Were all werewolves as well endowed as Daniel and McCain? She forced her attention up to this face. "So, how's it hangin', McCain?"

The shifters broke into laughter, clapping their neighbor on the shoulder and snickering comments under their breath. Naked McCain continued to grin. "Why don't you tell me?"

She feigned an "oh, I'd rather not" face and dropped her hand. "Um, do you know where Daniel is?"

McCain grew somber. "Actually, we'd like to know the same thing." He cocked his head at her. "Seems like I recall Daniel taking a female prisoner. A friendly sort of prisoner from what I heard. So tell me. Are you still his prisoner...or something else?"

"I'm his—" Lauren went blank. What was she to Daniel? A girlfriend? A friend with benefits? Or even worse, a fling on the human side of life? Now, however, wasn't the time to find out. Until she did, she'd fake it until she made it true. "I'm his girlfriend."

At least she'd managed to surprise McCain and his friends.

"Is that so?" He chuckled, pacing around her like she was a piece of meat, cooked and served up just for him. "I don't remember anyone ever referring to you as his girlfriend."

Lauren faked it some more. "Well, things changed. I'm his girlfriend now. Ask Tucker if you don't believe me. Where is Tucker anyway? I assumed he'd be with you."

McCain swept his arm around the room. "He was, and I would ask him, but he and the other human female went to find Daniel." His jaunty attitude changed, turning suspicious. "We sure do have a lot of human females hanging around. Way too many if you ask me."

How would an alpha's girlfriend react? Lauren was all in and ready to play poker—even if that meant taking more risks. "Oh, really? Too bad for you since I don't see anyone asking for your opinion."

"Uh-oh, McCain, she done whipped you good."

"Better watch out. This one's got a mouth on her."

The other werewolves added their two cents, but the consensus was the same. She'd back-talked McCain and now she had to take whatever came her way. Had she made him angry enough to hurt her? Or would he respect her courage? Lauren stayed quiet, ready to see which way he'd go.

McCain stepped closer, placing his nose—and a lower body part—mere centimeters from her. "Yep. You do have balls, girl.

But let me give you a word of warning. I happen to like sassy women. Others don't, so watch what you say." His smirk was a mix of humor and warning. "Not that you asked."

She had to hold back a huge sigh of relief. "Duly noted and understood." Since she was already in deep water, she took another plunge. "Which way did Tucker and Bobbie go?"

McCain paused and she worried that he'd changed his mind about her.

"That way." McCain pointed to a hallway behind him. "And if you find them, tell them—" he glanced at the hunters, "—that we're getting real hungry and might need a snack."

Lauren nodded, all too aware of the terrified pleas from the hunters. Pointing toward the hallway, she slipped past McCain and excused her way past the werewolves. Once inside the dimly lit passageway, she paused to let her frazzled nerves calm.

She stumbled along, cursing under her breath with each misstep.

"Ooh, ooh, oh, yes, ooh!"

Lauren heard Bobbie's voice and turned in that direction, taking a smaller hallway off to the left. Was Bobbie in pain? Or in danger? Who knew what Tucker might do to her friend. She picked up her pace, running through different plans to help Bobbie. Not that she had much of a chance against Tucker, but she'd give it her best shot.

"Ahhhh, oooh, no, no, no!"

"Yes. Now do as I say, woman."

What was Tucker forcing her friend to do? Anger stole her breath. Bobbie had said no, then Tucker needed to respect her wishes. No meant no. No ifs, ands or buts. Their voices grew stronger, louder. Lauren hurried forward, ready to come to her friend's defense. She whirled around a corner, curses on the tip of her tongue and sputtered in surprise. Tucker lifted a half-dressed Bobbie and pressed her to the wall. Bobbie, her face glowing with ecstasy, wrapped her legs around his naked torso and her arms around his neck.

"I can't believe—oh, my God—how big you are."

"I told you I could go deeper with you like this."

"I know, but, oh, God, I didn't believe—oh, hell yes!"

Lauren watched, mesmerized by the clenching and unclenching of Tucker's buttocks as he rammed into Bobbie. Hard muscles worked in his back, giving Bobbie ample leverage to cling to. She opened her mouth to tell them she was there, but decided against it. After all, who knew how Tucker would react?

Bobbie clung to him, her eyes closed, her mouth opened, letting soft squeaks of pleasure seep out with each of his pushes. Locking her ankles, she used her back against the wall to thrust her pelvis forward. Tucker lowered his head to take a nipple in his mouth and took her other breast in his hand. The couple fell into a steady rhythm, shaking the wall.

Hating to break them up but knowing Daniel might need her help, Lauren cleared her throat. The sex continued, Tucker and Bobbie both too engrossed to notice her. She cleared it again. Again, nothing. A third time was no charm so she did the only thing she could do. She tapped Tucker on the shoulder. "Excuse me."

Bobbie's scream sent Tucker into shift mode, his face contorting as he dropped Bobbie roughly to the floor and twisted toward Lauren. She scuttled backward, palms up in a futile attempt to ward off his emerging wolf. "It's me, Tucker. Lauren."

"Damn, Lauren." Bobbie tugged her jeans on and pulled her shirt down to cover her breasts. "You scared the total freak out of me."

Tucker growled, his wolf eyes hungry, and slowly changed back. "Are you trying to get killed, little hunter?"

Lauren leveled her frustration directly at those amber eyes. Standing up to werewolves was getting easier. "Trust me. I've already had plenty of chances to die." Who was this guy to get mad at her anyway? "McCain said you went to look for Daniel." At least he had the decency to look sheepish. "Somehow I don't think you're going to find him under Bobbie's shirt."

"Nope, I don't guess I will."

Bobbie slid her hand along his arm, exchanging a telling glance. "We used that as an excuse to get some, uh, alone time together."

"Aren't you afraid for Daniel's safety? Who knows? Maybe John or another hunter shot him?" Didn't Tucker care about his friend?

"Naw, he's fine." Tucker draped his arm over Bobbie's shoulder.

"How can you know? Have you seen him since you first got here?" Tucker's nonchalant attitude didn't score any points with her. "No? Then let me clue you in."

Tucker's acid tone belied the irritation on his face. "Oh, please do."

"John ran off and Daniel went after him." If he didn't grasp her worry for Daniel through her words, she hoped he'd get it through her anxious tone.

"Was John armed?"

She hadn't expected the question. Hell, she hadn't even thought about it. John had carried a rifle into the mirrored room when he took her there, but she couldn't recall if he'd taken it with him when he'd fled. Her concern for Daniel shot up another thousand degrees. "I don't remember. Shit, Tucker. What if John ambushes Daniel? Oh, hell, this is all my fault."

"It's not your fault."

Bobbie and Tucker spoke at once, then grinned at each other.

"Yes, it is. He never would've gotten involved with John if it weren't for me." Despair, cold and harsh left her weak. If anything happened to Daniel, she'd never get past the loss.

"Don't talk like a silly human, Lauren. Daniel and John would've run into each at some point after Mysta and Tyler. You just happened to facilitate matters." Tucker took Lauren under his other arm and led the two women back toward the pack. "Don't worry about Daniel. He can take care of himself."

"Okay. If you say so." But she remained unconvinced. Only seeing Daniel would ease her mind.

The ruckus of the pack startled them and even Tucker jumped at the howls and roars. He shifted, dropping to the floor on all fours, then dashed down the hallway.

"Get down and stay down." Daniel threw John to the floor. The pack howled their pleasure, adding snarls and comments as they formed a circle around their latest prey. The fresh shirt and bandages John had gotten at the clinic were stained with patches of blood and dirt.

"Good deal, Daniel. You brought the leader rat back to his nest of vermin." Devlin slapped his brother on the back.

"Did you bring us dinner, Daniel? Tucker said not to eat the others, but we can have this one, right?" A young shifter poked John with his gun. "He doesn't look very tasty, but he'll do for an appetizer."

Daniel let the others have their fun with the hunter. Their verbal jabs and the frightening growls from those in wolf form couldn't physically hurt the hunter, but it released some of their animosity.

The other hunters hadn't said a word to John, but that didn't keep him from pleading for their help. "Men, come on. Help me." He reached out, imploring the hunters. They continued to ignore him, averting their eyes and tucking their heads. He didn't give up, however, and attempted to crawl toward them, but the werewolves blocked his way.

"I don't think you're going to get any help from your friends."

Daniel almost felt sorry for the pitiful man. John's flight from the mirrored room hadn't gotten him very far, only making it to the outside of the fun house through a trap door. Daniel had loved the surprised expression on the hunter's face when he'd grabbed his rifle and cracked it in half. Hauling him back inside had proven the hardest part with John fighting and screaming the entire time. Hell, he'd have had less trouble if he'd just broken the man's neck and been done with him.

In fact, Daniel wasn't sure why he'd kept the man alive. If anyone deserved to die, it was John. He'd killed Torrie, killed other shifters and had tried to rape Lauren. The man was scum inside and out. But Daniel couldn't bring himself to do it. Every time he started to, he saw Torrie's and Lauren's faces, heard them asking him to spare the jackass. He'd leave John with his friends and get back to Lauren.

"Listen to me. I'm your leader. We can do this. We can take them." John's tone was timid against the bravado of his words. But his men ignored him. Crumbling to the floor, he let out a moan of despair.

"Shut up, hunter. Can't you see that your men—and I use the term loosely—don't have the stomach for a real fight?"

Daniel squatted beside John, then snatched him by the collar, forcing the hunter to look at him. "Hunters are such babies without their guns."

Tucker slid to a stop and morphed, changing into human form. "Don't I know it."

"Where have you been?" Daniel cocked his head in question at his friend. "Did you miss the fun?"

"Of course not. But I figured someone needed to track you down."

"Seriously?" Lauren strode past Tucker to take her place next to Daniel. His heart swelled, relieved to have her safely by his side. "Is that what you call what you and Bobbie were doing? Tracking?"

Although Lauren had seen him in the buff several times already, Daniel suddenly grew very shy. "A couple of you men run and get our clothes before I catch my death." From their expressions, Tucker and Lauren didn't buy his excuse, but they didn't say anything either. "So you and Bobbie, huh?" Better to change the subject than to bring more attention to his nakedness.

"Is that a bad thing?" An exhausted Bobbie finally emerged from the passageway and positioned herself next to Tucker. She wrapped her arm around him and squeezed. "Sheesh, you're fast."

Tucker's sappy smile told the whole story and Daniel was glad to see his friend happy. "He could do worse."

"That means he thinks you could do a whole lot better, Bobbie." Tucker took the clothes the men had retrieved and tugged on his jeans.

"I don't doubt that but, for now, you'll do." Bobbie kissed her finger and pressed it to his lips.

Dressed and ready, Daniel looked to Lauren and quipped, "You both could."

She leaned into him, running one hand over his stomach. "Hey, man, don't go getting any ideas. You're mine and, fortunately for you, I'm yours. The only question now is what are you going to do with them?" Her request for leniency was unmistakable.

Was he hers? The idea of Lauren claiming him was exhilarating. Almost as exhilarating as the idea of marking her and turning her into a shifter. They'd never talked about staying together, yet they'd fallen into an easy relationship. But could she accept his life? Would she want to run with the pack?

Devlin prodded John, making the hunter squeal. "Okay, Daniel, tell us your idea for this little piggie."

"Here's what I want to do." He made sure he had the full attention of the pack. "I want the pack to take the hunters' guns and cell phones, and destroy them." He got ready for the reaction he knew he'd get from his next proposal. "Then we turn them loose."

Tucker came to full attention. "What? That's it? I thought we were on the offensive now. Taking their toys away from them isn't going to make things right. We need retribution for what they've done."

"I feel the same way." Daniel glanced at Lauren, resolved to following her path. "But when does the fighting end? We get payback today, they get their revenge tomorrow and on it goes." The squeeze Lauren gave his arm spurred him on. "Besides, judging from what's happened today, I don't think many of them will keep hunting. Not now that they know how easily we can kill them."

Tucker scowled at him while Devlin quietly watched. "And what about their leader? Are you going to let him get away scot-free after what he did to Torrie?"

"No, I can't do that." He couldn't look at Lauren. If she didn't understand... "I'm talking about his followers. As for the ringleader, he deserves a different outcome."

"Well, do tell, boss dog." A relieved Tucker pecked Bobbie on the cheek. "We're dying to know."

His friend obviously had it bad for the diminutive receptionist. Almost as bad as he had it for her boss. The thought stalled him, putting the reality of his feelings into the light. He glanced at Lauren, her face glowing with love and knew, without a doubt, he'd fallen in love for a second time.

"Yo, bro. Earth to Daniel."

From Devlin's expression, Daniel knew his secret was out. Had Lauren figured it out, too? Did she know how much he cared for her? "If it's agreeable to my brother, I propose we take John back to the mountains with us."

"No! I'm not going. You can't make me." John tried to scurry away, but a snarl from a nearby werewolf curled him into a fetal position.

"Good grief. How old is he? Five?" Tucker knelt down, cocked his head to see John's face. "Do you need your mommy, little man?"

"Leave him be, Tucker." Daniel leveled his gaze at the rest of his pack. "Let the council and the pack decide his fate." A couple of werewolves mumbled their disagreement, but the majority didn't speak. He took their silence as their approval. "Besides, I've already given him a special punishment."

"And what would that be, dear brother?" Devlin poked the hunter in the ribs. "I hope it's something real good."

Daniel knelt beside John, wanting to see the hunter's face when he learned his fate. "I bit him. Not in the way we normally bite hunters, but in the way we do if we want to change someone."

Snickers mixed with gasps as werewolves and hunters reacted to Daniel's revelation. John's eyes grew wider as panic set in.

"Did you know there's two kinds of werewolf bites, Johnny? One kind is just a bite. Painful, yes, but nothing more. The other, however, includes an added ingredient that changes your entire chemistry."

"No. No-o-o-o." John shook his head, unwilling to hear the worst.

"That's right, Johnny. You're going to become the thing you despise. You're going to change into a werewolf." Daniel couldn't help the rush of delight filling him.

"Why the hell would you do that?" Tucker looked to the rest of the pack for confirmation. "We don't want him in the pack."

"Because, my fellow pack mates, I'm going to recommend to the council that they send Johnny to Chicago."

A stunned silence spread over them. Tucker chuckled. "Damn, man, when you lay down a punishment, you lay it down hard."

Lauren took his arm. "What's in Chicago?"

"Chicago is well known for its huge and nasty pack. They don't like intruders. Add a very active hunters' group to the mix and that city isn't a good place for visiting werewolves. In fact, I've never heard of an outsider werewolf going there and surviving."

"Lauren, please, don't let him do this to me."

Lauren, however, backed away from John. "I'm sorry, but you deserve whatever you get. At least they're giving you a fighting chance. That's more than you gave the shifters you killed."

"Devlin, what do you think?"

His brother took his time, thinking over the idea. "It's a different approach than I would've taken, bro. But let's do this your way."

"Good. Will you take him? I have something I need to do."

Devlin nodded, then barked orders to the rest of the pack. Daniel took Lauren's hand and led her to a corner of the room, away from the others. "Do you feel up to taking a walk with me?"

Chapter Thirteen

Lauren welcomed the yellow glow of the sunrise, lifting her face to enjoy the warmth. She wouldn't mind if she never saw another fun house again. "Did you want to talk to me, Daniel? Or was that an excuse to get out of that place?"

Daniel took her hand, a simple gesture that melted her insides. "Both."

He led her to the rundown carousel and lifted her, placing her on top of a horse with a black mane and tail. Most of the glitter that had once covered the wooden animal was gone and the paint had faded.

For a moment, Lauren indulged her imagination and pictured the horse as a beautiful white steed and Daniel as her charming prince. But soon reality forced her to ask, "What did you need to tell me?"

"We'll talk, but first I need to do this."

Daniel stepped on the edge of the horse's platform, leaned over and kissed her. Lauren closed her eyes, reveling in the softness of his lips on hers. The softness, however, didn't last long, his lips growing more intense, more demanding with each second. She cupped the back of his neck, holding him, and took his tongue inside. His tongue circled hers, making her head swim. His kiss, so simple, gave her chills, but these chills heated her body. Answering the fire he'd stirred within her, she arched her back to press her breasts against his chest. She yearned for him, ached to have his hands discovering every secret curve and valley. His kiss demanded more and she wanted to give that to him.

When he broke apart from her, she almost fell off the horse. "No. Don't stop."

His eyes boasted golden flecks and the desire she saw sent her own lust soaring.

"If I don't stop now, I won't stop until I've had you." His jaw clenched, a thrilling sight that signaled his need. "I want you, Lauren, in every way that I can have you."

She couldn't, wouldn't, contain her delight. "Don't you know I want you just as much? I don't want you to stop. Ever. I want you right now."

He closed his eyes, the struggle to restrain his lust decorating his face. Taking a deep breath that shuddered through him, he opened his eyes. "No, we can't. Not yet. We have to talk first."

Lauren tilted her head and batted her eyes, deliberately teasing him. "I'd rather you take me first and then talk."

"You, woman, are the real animal."

"You think so? Then tame the beast in me, Daniel." She crossed her arms over her chest and pulled up her T-shirt, ready to tug it off.

"Damn, you drive me crazy." Daniel smoothed out her shirt and shook his head. "Come on, Lauren. Don't make this harder than it already is."

She gasped, unready for what lay ahead. Had she misinterpreted his signals? She knew he wanted her, but was something else going on? Did he want her in every sexual way, but not in the way that mattered? She giggled, then slapped her hand over her mouth. If she could ever learn to control her nerves, now was the time. "Daniel, are you breaking up with me?"

At least his confused look reassured her. Still, had they ever been a real couple? Or had that been a wild dream?

"You sure ask me that a lot. Hell, no, I'm not breaking up with you. In fact, I'm trying to do the exact opposite."

"You are? And the exact opposite would be..." She couldn't finish the sentence. Not with fear mixing with anticipation to build a logjam in her throat.

Daniel slipped her off the carousel, then carried her to a grassy area decorated with rotting picnic benches and rusted grills. Unsure of what to make of the gesture, Lauren laid her head against his chest, her hand placed over his heart. She listened for the beat of his heart. Was his heart beating as fast as hers? He gently lowered her to the grass and sat down beside her.

Lauren bit her lip, silencing the nervous giggles. If she weren't so afraid of what he was about to tell her, she would've enjoyed the quiet peacefulness and the slight breeze blowing his hair around his strong face, like soft grasses framing the side of a mountain. Instead, she couldn't help but feel like a condemned prisoner ready to hear the judge's decree.

"You know how much Torrie meant to me."

She nodded, although she doubted he noticed. He continued to stare straight ahead.

"She was my mate, my lover, my everything."

Lauren understood how much he'd loved Torrie, but hearing him put it into words nearly tore out her heart. If only he'd turn to her and take her in his arms. She needed to have his embrace around her, needed him to tell her that he loved her, too. Giving herself the hug she wanted from him, she drew her knees to her chest and wrapped her arms around her legs.

"I thought my world ended when she was killed. And I blamed myself. If I'd made her stay home, or gone with her, then nothing would've happened to her. John wouldn't have murdered her."

Did he still blame himself for Torrie's death? Did a part of him still blame her? She hadn't killed Torrie, but she'd had a part in it. She'd attempted to kill her. Lauren glanced at him out of the corner of her eye, but his unreadable expression remained the same.

"I wanted to find the hunter who'd taken her from me. I wanted to tear him apart, make his loved ones grieve the way I did. For Torrie and for me. I thought that would rid me of my guilt."

Lauren couldn't allow him to continue to torture himself any longer. "You can't blame yourself. She wouldn't want you to. No woman would want the man she loves to live with that kind of pain."

Tension tightened her neck. *Please, get on with it. Tell me to leave. Tell me you don't care for me the way you cared for her. But don't torture me. Don't make me wait for the axe to fall.* But she wouldn't hurry him. He needed to do this in his own way, in his own time. If he wouldn't take her heart, she'd give him time.

"I know. And I don't any longer. You made me see that my guilt solves nothing. But then when I thought you'd shot her..." He twisted to look at her, his eyes filled with the emotion he'd kept from his face. "I didn't know what to think."

"I know, Daniel. I wish I could take it back. I wish I'd never met John or gone on a hunt."

"I was torn. Part of me wanted to see you die, to see you slowly bleed to death."

Lauren trembled at the thought and, for a moment, feared him. "I don't blame you. Wouldn't blame you."

Daniel placed his hand on her arm. "But another part of me, a stronger part of me, wanted you in my arms and in my bed. I tried to fight it, but I had to give in. At first, I thought if I took you, without love, without feeling, I'd get you out of my system."

What was he telling her? Could he forgive her? She hoped he already had, but now she wasn't certain. Had he changed his mind about her?

"But having you only made me want you more. I let that other part, the stronger part, take over."

A flutter of hope lifted her spirits. "Are you sorry that you did?"

A soft smile tweaked the corners of his mouth. "No. I'll never regret being with you."

The tension building inside her broke apart, flowing out of her in waves of relief. "Can you forgive me, Daniel? Will you?"

He shushed her, placing a finger to her lips. "I forgave you a long time ago. Even when I thought you were the one who took her from me. Then when John told the truth, that your shot wasn't the one that killed her, I had the strangest sensation. I was happy for the first time in a long while. Happy that I no longer had to think of you in that way."

She swallowed, cautious to ask, "You were happy?"

"At first. Then the anger, the hatred came back and I wanted him dead."

Daniel lay back and she did the same, stretching out beside him. "Why didn't you kill him? You had every chance to."

He pulled her against him, soaring her delight.

"Trust me, I struggled with the decision, going back and forth trying to decide. But every time I started to, I saw Torrie's face. Torrie wouldn't have wanted me to hurt him." He skimmed his fingers along her hair. "After I'd gotten to know you, I found that you're a lot like her. You're loving, caring and forgiving." He tunneled his fingers through her hair. "What choice did I have? You and Torrie would've wanted me to keep him alive. Killing him would've felt like a betrayal of both of you."

"Are we that alike?" Lauren fidgeted, unsure of the answer she wanted. Although she was glad he found qualities in her that he liked, she wanted him to want her for who she was. Not because she reminded him of Torrie.

Daniel cupped her chin, making her look at him. "I'm not replacing her with you, if that's what you're thinking."

She wanted more, needed to hear more of an explanation. "But, like you said, we're a lot alike." Did she really look like Torrie as well? Perhaps too much like her? She wished she'd seen the female werewolf in her human form.

Daniel propped his head on his hand and frowned. "Do you believe me? Do you think I'm using you as a replacement?"

Lauren couldn't speak and her silence served as her answer.

"Lauren, I thought you were smarter than that."

Did he just insult her? Irritation welled inside her, giving her the strength to glare at him. "Look, if you're going to keep telling me how dumb I am, then I'll get the hell out of—"

His mouth crushed hers, cutting off her last word. Heat, passionate and real, scorched from his lips to hers. She moaned, wanting everything, anything he would give her. The kiss went on, sending the fire from her lips to the cleft between her legs. She ran her hands along his shoulders and toward his back, her fingers dancing over the muscled curves.

Daniel broke off the kiss, then touched her swollen lips. "I didn't mean to insult you. But can't you tell that you're more than a substitute for Torrie? Can't you tell how much you mean to me?"

"Well, I—"

"Lauren, you and Torrie share a lot of similarities. Both of you were very lovable, very sexy and all woman. But you're also very different. You're spunkier than she was and I like spunk. I didn't know how much until you came along, but I do. Plus, Torrie wouldn't have put her life on the line to save random hunters. Not that she wouldn't have cared about them. She did. And she wouldn't have wanted to see them hurt. But she wouldn't have had the courage to do what you did either."

Lauren fought to hold back the tears. Not only was she different, but he thought she was brave. And spunky. Hell, she liked that she had spunk, too. "Go on."

Daniel's chuckle was as warm as the sun. "You're funny, too. Smart—at least most of the time." He dodged her halfhearted attempt to swat him. "And you're witty, too. Comparing Torrie and you is like comparing a summer breeze to a windstorm."

"Are you calling me a big bag of wind?"

Giving her a quick peck on the tip of her nose, he added, "I'm saying that I like having a feisty woman like you. I'm saying you're very much your own woman. Lauren, I fell in love with you because of who *you* are, not because you sometimes remind me of her."

The heat his kiss had started flickered into a low fire that promised to burn hotter with each kiss. A fire only he could put out. Searching his velvet eyes, diving into them, into his soul, she watched as his irises sparkled with amber. Her stomach fluttered with anticipation. "Does the animal inside you always come out when you're turned on?"

"The animal and the man are one and the same. You can't have one without the other." He trailed his tongue down the side of her neck, the licks soon turning to kisses. "Does that frighten you?"

"No. Not anymore," she answered in a breathy voice. His attentions took her over the edge, driving any reservations she'd had away. "Daniel."

Reaching behind her, he slipped her shirt over her head, then moaned at the sight of her naked breasts. Their clothes soon lay strewn over the grass, the light skimming on their bodies as the sun lifted into the sky. He gripped her sides, lifted her and placed her on top of him. His already large erection pushed at the wetness between her legs.

"What if the others come out and see us?" Lauren feathered her fingers on his bare chest and pushed her breasts together, plumping them for his satisfaction. She tossed her hair, the tips tickling her shoulders.

"Then they'll know I'm one helluva lucky man." Daniel suckled one breast and fondled the other.

She leaned forward, closing her eyes to revel in the delicious sensations racing through her. The warmth from the sky heated her back but it was no match for the warmth testing the boundaries between her legs. She rubbed, sliding over him in a sexual tease and heard his groan of frustration. "Easy, big boy. Easy."

"I can't take it easy. I need you now."

He gripped her neck, holding her head still, startling her. He could kill her with one squeeze, but she knew she was safe in his hands. "Tell me what you want, Daniel."

The bits of amber in his eyes suddenly grew, taking over most of the brown.

"I want to eat you."

"I want you to eat me." She removed his hands, twisting around to place her pussy over his head. "But fair's fair."

His growl, deep and masculine, sent more juices flowing. Seizing her buttock cheeks, he guided her to his mouth. His tongue swept over her and, although she knew what was coming, surprised her with the ensuing surge of desire. She mewed and lowered to cup his cock in her hand.

Their bodies molded together, each matching the rhythm of the other, moaning their pleasure to each other. His mouth on her sex lips sucked and teased, and she mimicked him, giving him as much ecstasy as he gave her. Her legs quivered as wave after wave of release rushed though her, but she held on, stroking him, licking him, sucking him.

"Damn, Lauren, you're going to make me come."

A warmth of delight surged through her and she chuckled, liking the way his shaft jerked as the hot air spread over his wet cock. "Isn't that the point?"

"No. I want to be inside you when I come. Not like— Ah, shit, that's good."

Lauren took him inside her mouth, sliding him in until he couldn't go any farther. She swallowed, tugged, pulled, then repeated the movements over and over. He moaned, leaving her pussy to encourage her with sweet words, then returning to treat her. At last, however, he reached his peak.

In one quick move, he had her on her back, then lifted her torso until only her shoulders, neck and head touched the ground. A low rumble echoed through his chest, into his shoulders and into the inside of her thighs. Staying on his knees, he yanked her bottom upward, positioning her legs over his shoulders, higher still until he pressed his mouth to her throbbing clit.

"Oh, oh, oh. Yes!" Breathing became more difficult, thinking impossible as he savored her, drawing every ounce of flavor from her body. Unable to grasp any part of him, she writhed on the ground, clutching the grass and tearing it out in handfuls. "Daniel. You're going to make me— Oh, shit, please, please."

"Please what, Lauren?" His golden eyes blazed into her. Almost as though meaning to torture her, he sucked harder, then swiped his tongue across her tender skin and sucked more.

"Fuck me. Now." Her body trembled from the multitude of climaxes racing along her body, her mind closing down until only the primal part of her consciousness remained. She shut her eyes and reached out, fighting to find his manhood, desiring him deep inside her. His tongue, his wonderful tool of torture, left her spent, yet ready for anything.

Lowering her, Daniel rubbed his shaft against her, wetting his tip, taunting her to make her plead even louder, longer. Unashamed, she did, adding the plea to her eyes. "Daniel, please." The ache in her tone couldn't match the yearning inside her.

Daniel rested her buttocks on the tops of his knees, massaging her weak legs. Licking his upper lip, he helped her wrap her legs around his waist. "Now?"

"Are you freakin' kidding me? Yes, yes, yes!"

Daniel shoved into her and Lauren screamed in joy, energized by his attack. She thrust her pelvis upward, her wall to his battering ram. She grabbed his hands and placed them on her breasts, urging him to fondle them. He groaned, keeping his eyes locked with hers. They moved as one, each reveling in the pleasure they gave each other.

"Play with yourself, Lauren." He glanced down, his body tense, sweat running down the rivulets of his chest to the toned abdomen and, finally, into the valley their union formed.

Using her middle finger, she toyed with her swollen nub, taking joy in the way he watched her hand move. She tried to hang on, to keep the delicious agony going, but his thrusts were too much. Nothing else mattered except the sensations coursing through her, the heat making the sweat seem almost cool against her skin. She watched his face, a study in restraint, and pushed against him. Another climax wracked her until she was sure she would pass out. "Oh, God, Daniel, I don't know how much longer..."

"Lauren, I have to..."

She couldn't think, not with him deep inside her. "Have to...what?" He stopped, the abrupt cessation shocking her. "No, Daniel, don't stop."

Daniel opened his mouth. Fangs, sparkling in the bright sunlight, slid from behind his lips. "Lauren, do you want me to? Quick. Tell me. If I go much further, I won't be able to stop."

"Do it, Daniel. Make me yours."

Howling, he shook his head, his features changing seconds before he bent over her and sank his teeth into her neck.

She felt his fangs tear into her skin and panic seized her. Yet before she could even rethink her decision, she succumbed, clutching the back of his head and hugging him close. A liquid burn, hotter than a branding iron, spun into her neck, into her veins to scorch down her body. She screamed, her body bucking under his, and still she held on.

At that moment, his body tightened, and his features changed, returning to the Daniel she loved. Howling again, he gave into his release, taking her along with him, his shudders smoothly flowing into hers.

Daniel lay next to Lauren, his eyes closed, enjoying the cooling breeze flowing over his love-worn body. Her shoulder grazed his, tantalizing him, awakening another burst of desire. If they didn't move soon, he'd take her again. Not that he wouldn't love to do exactly that. But they needed to address other matters first. "Lauren, are you all right?" He peered at her wound, already beginning to heal.

Eyes closed, she snuggled in the crook of his arm and ran her hand over his chest. "Hmm?"

"Do you know what just happened? What that bite meant?" Had she understood? Or had he been mistaken?

"You marked me."

Did she sound angry? She didn't look angry. In fact, she seemed very relaxed, satisfied, even happy.

"Yes, I did." A bee buzzed between them, the only sound disturbing the silence. Wouldn't she act upset if she hadn't wanted him to mark her? "I know neither one of us has mentioned this what with all the problems going on. Then John, the hunters—"

"Daniel, just spit it out." She was suddenly alert and, propping her chin on his chest, arched her eyebrows at him. "What is it?"

Her hair felt like silk in his hands. Did he dare ask her? If she turned him down, could he stand it? "I know your life is in the city, but would you ever consider—"

"Yes." She laughed, then buried her face against him. "I'm sorry. I know I should've waited for you to ask, but you're taking way too long to get to it. So I figured I'd help you out."

"How do you know what I want to ask you?" His heart lurched at the idea. What if she didn't know? What if she'd assumed incorrectly?

She sat up, her eyes wide. "Uh, I guess maybe I don't. And maybe I should've kept my big mouth closed."

He tried to get her to look at him, but she turned away. "You? Keep quiet? Come on." He winced, fearful that he'd made a mistake when she didn't laugh at his joke. "Lauren, we've gone from enemies to…"

When she turned to seek his eyes, he found he couldn't meet them. When had he ever gotten tongue-tied? But the question he had to ask was too important. If he didn't ask her the right way, she might refuse him. Hell, she might refuse him anyway.

"What are we now, Daniel? I thought since you marked me, that made us…together."

He sensed she wanted the same answer he did, but fear made his words stumble from his mouth. "You're right. We're, I mean, we're good together." He took her nod as a positive sign. "Uh, not sexually—I mean, not *just* sexually—but…" He studied her, readying for her reaction. "You do realize that you're going to change, right? That you'll become one of us?"

She smiled and ran her palm along his cheek. "Yes, I know. And I'm happy about it."

He relaxed a little. "Good. But I want you to know that just because you're going to change, it doesn't mean you have to come with me. You can still choose." Why couldn't he get the words out? "Lauren, I'm trying to ask you if you'd go, I mean, come. Oh, hell, I'm not saying any of this right."

"For the sake of the pack, man, will you just ask her?"

Daniel followed Lauren's stunned gaze and found Tucker standing at the edge of the picnic area. She gasped and hid as much of her body behind his as she could, reminding him of the other time at the mansion. Talk about déjà vu. "Tucker, what the hell are you doing here?"

Tucker's grin said it as well as his words did. "I'm watching a terrific show. In fact, I think you two should make a video and submit it to one of those amateur porn websites."

Daniel heard Lauren's quick intake of breath, felt her bump against him as she hurriedly pulled on her clothes. She remained behind him, probably hiding from embarrassment.

"How long have you been standing there? And why didn't you let us know you were there?"

"What and cut the show short? If anything, I'd like to see more."

Daniel held back his anger, knowing Tucker would take it as a sign to further bait him. "Did the others take John?"

"Yep. The rest of us are escorting the hunters to the edge of town. Minus their guns and cell phones, of course. Devlin's escorting the big white hunter to his trial with the council."

"Good. Then you can get on your way, too." He flicked his hand at Tucker, motioning for him to leave.

"Hell, no. I want to hear her answer."

Daniel gritted his teeth. "I haven't asked her anything."

"Shit, man, why are you such a slowpoke? I can't wait around here all day. Lauren, darlin'?"

Daniel glared at Tucker, but that didn't intimidate him.

"Yes?" Lauren's tone was soft, tentative.

"What this clod is taking his god-awful time asking is this: Will you come home with him? You're his mate now. You're one of us now. Of course, that also means you're stuck with this tongue-tied clod, but, hey, at least you'll get to run with the pack."

Daniel longed to wrap his hands around Tucker's neck but, in order to do so, he'd have to move, exposing Lauren.

"So even after I said yes to your bite, you're still afraid to ask me to live with you?" She arched an eyebrow, her lips pulled into a smirk.

Daniel held up his hand, silencing Tucker. "Yeah. But only if that's what you want. I don't want to pressure you." Much less kidnap her. Would she hold that against him? He doubted it, but who knew? The silence, however, was deafening.

Tucker, however, wasn't finished mouthing off. "Say yes, darlin', and you'll gain an instant family, too."

Aw, hell. If he'd wanted to strangle his friend before, now he wanted to skin him alive, then boil him in oil. His and Torrie's children were the great joy of his life, but that didn't mean Lauren wanted a ready-made family. Especially a ready-made shifter family. He'd planned on easing into the topic of his children, but Tucker had blown his plan apart more effectively than a block of dynamite. Now he'd have to forge ahead and hope for the best.

"You have children, Daniel? Torrie's children?"

He had to see her, to interpret her emotions before she made a decision. Facing her, he studied her expression, her eyes, her body language. She stayed close to him, meeting his frank perusal with her own, her body tucked into a tight ball. "I have two great kids. A girl and a boy." He couldn't help it. Just thinking about his children always made him smile. "Lance, he's six, and he's all boy, all shifter, and loves to stay in wolf form. Tracey, who's three, is just like Torrie. She's beautiful, caring, loves everyone and everything which, of course, worries me."

She touched his hand, giving him the reassurance he needed. "You're afraid she won't see danger when it comes at her. Like her mother."

"I know I should have mentioned them before I marked you, but..."

"I understand. We both kind of jumped into this."

"In a way, but I've wanted to make you mine for a while now." He choked, relieved that she understood. "They're great kids, Lauren. But I understand if you don't want to get involved with someone with children. If you want me, if you want to come with me back to hills, then you'll have to accept them, too. It's like they say: We're a package."

Her eyelids fluttered, waving her lashes at him. The simple unconscious action zipped lust into his abdomen and, if Tucker hadn't been watching, he would've pushed her on her knees and had her again.

"They sound terrific." She bit back a giggle. "I'd ask to see photos but, under the circumstances—" her gaze fell below his stomach, "—I doubt you have them on you."

Her light joke spurred him on, hope filling him. "I don't need photos if you decide to come home with me. Once you meet them..." Could he really expect her to fall in love with them that fast?

"I'm sure I'll love them." She saw into his very soul with that one look and said the best words he could ever hear. "If they're anything like you, I'll love them. But will they like me? Will they accept me?"

He had to warn himself not to shout his happiness to the world. "In time. How could they not?"

"Damn, you two are getting downright lovey-dovey." Tucker shook his head at them. "I'm getting the hell out of here before I upchuck from all this sticky sweetness. Daniel, I'll see you later for sure. Lauren, as far as I'm concerned, you can run with the pack anytime you want. Now, if you'll excuse me, I have some hunters to boss around and a lady friend to take home." He tossed her a grin and strode away.

Daniel's joy exploded and he pulled Lauren on top of him. "So, just to make sure I've got this right, you'll come with me and be my mate? I marked you, but that doesn't mean you have to go. But say the words, Lauren. I need to hear the words."

"Yes, Daniel Cannon, I'll come with you. I love you, ya big wolfman." She tugged her shirt over her head and tossed it away. "However, I'll only come with you on one condition."

He struggled to tear his attention away from her breasts and failed until she tilted his head up to meet her sultry expression. "Yeah. One condition. Name it."

"I'll come with you and I'll be your mate, if you make love to me again. Right now. Right here."

The breeze blew her soft curls, making her seem like an angel in flight. Pulling her down to him, he nuzzled his face in the curve of her neck. "You've got a deal."

Epilogue

"Lance Cannon, if you pull your sister's tail one more time, I'm going to give you a consequence you won't soon forget." Lauren made her "mommy's mad" face and pointed a finger at the precocious werewolf. His pretty sister, Tracey, giggled and pointed her own finger at her brother.

The young werewolf shot her a fang-filled grin, wagged his tail and sat on his haunches, the picture of innocence. He cocked his head, reminding her of Daniel's gesture, his question silent but unmistakable.

"You're wondering what the punishment is, aren't you?" He nodded, sticking to the silent routine. "If you pull your sister's tail again, I'll make you stay in human form for the rest of the week." She almost laughed at the horrified expression on the young shifter's face. "Have I made myself clear?" Lance yelped, then twirled around twice, pretending to chase his tail. Lauren chuckled, knowing he played the fool because she thought his antics were funny. "Now off to spend the night with your Aunt Sydney. Both of you."

Strong arms slipped around her waist. Recognizing the familiar scent, she leaned into Daniel, liking the way he supported her weight. "Ah, there you are." She sniffed again, loving one of the perks of being a shifter. Soon after coming to the pack's home in the mountains, she'd gone through the

Change. She loved staying in the magnificent caves where most of the pack lived. "Where have you been?"

As if she didn't know. She could smell Tucker's aroma on him, knew the two men met every day to discuss pack business. But she could sense they'd discussed more than the everyday matters of the pack today. She'd known something was up ever since the council had made their decision about John, sending him to Chicago to face whatever happened to him there.

"Talking with Tucker." Daniel turned her to face him, buried his hands in her hair and kissed her deeply, lovingly. "But I figured you already knew that."

She sighed, contented and blissful. "Uh-huh. And what kind of trouble are you two brewing up?"

He feigned shock, but she knew better.

"Well, if you must know, nosy woman." He ducked away, narrowly missing her playful swipe at him. "Tucker wants to go out on his own."

She'd suspected something different about Tucker in recent days, but she hadn't expected that. "What do you mean out on his own?"

"He wants to start his own pack."

A werewolf starting his own pack was rare and dangerous, especially in an area that already had several packs. Most pack leaders wouldn't hear of it, would consider it a challenge to their authority, but did Daniel? "And what did you say?"

"I told him to go for it."

Her mate never failed to surprise her. "You did? Aren't you worried for him?"

"He understands what's involved. Besides, he's leaving the area." Daniel played with a strand of her hair, a sure sign he wanted sex.

"Where's he going?" Tucker was such an integral part of their pack that she had a hard time thinking of the pack without him.

"He wants to see what Oklahoma is like."

The surprises just kept on coming. "Oklahoma? Why does he want to go there? Are there any mountains, any forests there? Daniel, has he really thought this idea through?"

He lifted her, carrying her toward their cave, and she locked her hands behind his neck.

"He wants a city pack. But they have enough unoccupied land that they can run when they want to."

She slapped his hand away from her breasts, intent on finishing this conversation first. "Daniel, stop. Talk first. Then sex."

He dropped her, exasperation showing in his features, in his demeanor. "Fine. Let's get this over with. Tucker is going to Oklahoma and I support him."

"And your brothers? Do they support him, too?" Jason would more than likely go along with the idea, but Devlin didn't like losing pack members.

"I'll talk them into it." He paused, waiting for her next question. "Are we good now?"

She nodded, figuring she shouldn't push too hard. "For now. But we're going to talk again later. Okay?"

"Anything you say, my love."

Easing her onto their bed, she watched as her sexy mate quickly lost his clothes, then removed hers. Her gaze slid hungrily down his chest, over the hard stomach to rest on the object of her lust. "You're just saying that to shut me up, aren't you?"

His answer, however, was muffled as he dove between her legs.

About the Author

To learn more about Beverly Rae, please visit www.beverlyrae.com. Send an email to Beverly at info@beverlyrae.com or join her Yahoo! group to join in the fun with other readers as well as Beverly! http://groups.yahoo.com/group/Beverly_Rae_Fantasies/.

GREAT CHEAP FUN

Discover eBooks!

THE FASTEST WAY TO GET THE HOTTEST NAMES

Get your favorite authors on your favorite reader, long before they're out in print! Ebooks from Samhain go wherever you go, and work with whatever you carry—Palm, PDF, Mobi, Kindle, nook, and more.

WWW.SAMHAINPUBLISHING.COM

CPSIA information can be obtained at www.ICGtesting.com
Printed in the USA
LVOW080316201211
260252LV00002B/5/P